THE MEDINA DEVICE

T.J. CHAMPITTO

Black Rose Writing | Texas

ISBN: 978-1-68433-490-2
PUBLISHED BY BLACK ROSE WRITING
www.blackrosewriting.com

Printed in the United States of America
Suggested Retail Price (SRP) $19.95

The Medina Device is printed in Calluna

For my father.

ACKNOWLEDGEMENTS

Thanks to my biggest supporter and sharpest critic, my wife, Tisha. To my agent Linda Langton who made all of this possible, and had the foresight to believe in this project with as much heart as I did. Reagan Rothe at *Black Rose Writing* for taking a chance on an unknown writer and finding the forest in the trees. And to my amazingly talented editors for their astute advice; Jason O'Toole in Ireland, Ashley LaChance in Canada, and Karen Wise in the United States.

THE
MEDINA
DEVICE

CHAPTER ONE

Qaluyu, Bolivia

An aging professor leaned through the arched passage of a mysterious tomb. Halogen spotlights exposed a thick cloud of dust hanging effortlessly in the air of the underground tunnel. He inhaled deeply, allowing the smell of freshly unearthed history to overwhelm his senses. It was the smell of victory. The taste of success.

Dr. Ricardo Diaz and his team had been working the dig site off-and-on since last spring. Located five miles from the Incan ruins at Puma Punku, Diaz's site on the southern mountainside of Qaluyu had shown more promise than any of his previous expeditions.

Deep below the ground, standing before him and his small team was an ancient tomb, enclosed on three sides with limestone walls. Unlike the sandstone ruins found at nearby Puma Punku and Tiwanaku, the rare limestone located here had immediately caught their attention. The nearest limestone quarry was thousands of miles away.

Diaz's team, funded by the Argentina Foundation for Historical Studies, had discovered the twelve-by-twelve room two days ago, thirty feet below the surface—their reward for weeks of exhaustive digging with no more than buckets and shovels. Every five to ten feet, the team unearthed new

Incan artifacts—shards of pottery, carved stone and other menial objects. But at twenty feet, they began mining items that were increasingly less and less Incan. At thirty feet, the engineers reached a man-made subterranean corridor that led directly to the tomb entrance where they now stood.

Diaz felt certain they were closing in on evidence of an ancient, unknown civilization—one that seemingly pre-dated the Incan Empire.

He stepped through the wide entrance with his headlamp darting its beam of white light through the thick, musty air. He scanned up and down the wall to his right as the team began to gather around him. The hieroglyphs carved vertically into the walls couldn't be deciphered by any of his on-site experts. The team's inability to make sense of the glyphs added a touch of drama to the moment at hand. With an immediate translation impossible, the best Diaz could do was photograph everything and send it on for further analysis to the University College London's Institute of Archaeology.

Atop a small stone altar in the center of the tomb rested an ossuary. It was a rectangular box no more than three feet wide. Diaz took a deep breath and tightened his gloves, then reached toward the stone box to wipe away a collage of cobwebs and debris from its limestone shell. Two assistants hurried to his side to lend a hand.

As the ossuary's esthetic details slowly came into focus, it revealed a flawlessly chiseled framework of symbols and glyphs. The professor took his time, examining every inch of its exterior. The glyphs proved to be as unrecognizable as those etched into the walls. But one symbol stood out to Diaz—it was the stamp he'd spent the last six years searching for.

A slow grin appeared through his salt-and-pepper beard as Diaz shifted his focus from the side of the ossuary to its sealed cover. For a moment, he questioned whether to open it immediately or to carefully pack it up with the rest of his finds. It was a question he quickly answered. No, this discovery could not wait, he told himself.

At Diaz's command, a young field assistant made his way to the center of the tomb with a handheld wet saw and began meticulously cutting away the cover of the time capsule. Moments later, the slab of limestone was carefully detached and removed. The team anxiously held their breath, allowing the professor to be the first to lay eyes on his treasure.

Ricardo Diaz inched closer to the altar and peered cautiously into the ossuary. His gaze remained frozen for what seemed an eternity.

"*Todos fuera. Ahora*," he shouted, waving with great urgency for everyone to evacuate.

CHAPTER TWO

Providence, Rhode Island

Cameron Lyle looked like a zombie. His plane had just touched down at Green Airport and after a four-hour flight from New Orleans, with a breakneck layover in D.C., Cam glanced down at his wristwatch and noticed his flight had arrived seven minutes early.

He lumbered through the jetway with wrinkled khakis, a loosened tie and the look of a man who hadn't slept in many days. With a backpack slung over his right shoulder and a briefcase dangling at his side, the thirty-eight-year-old defense consultant finally made it to the gate lobby—the home stretch.

On the heels of a weeklong business trip to Louisiana, Cam was relieved to be back in Rhode Island. It had been an agonizing mission rubbing elbows with private military executives and contractors. As a tactical combat strategist, his trip to the annual defense conference allowed him the opportunity to pitch potential clients. Weeks like this made him feel cheap.

With no checked baggage to claim, he swiftly exited the airport terminal to the transportation depot. He stepped into the clear, northeastern air and jumped into a shuttle, which loitered on the curb for fifteen minutes before whisking him to the parking deck.

It was the end of a harsh season and Providence was taking the brunt of a small storm—winter's final encore. After a painstaking forty-five-minute drive through a frozen rain, Cam pulled into the driveway of a modest four-bedroom home in the suburbs. While happy to be home, he sighed with a sense of disappointment because it was late and the girls were surely asleep. Cam quietly made his way upstairs and slipped into bed next to his wife, Hannah. He admired her beauty before kissing her on the forehead and collapsing against his pillow.

The next morning, Cam slept in late. Hannah had gone out of her way to keep the two girls quiet during their normal routine. "Daddy's been working hard," she told them, "he needs the rest."

Upstairs, Cam's eyelids slowly unpeeled. He sat up and planted himself on the edge of the bed. It was Thursday morning and he had nowhere to be, a thought that comforted him. His next consulting project wouldn't begin for another two weeks and his subsequent hunt was still months away. Just then a familiar voice shouted from the hallway.

"Daddy!" called out his oldest of two daughters. She charged through the bedroom and into his waiting arms. This was the first time Abigail had seen her father in eight days—a millennium for a little girl.

"How's my princess?" he muttered, snatching her up onto the bed next to him with a kiss on her cheek.

"I missed you. Did you have fun on your trip?" she asked in a tiny voice as she pulled her long brown hair into a ponytail.

"I *did* have fun on my trip," Cam replied with exaggeration. "And I missed you and your sister very much."

Lindsay, the six-year-old with a head full of blonde tangles, bounced into the room like a missile and landed successfully in his lap. The direct hit forced a deep moan from Cam's gut. It was good to be home.

Hannah stood quietly in the doorway holding a cup of coffee in an over-sized mug. She was happy to have him back and could spend eternity watching her husband frolic with the girls. But she had been up since dawn preparing for day six of her trial, and it was time to get dressed and ready for court. Cam would be responsible for getting the girls ready for school over the next few weeks—a chore Hannah was somewhat thankful to be temporarily relieved of.

She was an assistant prosecutor for the state of Rhode Island and had a strong track record of convictions. She excelled at law and liked nothing better than sending the bad guys to jail. It was very much a career that suited her rigid, hyper-organized lifestyle.

Twenty minutes later, Cam was plating the last of the toaster waffles when Hannah made her way down the stairs with all the grace of a lawyer running late for a trial. She slid her way into the kitchen and kissed both of her children—now seated and fighting over syrup—on the cheeks.

"Love you, Cam," she finally got around to saying. "I should be home by seven, I'll pick up some dinner."

"Love you too, babe. Stick to your guns out there, and you can tell me all about it tonight over a glass of wine."

She replied with a knowing grin and a roll of her big, blue eyes. Cameron then walked her to the foyer and was rewarded with a quick kiss. He shut the door behind her, sneaking one last look at her blonde hair and flawless curves as she paraded down the steps and disappeared around the corner to the side driveway.

They'd met twelve years ago and it was love at first sight for Cam. It was a chance encounter at an airport bar that sparked a romance that would ultimately change both of their lives forever. At the time, he was a special forces operator from Delaware and she was an ambitious Penn State grad from Chicago.

Cam knew she had been struggling with her current case, but until now he had been too preoccupied to show much interest in it. He'd missed her over the last week and was determined to spend a relaxing night sipping pinot noir, listening to her champion through the finer details of the case. He could be a brilliant listener when he wanted to.

After breakfast, Cam ushered the girls outside and down the sidewalk, where their school bus awaited with open doors. He hugged them both with his burly arms and watched them board. Abigail and Lindsay both waved through the window before the bus disappeared around the corner. The smile remained on his face long after they were gone.

It was one of those moments that could tug a parent back to their own childhood—to a time when he and his brothers would wave goodbye like this to their father.

Cam was the middle child of three boys. He'd joined the Navy out of high school and breezed through boot camp. From there, the strapping young athlete completed BUD/S training and SEAL Qualification Training (SQT). After earning his Trident, he was assigned to SEAL Team 8 and served in the Middle East for ten years. He went on to become a training officer with the Naval Special Warfare Command in San Diego, before finally retiring from the Navy. His work as a tactical combat consultant had seen its ups and downs but afforded him more family time.

Just as he made his way back to the front door his cellphone rang.

It was his younger brother, Michael.

"What now?" Cam sarcastically answered.

"You know exactly why I'm calling," Michael chuckled. "It's time."

There was a long pause before Cam responded. "Of course. When?"

"Seventy-two hours from now."

"Fine," he huffed. "I'll pick you guys up in Philly. Make sure your target packs are ready."

CHAPTER THREE

FBI Field Office, Las Vegas, Nevada

It was just before midnight. The last remaining sign of life in the building leaned over his laptop, squinting at the words staring back at him. With his face illuminated in the dark office bullpen, he scanned through digital documents. The night's research had provided a treasure trove of new, useless information regarding one of Special Agent Rand Kershaw's most frustrating cases.

Other agents from the Las Vegas field office had written the Wynn casino heist off as an "unsolvable wild goose chase." While the FBI would never publicly throw in the towel on any criminal investigation, it often did.

The heist had become a giant stain on the FBI. It had been almost a year since three masked men stormed the casino, and Kershaw seemed to be the last agent left with any intention of solving it. The case had driven him to drink, as evidenced by the half-drowned bottle of cheap whiskey sitting on his desk. Having long ago given up on soda mixers and cocktails, he rifled through a collection of discarded Dixie cups until he found a relatively clean one and poured another straight whiskey. Even if any superiors had been there, they likely wouldn't have noticed, or cared, about his behavior—neither did he.

At thirty-five-years-old, this was Rand's first unsolved case and he had chased this rabbit down the hole into depression and a growing list of anxiety disorders. Yet he continued grinding, chasing the ghosts that haunted his dreams.

Rand Kershaw was a handsome man, never married and single for reasons he couldn't explain. He had a medium-build and dark hair, with eyes that could burn a hole right through a person.

The special agent now stared intently at a computerized map, which outlined the path of the robbery, or at least the small patch of ground the FBI could account for. He opened a new tab, then pulled up several security cam videos and began cycling through them. The black Jeep Cherokee used in the heist was caught on traffic cameras heading south on Las Vegas Boulevard moments prior to the robbery. Property cameras at the Wynn resort showed the vehicle pulling up on a hotel side street just north of the main entrance. Three masked men armed with M4 machine guns exited the Cherokee with its engine running and the hazard lights on. They disappeared on foot behind the adjacent parking garage.

One minute and seven seconds later, they broke into the rear of the Wynn Theater, which was empty at the time. The ghosts pushed across the theater and the other side, where security footage showed them spill out into the northwest corner of the casino, a mere twenty yards from their target—the Main Cage. Just down a hallway, they quickly disarmed a gated door with three deliberate, well-placed rounds of .223 Remington bullets and kicked it open with the heel of a boot.

Agent Kershaw clicked *play* on the next grainy, black-and-white security footage from his hard drive. He watched, for the thousandth time, a twenty-two-second clip of his ghosts as they flawlessly entered the main cage and secured what they had come for—$3.6 million in untraceable cash being prepared for transport. The armed pick-up guards were scheduled to arrive only three minutes later to collect the cash load. It was all done with perfect military timing.

That's all it took. Twenty-two seconds, Kershaw thought to himself.

He switched back to the outside property footage of the Jeep parked on the side street, its hazard lights still flashing. Seconds later the three men, now carrying large duffle bags, calmly piled into the SUV. Rand knew they drove southbound again onto Las Vegas Boulevard, then west onto Spring Mountain Road, which granted them immediate access to the Las Vegas Freeway. From there, they simply disappeared.

Rand tightened his jaw in anger. *They kept the damn hazards on. Who does that?*

He took the last sip from a Dixie cup and crumpled it in his hand. A dramatic hook shot fell short of the nearby trashcan, where several other wads of paper had met the same fate.

Rand had looked at this heist from countless angles over the past nine months. He now caught himself spinning his wheels again. He tried to rein in his wandering imagination and shift his anxious attention elsewhere. Frustration and focus had become his worst enemies.

Reaching for his messenger bag, Rand decided to take a few files and get out of the office, maybe stop by Callahan's on his way home for a nightcap. He thumbed through a few folders that littered his desk and zeroed in on one in particular that had caught his attention earlier that day. *Some fresh blood would be good,* he decided, and threw it into his bag. The weary agent placed the whiskey bottle in a desk drawer and turned off his laptop. It was midnight.

A half hour later, Rand lumbered into Callahan's Pub—a small, dark bar on the south-side of town outfitted with all the decor of a mid-century storeroom. The FBI agent in him instinctively checked the place from left to right before making his way to his favorite stool. Rand Kershaw projected an air of intelligence, but carried an unwelcoming sense of professionalism that often rubbed people the wrong way. The bartender, known only as Big Nick, had a whiskey-on-the-rocks already poured and waiting on the bar by the time Rand landed on his stool.

The half-drunk agent stared endlessly into the ice cubes floating in his highball glass, watching them slowly melt into the cheap booze. He caught himself daydreaming about the file he'd grabbed from his desk and, more importantly, where it would take him when he dove into it later that night.

It was a silly hunch, really. A hunch that relied heavily on the age-old tale of Robin Hood—a band of criminals stealing from the rich and giving to the poor. As ridiculous as it sounded, it was a theory that provided answers to all his questions.

The thin folder tucked away in a messenger bag in the back seat of his car contained articles and documents pertaining to several large, anonymous donations that had been made in the months following the heist. Written on the front in black ink were the words *Robin Hood.* And tonight was as good as any to peel back the layers of a long shot theory and get lost down another rabbit hole.

Rand knew that the story provided entertainment value and cultural symbolism. The tale of Robin Hood was no more than an attempt to denounce the foundations of the ruling class and give the "people" a hero— someone who kept their hopes alive in an otherwise hopeless world. But there was just one problem; when Rand viewed his theory through an investigative lens, he couldn't help but ask himself: *Why would a guy take so many risks for a return that yielded no real value or reward for himself, yet reaped life-changing rewards to others? To complete strangers, no less.*

It had to have been Rand's one-hundredth eureka moment since the investigation began.

Vigilantes like Robin Hood didn't actually exist, did they? he wondered as he sat upright in his bar stool. *The laws of psychology would probably say no,* Rand reasoned. *In the conscious of most modern humans it is extremely rare that our natural instincts would allow us to follow through on an action with such an unrewarding projected outcome. It was basic biology—people just weren't wired up that way.*

The thoughts spun wildly in his head. After one more drink, Rand left Callahan's and, by two in the morning, he was sitting alone in the cluttered living room of his small apartment in Henderson, just south of Vegas. The place was well-furnished and upscale, carrying all the hallmarks of an overworked bachelor.

Seated on a black leather couch, he leaned in to have another go at the file. Three receipts rested on the coffee table: a $400,000 anonymous donation to the U.S. Hunger Relief Organization; an untraceable donation of 6,000 laptop computers made to a dozen school districts in southern

Alabama; and an anonymous $3.24 million donation to St. Jude Children's Research Hospital.

The latter stuck out for obvious reasons—it was by far the largest of the group. But there was more about the St. Jude's donation that caught his attention. With a single sheet of paper in one hand and a glass of bourbon in the other, Rand squinted through floating eyes at the receipt. He distinctly remembered the donation from the news cycle earlier that year. The incredible act of humanity had created a feeding frenzy for the media, who hailed the anonymous donors as heroes. Undisputed praise littered social media for weeks. It was the stuff of movies. But something else suddenly stood out to Rand: the donation was exactly ninety percent of the amount stolen from Wynn. The percentage was insignificant in the grand scheme of things, and the agent feared he was finding logic where logic didn't exist.

Rand had hit the wall, physically drained and very drunk. With a deep sigh, he got up and sluggishly wobbled his way to the bedroom. Tomorrow he'd dive into the St. Jude donation with a recharged battery.

CHAPTER FOUR

Cameron Lyle sat comfortably behind the wheel of a rented BMW X5 as it roared up the open country road. There was a certain energy in the air as they made their way north through the Pennsylvania foothills. He darted a wincing smile at his passengers. His brother Michael was already buzzed from a bottle of Scotch he'd picked up at the airport. In the backseat, buried in his smartphone, William "Trip" Montgomery III was shaking off his jet lag and sifting through technology headlines he may have missed while trapped in the air. The self-taught hacker had flown cross-country from San Francisco to Philadelphia, where he met up with Cam, who had drove down from Providence, and Michael, who had raced up from D.C.

That was a half-bottle of Scotch ago.

"We're about an hour out," Cam announced, trying to yell over the Van Halen track blasting through the speakers at Michael's insistence. "I'm stopping at North Bend for supplies. You guys need anything?"

"Booze. Lots and lots of booze," Trip called from the backseat. "I gotta catch up with your idiot brother."

At just twenty-nine-years-old, Trip was the youngest of the pack. He grew up in Lodi, Texas, on his family's farm. Both his parents died in a car accident while he was a teenager, leaving him to be raised by his older brother, who was later killed in action while serving in Afghanistan.

It was an annual tradition for Trip, Michael and Cam to spend a week at the Lyles' cabin in Susquehannock State Forest, nestled in upstate Pennsylvania. The place was originally built by Elliot Lyle back in the Sixties, but as time passed Elliot's sons eventually took it over as their own. It was a rugged, four-bedroom that sat high on a cliff overlooking the lush wilderness below.

The SUV pulled into a convenience store just off the main drag that ran through the sleepy mountain town of North Bend. Cam got out and inhaled the fresh air as he had a cursory glance at his surroundings. The cabin was stockpiled with everything the guys could think of, but it never hurt to pick up a few additional items on the way. He entered the dusty, old country store and minutes later emerged with two bags brimming with charcoal, steaks, eggs, two cases of beer and a gallon of off-brand whiskey.

He topped off the gas tank at the pump outside, and moments later the SUV pulled back onto the two-lane, scenic highway to begin its final ascent into the mountains. Before long they would be stoking a fire and lining up shots of liquor in the cool Appalachian air.

As the BMW climbed, Cam pinched his lips and stared blankly beyond the steering wheel at the colossal pine trees zooming by. The weather was overcast and gloomy, but Cam found beauty in the vast surroundings of the foothills and was excited about a week of testosterone-filled banter, high-stakes drinking games and war stories.

The three guys had been coming to the cabin together for the past four years. Before that, when Cam was home on leave, he and Michael would meet there with a handful of rowdy childhood friends from Hockessin. But as time went on, each year brought fewer of those friends, and eventually it was just the two youngest Lyle brothers. Until that fateful night four years ago, when Cam and Michael invited Trip on their annual getaway. And *The Huntsmen's Club* was officially born.

The memory brought a soft smile to Cam's face. He peered into the rearview mirror at the young hacker in the backseat.

"What?" Trip finally asked, sensing the steely eyes lurking at him.

"Sorry," Cam replied with a grin. "You remind me of your brother sometimes."

CHAPTER FIVE

As the gang embarked on their big week in the Pennsylvania foothills, Special Agent Rand Kershaw sat quietly at his desk at the FBI field office in Las Vegas. He had spent the previous night laying out his Robin Hood theory and was now ready to present it to Special Agent in Charge, Steve Brodsky. Rand had struck out so many times in previous attempts at selling Brodsky on his theories. He was nervous, knowing damn well his boss had become skeptical of almost everything that spilled out of his mouth.

With a deep breath of confidence, Rand grabbed his case file and marched down the hall, then briefly paused to gather his thoughts before jumping in. He opened his eyes and rapped his knuckles on the door.

"Steve, you got a sec?" he asked, leaning into the doorway.

"Sure thing," Brodsky replied, removing his bifocals and closing a folder on his desk. "To what do I owe the pleasure, Agent Kershaw?"

"The Wynn case. I've got something. Thought I'd run it by you if you have a moment."

"I can always make time for a hard-working agent. Take a seat."

Rand sat sheepishly in the worn-out chair in front of his boss's desk. He placed the file in front of Brodsky and leaned back into the chair.

"I've been looking into some large, anonymous donations that took place in the months following the heist," he began.

Brodsky narrowed his eyes and opened the folder. The bifocals quickly returned to his face as he peered at it inquisitively.

"Of course, I found several," Rand continued. "But one in particular stood out to me. It was a $3.24 million-dollar donation to St. Jude."

"No shit?" the Special Agent in Charge contemplated. "That's a lot of dough."

"Yeah, it certainly caught my attention. I have a feeling these guys are...well, it's just a hunch..."

"Spit it out," Brodsky scoffed.

"The thing is, it was such a *large* donation. All our usual suspects for anonymous donations—Brockman, Gates, Buffett—would never make this large of a donation without the charity having some inkling of who it was. They simply haven't got one iota here about who made this donation. I mean, this is 'throw a gala and a press conference' type of money—and even if it was supposed to be anonymous, the media would have named the philanthropist."

"I'm not biting, Rand. But go ahead and walk me through the scenario. You've got me on pins and needles." The sarcasm was thick.

Sensing defeat, Rand pressed on. "So, three guys steal $3.6 million from the casino, completely untraceable. They keep ten percent to pay for expenses and donate the rest—$3.24 million dollars—to one of the largest cancer research charities in the world."

"I'm done, Rand." The bifocals were off again. "This is another bullshit goose chase and I won't go on it with you."

Rand hated seeing Brodsky clearly disappointed and annoyed like this.

"But, Steve..."

"Don't 'But Steve' me. You're just bringing me more garbage because, at the end of the day, you have absolutely nada, hombre. Absolutely nothing here." Brodsky waived the useless folder around in the air as his football-shaped belly pressed against the desk.

"No," Rand shot back. "I need you to hear me out. Please."

"You're not letting go, huh? Fine, you have two minutes. Rapido. Let's hear it."

"The donation was exactly ninety percent to the dollar of the total taken from Wynn. It was made exactly three months to the day after the heist. Nobody, and I mean no one, was ever able to identify the donors. These guys unloaded the cash without any trace of origination. The donation was made by a dummy corporation from San Pedro: Boro Industries. That piece of information was leaked to the press, who then tried hunting down anyone they could find from Boro Industries. All the newspapers had was an address to an abandoned warehouse in the valley and a debunk website hosted from China."

"What else?" asked Brodsky, still clearly unimpressed.

"My profile is three males, late-twenties to mid-thirties, possible military training and absolutely no interest in the money, or obviously any attention. They're driven by pure adrenaline. The thrill of the hunt."

"The thrill of the hunt," Brodsky repeated, now seemingly ready to play along.

"Chasing adrenaline can become addictive," Rand pointed out.

"They're not called adrenaline junkies for nothing."

"Exactly. So, when people get addicted to things, they crave it—and do it over and over again. Let's pretend for a second I've profiled them correctly: What are the chances that the Wynn casino isn't the only heist they've pulled off?"

"That's an interesting observation, Kershaw. A robbery like that could take up to a year to plan. Maybe there were more before this." Brodsky was thinking out loud now. "Three men with the right resources could potentially pull one of these off every year."

Rand gave his boss a moment to process it.

"So, let's play ball. What's your next move?" Brodsky asked.

"I'd like to dig into a few other high-profile heists followed by high-profile anonymous donations. You're right, there may be a string of these things that lead up to the Wynn job."

Steve Brodsky nodded in agreement. "Set your timetables roughly a year apart and see if you can't connect some dots. But don't bring this shit back to me until you do. Otherwise, I don't want to hear any more crazy tales of a modern-day Robin Hood and his band of merry goddamn men terrorizing the country for no other reason than to cure cancer. Got it?"

"Yes, sir." Rand's mind was already racing with the idea of serial criminals on a mission to save the world. He loved it. He needed it.

"And get some sleep for Christ's sake! The bags under your eyes are embarrassing."

Rand replied with a distracted smile and left. He hadn't even reached the end of the hallway when it hit him like a ton of bricks: The Hamilton hack, if that wasn't a high-profile heist than nothing was. It was almost too high profile. The cyber security hack on Hamilton Entertainment two years ago had been one of the biggest robberies since the 1978 Lufthansa heist. Everyone in the world knew about it, it had made the international news and become the stuff of hacking folklore. The thieves had stolen six million dollars, all without ever setting foot on Hamilton property—the cyberattack was executed remotely, and the hackers were never identified. *The timing would have lined up perfectly*, he thought to himself. *Almost a full year before the Wynn robbery.*

As he considered his next move, the young agent shuddered at the idea of connecting his casino case to one of the largest thefts the bureau had investigated in the last twenty years. He drifted back to his desk and tried to organize his thoughts. After a moment, he was already trying to poke holes in his own theory, because that's what good agents do.

If they're adrenaline junkies, then why would they launch a robbery from behind a computer screen? What's the fun in that? Or maybe the adrenaline they're chasing isn't the physical rush of guns and getaways but simply the rush of stealing. Or, more importantly, giving.

Rand caught himself slipping off track. *No, no, no, you do this every time.* He closed his eyes tight, knowing he had an unhealthy tendency to obsess and fantasize—to take the tiniest thread of information and build it into something crazy. He leaned back in his chair and rubbed both hands down his face. *Relax*, he told himself. *Start from the bottom and work your way up.*

Rand opened his laptop and began an exploratory mission to identify all high-profile robberies from the last two years and pick them apart case by case. He would then do the same with anonymous donations. It was going to be another long and sleepless couple of nights.

Chapter Six

Susquehannock State Forest, Coudersport, Pennsylvania

In a rustic cabin on the northern tip of Susquehannock Forest, Cam poured a glass of bourbon and stared through the kitchen window into an endless abyss of towering pines, littered with groupings of red cherry trees. The sign above the adjacent wet bar was artistically hand-carved and etched with an inscription— *The Huntsmen's Club.*

The cabin was their lair, a place they could never be traced to, where cellphones were never turned on, and, more importantly, a place where they could escape the stresses of their daily lives.

Trip and Michael were getting riled up in the living room over a game of blackjack that incorporated regular shots of rum into the rulebook. It was the calm before the storm, Cam thought. Each year they would convene at The Huntsmen's Club and run through possible options for their upcoming hunt. And for the rest of the week—in between skeet-shooting tournaments and fishing—they would identify the pros and cons of the multiple heists that had been put on the table. Their final target wouldn't officially be chosen for weeks, but this was the place where the wheels were set in motion.

Cam's deep stare into the wilderness was interrupted by the sound of a shot glass shattering against the stone fireplace and the roar of Michael's victory cry.

It was their cue—time to get down to business.

With an outburst of laughter and some unsportsmanlike ribbing, Michael and Trip made their way to the kitchen table.

"Alright, ladies, let's get to work," Cam finally announced. "Who's first?"

"The floor is yours, big brother," replied Michael.

With a subdued grin, Cam pulled three dossiers from a nearby backpack and handed them out.

"Alright, I've been debating this for months, but here it goes," he began. "My choice for our next target is Pacifico Logistics Partners. They are the financial backer for over a dozen new pipelines set to run through national parks, wetlands and native American burial grounds."

"So, you want to do battle with Big Oil?" Trip interrupted. "You'll never be able to stop the pipelines, Cam. It's a pipe dream, no pun intended."

"If we can cripple these guys where it counts, it might slow things down long enough—"

"Long enough for what?" Michael shot back. "We could steal a billion dollars from them and there'll just be another corporation with *two* billion more dollars to step in and keep it going."

"Understood," Cam conceded. "But, if we hit them in the wallet it just might offset the project costs enough to scare off other investors. Victory lies in forcing them to move these things off protected grounds, not kill it altogether."

"Alright, alright," Michael said with his hands spread out over the table. "While I like the idea of stealing from oil conglomerates, The Huntsmen's Club deals in millions, not billions. We wouldn't even put a dent in a four-billion-dollar pipeline project. And what's the take on an espionage mission? Nothing, that's what."

Cam waved off his stubborn brother. "Well, like it or not, that's my submission. Pacifico Logistics Partners. How we hit 'em and what we come home with is totally up for debate, but that's what I got."

"Months of theorizing right down the toilet, huh?" Trip teased. "Michael you're up. Whatcha got?"

Michael cleared his throat and leaned in. "I have a trifecta in mind this year." He pulled out a folder and opened it on the table.

"I like this already," his big brother noted, rubbing his hands together in anticipation.

"We all know Iran is supplying arms to terrorist organizations in Syria," he began. "I wanna intercept their next big shipment, sell it all at a deep discount to Nigerian freedom fighters currently outgunned by the jihadist militants Boko Haram. We then take the cash and deliver our standard ninety percent to a charity of our choosing. In the end, we steal from a foreign enemy, we help Nigerian citizens fend off terrorists, and we continue to flood money into charities right here at home. It's a multi-pronged hunt that has more positive effects than our last two combined. Besides, it's time we take this club international."

"I like it," Trip agreed. "Besides, we'd be in Cam's element pulling off a military-style mission. You got my vote."

"Hold on here!" proclaimed Cam. "What do you mean he has your vote? We haven't even heard *your* bright idea, Einstein!"

"That's because I don't have one," Trip fired back. "I knew you two boneheads would each put good stuff on the table. I mean, sure, I'd love to hack SVR mainframes and expose Russian intel officers around the world but that's a dangerous game, no need to get tangled up in international counterintelligence. So, I got nothin'." He folded his arms like a petulant child and leaned back in his chair.

"Lazy punk," Cam muttered under his breath.

His insult was met with drunken laughter.

"Alright!" Michael exclaimed. "We got two solid picks: Pacifico Logistics or a shipment of Iranian arms. I love our options."

Michael then placed three shot glasses on the table and filled them with one sloppy, sweeping pour from a one-gallon whiskey jug. They each snatched up a shot glass soaked in liquor and raised them high.

"To the next hunt!"

Later that night, Michael and Cam sat quietly on the tattered couch in the living room as Trip slept off his stupor on the floor at their feet, still clutching an empty beer can.

"Is this what we've become, Cam?" asked Michael through a slurred tongue.

"What do you mean?"

"You spent all those years fighting faceless enemies, all in the name of American capitalism and freedom." Michael drew a deep sigh from his belly. "I, on the other hand, have been all over the world, jumping off cliffs and racing through rapids just so rich dentists and CEOs can feel alive. Yet here we are—stealing from the very people you kept safe, the same assholes I make a living off of."

"Don't overthink it, bro."

"Easy to say. But one day we'll be on our deathbeds, and we'll have to face judgment. Not from some god but from ourselves. What will I tell myself?"

"The world isn't so black and white," Cam offered. "Times change. People change. The rules change. Regrets are real but even those change. So who knows, by then you might not give a shit."

Michael pulled a shot glass to his lips, then reconsidered with a look of disdain and placed it back on the end table at his side.

"But what about the demons that eventually come out? We've all got 'em, Cam. What are yours?"

Demons were something Cam rarely considered, so instead, he found a tiny smile as he thought of his girls. "All I want is a better world for Lindsay and Abigail. And I hope that I've done enough in my lifetime to make that happen. I'd give anything and everything to make sure they see a world that's more compassionate and pragmatic than this one. And I'm willing to die for it."

"Captain America," Michael scoffed as he brushed the wavy brown hair from his face.

"Yeah," Cam replied with a grin. "Captain fuckin' America."

"When I blew out my knee senior year, I thought my life was over," Michael confessed. "I lost my scholarship and friends. I cried that night in the hospital, ya know. Not because of the physical pain. It was the first time I actually *felt* something. The first time something happened that put the rest of my life in jeopardy. I was scared."

Michael snatched the shot glass and poured it down his throat, wincing in disgust.

"Your life wasn't over, it was only beginning."

"Yeah, I guess you're right," Michael agreed. "As soon as I healed, I booked the first one-way flight to Europe. I just wanted to run. But I'll tell ya something, that year with nothing more than a backpack and a few dollars somehow reinvented me. It made me whole again. And now this—being able to give so much to people who have so little. It's done something to me. Something good. I can't thank you enough, Cam."

"*Thank* me? You're shitfaced out of your mind. You two morons begged me for months to bring you in. Don't thank me, you brought this on yourself."

Michael's mind drifted back to three years ago, when Cam got very drunk and confessed to his little brother and Trip how it was his life's mission to put together a small team of bandits to steal, as he put it, from the greedy and corrupt and give to the tired and weak. It was a silly ambition. But the more Cam went into detail about military strike tactics and the extreme vulnerabilities of casinos, banks, network security and infrastructure, the more Michael and Trip's eyes widened. They wanted in. And they got it. A year later, they were launching a cyberattack on a multi-billion-dollar corporation. A year after that they were rushing the main cage at Wynn casino with machine guns and masks. The rest was history—a meticulously woven trail of choices and circumstances that led to now.

Michael brought himself back to the moment—drunk on the couch with his brother.

"Trip and I are too stupid to understand the risks we take every year," he finally confessed. "I'm just here for the free coffee and adrenaline rushes. Trip, though, I don't know why he's here. I guess some time in prison will lower your ambitions."

The brothers shared a smile, remembering Trip's stint in Leavenworth for downloading classified documents from State Department servers.

"He's too smart for his own good," Michael joked. "We all are. One day, it'll get us killed."

"That's not funny," Cam quietly snapped.

"You've killed a bunch of people. What's that like?"

Cam snorted at the question and leaned his head back against the couch. "Why do you always ask me that?"

"I've never really meant it. I never expected an answer. But, now seems like a good time."

Cam paused, thoughtfully choosing his words. "I took an oath to serve my country. And in order to follow through on that, to be good at what you do, sometimes you're forced to pull the trigger. But killing another man isn't what stings. What stings is not being able to save your guys—your friends, your family. Guys like Trip's brother."

"I didn't mean to bring up Mark," Michael said with a touch of remorse.

"It's okay. A lot of good men put their lives in my hands, and I failed some of them."

An awkward silence filled the room.

"You never talk about what happened," Michael said.

"And I never will." Cam leaned over and looked down at Trip, still asleep on the floor. "They were close. He talked about Trip all the time. About what a fuck-up he was and how much he loved him for it. They lost both their parents. I wish I could have brought Mark home—for Trip." Cam took a moment to gather his emotions. "And now I'm putting him in the same danger I put Mark in. What the hell is wrong with me?"

"You're not Trip's protector and you can't carry that around all the time," Michael said with an air of wisdom. "Look, how many guys did you train while you were in San Diego? Guys whose lives were determined by how well you prepared them?"

"Hundreds. I have no idea how many saw combat. Or how many never came home."

"And are you at fault for the guys that didn't?" Michael asked.

"No. I guess not. We gave them the tools to survive. How well that served them—who knows. But sometimes skill isn't enough, being a good frogman isn't enough. IEDs and snipers don't give a shit how talented of an operator you are. Sometimes circumstance alone is enough to get you killed."

"Just know that for every guy that never comes home—for every Mark— there are hundreds that owe their lives to men like you. All you can do is take comfort in that and let the Universe sort out the rest."

"Sounds about right," confirmed Cam.

Michael could barely keep his eyes open now. "Do you worry about getting killed on any of these hunts?"

"Legacy can be a cold, hard bitch," Cam grumbled. "As much as I want my girls to see a better tomorrow, they may not like the things that had to be done to get there. Things get messy when you try to save the world. As much as I feel responsible for the safety of you and Trip, we all made the choice to throw our legacies out the window the moment we walked into that casino."

The two brothers shared a solemn, tired moment of levity before toasting another round and calling it a night.

• • •

The next morning at sunrise, Cam fumbled anxiously through the kitchen for coffee filters. Bacon, eggs and beer were on the table by the time Michael and Trip awoke. It was fly fishing day. And there could only be one winner.

By noon, the guys were huddled together on the rocks along Hopper Run Creek eating pre-packed ham sandwiches. Michael was up by three trout.

"This happens every year," Cam quietly noted.

"What does?" his brother snapped.

"You win."

Trip, meanwhile, watched eagerly as a pod of brook trout danced downstream. "The day's not over yet, boys."

The sandwiches were dry and tasteless but provided a good source of energy for the afternoon challenge.

Hopper Run was the spot Michael and Cam had fished as kids with their oldest brother, James, and their father. It was quiet and peaceful, far from the Susquehannock River and any outlying lodges. The leaves had changed months ago, only a few random specks of brown remained on the northern hardwoods. A few cherry trees peppered the surrounding woods, still holding their brilliant red flare.

"This place hasn't changed a bit," Cam noted.

"Nope, not one bit," Michael agreed as he gave the forest a quick glance. "Dad still loves this place. Comes up every spring."

"Remember that time he got so excited about a catch he stumbled over a rock and fell face first into the creek?"

They chuckled.

"How about you, Trip? You guys do much fishing in Texas?" Cam asked, trying to draw him into the conversation.

"Sure. But we're mostly hunting folk," the young hacker joked. "Always been better with a rifle than a rod."

"What'd you hunt?"

"Deer mostly. You know, I was a better shot than Mark. He couldn't hit the broad side of a barn from five feet back then."

"I believe it."

"I don't know why you SEALs let him become a sniper...never sounded right to me."

The three shared a spirited exchange of grins.

"I wish I had a chance to meet him," Michael said.

Trip's jovial spirit morphed into a flash of happy memories. "He was a protector. The big brother who always had your back. A brilliant decision maker. He would have hated you."

A flow of laughter echoed along the riverbed.

"Fair enough," conceded Michael. "So where does Elena think you are this week?"

"She knows I'm out here."

"Brave man," Cam said.

"She's a good girl," Trip explained. "Probably out of her mind to be with a guy like me, but I guess that's why I love her."

"You trust her?" Cam asked.

"I do. She'll be my wife soon. And while she knows I'm with you guys, she doesn't exactly know what we're planning. It would ruin us," he said with a sobering tone of truth.

Cam stared down at the rocks beneath him. "We don't have to do this forever. I never want these hunts to come between you and Elena, you know that right, Trip?"

"I do."

"You just say the word...and this all ends."

"How about we just burn that bridge when we get to it?"

"Deal."

They rose to their feet and cracked open their cans of beer, taking in the mountain air that drifted through the valley. With one last toast, the tournament's second phase got under way.

The next few days passed with scenic hikes and drinking games. Their weeklong getaway had been a complete success.

CHAPTER SEVEN

The cabin hangover lingered for a few days.

Their specific target, including logistics and tactical plan, wouldn't be set for another month or so. But the votes had been tallied; they would be hijacking a mass weapons cache at the Syrian border. It was going to be a huge adrenaline rush, Cam could already feel it in his bones. It was the type of mission he had trained for a hundred times over. But it was hardly going to be a proverbial walk in the park. It never was; danger always lurked on even the most simple of missions.

It was Monday morning and the girls had left for school an hour earlier. Cam sat in the kitchen, ravaging a breakfast burrito still steaming from the microwave. With no work on the day's calendar, he had time to clear his mind at the shooting range.

Iran would be a tough egg to crack, he thought. Standard back-channels were rare and getting the information they needed could take months. Luckily, Cam had a huge network within the intel community and Trip was still in contact with a collective of vigilante hackers who had proven they could deliver top secret information.

But even with all their resources and bravado, Cam understood they had to be willing to scrap a mission without hesitation. And with so many moving pieces involved in an operation like this, it would only take one to go wrong and derail the entire thing.

He spent the afternoon at Massasoit Gun Club keeping his aim sharp. Afterwards, his cellphone rang while he was walking back to his truck.

"Mr. Lyle, have I caught you at a good time?"

"Is there ever a good time? Who's this?" he asked, unable to identify the voice. White male, mid-sixties with a British accent, he noted.

"My name is Mr. Hall and I'd like to speak with you about a job opportunity," the man politely stated.

"I already have a job, Mr. Hall. What exactly do you need help with, maybe I can recommend someone?"

"That won't be necessary. I understand you and your team have a particular skill set that may be of value to our organization."

Cam hesitated, then looked over his shoulder at the surrounding parking lot. "My team? I don't understand, I'm a defense consultant—I work with a lot of teams. Which one are you referring to?"

There was a dramatic pause.

"The Huntsmen's Club, Mr. Lyle."

Cam's face fell with shock, blood quickly rushed to his gut. His first instinct was to hang up, but whoever was on the other end of the line already had his contact information and probably even his home address.

"How did you get this number?" he whispered as he jumped into the driver's seat of his pickup.

"That's irrelevant."

"I have no idea what you're talking about, you got the wrong number, buddy."

"The offer I have will set you, Michael and William up for the rest of your lives. Abigail and Lindsay will be able to attend any university they want, and you can live out your days sipping cocktails in the French Riviera. I highly recommend you hear what I have to say."

Cam's emotions quickly shifted from fear to anger.

"Listen to me very carefully, you son of a bitch," he warned, trying his hardest not to shout. His eyes frantically continued to scan the parking lot for anyone suspicious. "I don't know how you got the names of my family, or how you got my number, but I will tear you apart—"

"Cameron," the voice calmly interrupted. "All I ask is that you consider my proposal. You can text this number back with a time and location of your choice and I will be there. Alone. You have my word. Please don't make this difficult."

The line went dead. Cam got out of his truck and paced in a circle with his hands above his head. The club had a protocol in place for this type of scenario—shut down everything; wipe all computer devices and cellphones; empty the bank accounts... and abscond to some far-flung location. All he had to do was send the signal and all three men would be in the air within ninety minutes, each heading to a different destination under fake passports. He pulled out his cellphone and brought up a text to Michael and Trip. He then typed in the code phrase:

The weather in Florida is unseasonably warm.

His thumb danced over the send button. Once the signal was sent, there was no turning back. No follow-up calls. No questions or explanations. It would immediately set into motion a series of life-changing events with no way to stop it. Years would go by before they ever spoke again. Cam took a deep breath and tried to regain his focus. The realization suddenly hit him that whoever had just called probably had the surveillance resources to follow him and his brother, as well as Trip, to their escape destinations.

Cam's mind raced in circles. He deleted the code phrase from his phone and replaced it with a request for Trip to setup an encrypted video conference for later that afternoon. His cellphone had clearly been compromised.

The black Chevy truck quickly exited the parking lot onto a side street and drove toward Providence. He had an hour to get to his laptop.

•　　　•　　　•

Meanwhile, Trip sat at his desk in Silicon Valley. In his office, on the fourth floor of Spartan Cyber Security, a tattered American flag from a World War II battleship hung on the wall above a small leather sofa, flanked by a collection of his brother's military medals and a photo of his parents. On his desk, watching him with love, was a photo of his fiancé, Elena. Trip had asked the beaming brunette to marry him just two short months ago. There were tears of joy in her eyes when he got down on one knee and produced the ring.

He leaned back in his chair and stared at Cam's text message. Something was off. It was too soon for the club to start discussing the upcoming hunt, and it was standard protocol to wait a couple weeks before scheduling meetings. No, now was a time of contemplation and decompression after a week at the cabin. Something had gone wrong.

Trip stood up to close his office door, then shut the blinds and made his way back to the old leather chair behind his desk. He set up a secure video channel for the guys to meet on, then sent the link to encrypted email addresses that Cam and Michael only used when all other forms of communication were off the table.

What's going on, Cam? Trip wondered as his fingers worked the keyboard with dizzying speed.

An hour later, the three sat in front of their laptops, live streaming a video conference feed.

Cam wasn't in the mood for small talk. He got straight to the point.

"Sorry to raise the alarm, guys. We've got an issue. Our cover's blown."

"Fuck!" blurted Trip.

From his shop in Washington, D.C., Michael put his hands over his face. "Please tell me this is a goddamn prank, Cam."

"I wish it was. Got a call today from some British spook. He knows our names, he even referenced the club."

"British? That seems strange. Who do you think it is?" asked Trip.

"Who knows!"

"What's he want?" Michael pressed with agitation.

"He wants us to pull off a job, I think."

"What? We're not hired guns, Cam. We made a pact," his brother reminded him.

"I know, I know. All he said was...we'd be set for life. He called my girls by name, for Christ's sake."

"So, what do we do?" asked Trip.

"He just wants us to hear him out."

"If it's the Feds, they're trying to draw us into the open and get us all in the same place. It sounds like a trap," Michael guessed.

"It's not the feds," corrected Trip. "If they have our names, we're obviously not that hard to track down. Hell, my name's written on my office door and Cam's one of the most renowned military strategists in the country."

"And what am I, chopped liver?" asked Michael.

"Save the ego, little bro. We need to figure out our next move. Guys like this don't just go away."

"So, what's the channel? How do we set this up?" Trip wondered.

"You guys are not seriously considering this shit!" Michael was clearly spooked.

"We don't have a choice," Cam shot back. "The only thing we can do is keep the tactical advantage and be ready for a fight. Our mystery man wants me to text him a time and place. I suggest all three of us be there. I'm not going into this alone."

Trip thought about that last statement. "But what if he thinks you are."

"I like where your head's at," agreed Cam.

"I don't like any of this at all," argued Michael.

Trip pulled up a satellite map on a second monitor and narrowed his eyes on the screen, then zoomed in with a few more clicks.

"Set it up, Cam," he demanded. "We'll head down to Michael's neck of the woods. The wine cellar of Fiola Mare in the Washington Harbor district. Two days. Tell him you're coming alone."

"Done."

• • •

Fiola Mare loomed over the Potomac River from the southern end of Georgetown. The upscale restaurant served as a hotspot for Washington's political elite. Known for its five-star seafood and endless wine list, Fiola Mare offered a panoramic view of the beltway. The White House illuminated as a backdrop to the north, the Roosevelt Bridge to the south.

It had been two days since he received the mysterious call from Mr. Hall. Cam paced the sprawling wine cellar awaiting his guest, half hoping the guy wouldn't show. It was just after eight o'clock in the evening and Mr. Hall was supposed to be here at any moment. A tiny earpiece rested in Cam's left ear, awaiting the update from Michael that their guest had arrived.

Cam took a deep breath and sat at a small wooden table in the middle of the cement floor. Three random lightbulbs encased in steel frames cast an eerie ambience over the room. The walls of the cellar were hidden by dusty wine racks containing some of the most expensive bottles on the East Coast—a remarkable collection beneath one of D.C.'s most prestigious restaurants.

The muzzle of a silencer rested comfortably inside one of the many triangular wine rack openings. At the other end of the M4 rifle stood Trip, hidden just behind the dark, wood-stained rack. From his hide, he had a clear view of the entire cellar. Trip gently massaged his finger on the trigger and awaited his target. At the first sign of trouble, he would put a two-round burst into the man's chest. From there, they would prepare the body for its final resting place at the bottom of the Potomac. Trip chose this restaurant for a multitude of tactical reasons, its close proximity to the river being one of them.

He and Cam had been lying in wait for over an hour and the moment of contact had finally arrived. Michael, positioned upstairs in a sous chef uniform, would remain on the kitchen's salad line only feet from the cellar door, ready to pounce at a moment's notice.

The peculiar sous chef kept his head down as Mr. Hall was escorted past him to the cellar door by a maître d'. Dressed in a crisp, black tuxedo, the mystery man entered the stairway and began his descent to the cellar.

The ominous sound of footsteps echoed down to Cam. The man was older, in his late seventies, Cam presumed. He stood roughly six feet tall with a full head of silver hair and cleanly shaven face. Once at the bottom, he and Cam locked eyes. A small grin appeared on the stranger's face as he examined his surroundings.

Cam didn't flinch. The soldier in him stood cold, gazing at the man who had the audacity to seek him out.

"Well-chosen location, Mr. Lyle," the visitor stated. It was the same soft British accent from that unexpected phone call.

Cameron didn't respond. Instead, he folded his arms across his broad chest as a show of authority. This mystery man, he told himself, had just made the biggest mistake of his life.

Mr. Hall took a few careful steps toward his host and calmly placed his hands in his pockets.

"Where shall we begin?" he politely asked.

"That's up to you," replied Cam, "but I promise this is going to end just as quickly as it began. We're not interested."

"Funny that you chose to meet me alone, Cameron. May I call you Cameron?"

"Don't call me shit."

"Spoken like a true American. I like that," the man confessed.

"I came alone because you don't scare me. And I'm not dragging my friends into whatever bullshit you're trying to sell us. Like I said, we're not interested. And now that I've got a good look at you, I think we're done here."

"Sit. The fuck. Down, Cameron," the man said in a surprisingly stern cadence.

Cam didn't budge, only narrowing his eyes at the dead man standing in front of him. With tensions already rising, he prepared himself for one of Trip's bullets to tear through the man's heart at any second. He smiled at the thought.

"Very well," the visitor said. "However, we are not done here. Quite the contrary, we are only beginning."

"Okay," Cam replied with a roll of his eyes. "Make it quick so I can tell you again that we're not interested. Where would *you* like to start?"

"I think honesty would be a good place. My name is not Mr. Hall, as I'm sure you've gathered."

"No kidding."

"And while I have no legal name, you may call me Rook."

"Okay, Rook, why did you contact me?"

"Well, first, I'll need an act of good faith from you. A small show of honesty, if you will."

"Sure, I'll play along," Cam said.

"I'd like to speak with all three of you—in a purely professional respect, of course."

"I told you I'm alone." Cam made sure not to show any physical tells of his lie—no twitches or wandering eyes. No increased pulse.

"Come now, Cameron. Let's start off on the right foot, shall we? Michael is upstairs preparing salads. Why don't you ask him to join us? And William," he called out. "You may come out as well. You'll want to hear what I have to say."

Cam shuddered in disbelief. *Who the hell is this guy?*

After a moment of consideration, Cam pressed into his hidden earpiece. "Foxtrot Two, come on down. You've been invited to the party."

"Roger that," Michael responded.

Trip emerged from behind the wine rack with his M4 shouldered and trained on Rook. He slithered from the shadows in his black cargo pants and black hoodie, pacing slowly from his hide into the open. His target seemed strangely unintimidated.

As Michael crept down the stairs with a pistol trained at Rook's back, Cam signaled for both of his teammates to lower their weapons.

The three huntsmen strategically surrounded Rook, closing in on him with tactical awareness. Rook remained at ease, with a sliver caution.

"Very impressive, gentlemen. Precisely why you were chosen," he softly granted them.

"Chosen for what?" asked Michael.

"As I told your brother, my name is Rook. I am a representative of the Knights of Medina. For more than eight hundred years, we have protected everyone from the Templars to the kings of Europe's greatest dynasties, to the brightest minds in the world and the most despised heretics in human history. We protect people, secrets and sometimes even objects."

"Great," scoffed Trip. "Another religious order with delusions of grandeur."

"Indeed," Rook replied with a tiny grin. "However, there is an artifact that was recently discovered by one of our Knights. And we'd like you to recover it."

"That doesn't make sense," said Cam. "If it was discovered by one of *your* people, why don't you just ask *him* for it?" He was pointing out the obvious.

"This particular Knight's sole mission in life was to locate this treasure on behalf of our organization. Unfortunately, he's been compromised and has decided to sell it to the highest bidder. As I'm sure you can imagine, we cannot allow that to happen."

With a calculated glance around the room, Rook slowly reached into his pocket and removed what appeared to be a piece of torn newspaper. He gently unfolded it and placed it on the table in front of Cam. Trip and Michael circled in and all three read the headline splashed across the top; *Research Continues Outside Puma Punku.* Below it was a black and white photo of several researchers standing in a deep hole on the side of a mountain in Bolivia. The caption read, *Dr. Diaz and his team inch closer to unearthing new information about the Incan Empire.*

A look of confusion eventually spread down their faces as Rook lingered at the table.

"I don't get it," Michael chided. "You could have picked anyone to steal back whatever this is. You must have mistaken us for Indiana Jones, pal. Why us?"

"We've been keeping an eye on you lads," explained Rook. "I chose you because you're the best at what you do. And I am certain the Knights of Medina can trust you."

Trip shook his head. "You chose us because you hope we're stupid enough to say yes. And you'll just kill us when this is over. That's what I'm certain of."

"You've seen too many Hollywood movies, William. I assure you; you will not be harmed. In fact, I plan on rewarding each of you handsomely."

"And if we don't?" Cam asked sharply.

"I'll make this easy," Rook continued. "I have a dossier in my office ready to be mailed to the FBI field office in Las Vegas, Nevada. Apparently, they are investigating an armed robbery at the Wynn casino. Let's just say that the dossier will blow their investigation wide open."

"Shoot him, Trip," Michael calmly instructed.

Without hesitation, Trip shouldered his M4 and stared down the barrel at Rook.

"If I don't make a call within the hour," the old Knight threatened, "that dossier immediately lands in a London mailbox destined for the FBI's Special Agent in Charge, Las Vegas Robbery Division."

"Blackmail," Cam quietly observed.

"Yes, make no mistake about it. This is blackmail," promised Rook. "However, my organization is willing to pay you fifteen million dollars in untraceable US currency. Half up front, the rest will be given to you upon the safe delivery of the target. Naturally, we'll supply unlimited resources to support your mission."

"And what's the target?" asked Michael.

"It is an ancient ossuary containing several artifacts. The contents of which are none of your concern and complete secrecy is for your own safety. If you don't know what's in the ossuary, you are not a threat to me or my brethren. Thus, we have no need to dispose of you."

"And if we open it?" Michael was gambling now.

"Don't," Rook coldly answered.

"This is ridiculous," Cam finally interrupted. "Maybe I'll just let my friend here put a bullet in your head. You can spend the night at the bottom of the river. Besides, intercepting a package from your London office before it gets to Vegas is child's play for guys like us. I believe you've overplayed your hand, Rook."

"And I believe you're bluffing, Mr. Lyle. Besides, the information can always be posted out again or even hand delivered to the agent in charge of this case."

Cam, Michael and Trip flashed stares of frustration between one another. With a quiet nod, Cam let them know this offer was indeed worth consideration. Fifteen million was a lot of money, and their attempts at intimidation were proving unsuccessful.

Understanding the silent agreement hanging in the air, Rook continued on: "The artifact is set to depart Arica, Peru, on a shipping freighter. Its destination is San Diego, California, where CIA officers will be awaiting its arrival. The asset, however, can never reach its destination."

"Whoa, whoa, whoa," complained Cam. "The Central Intelligence Agency?"

"Dr. Diaz has sold the artifact to the highest bidder. In reviewing the ship's manifest, a peculiar piece of cargo—our target—has been coded 'C-Level Juliett Six.' There will be eight, armed security contractors from Danika PMC aboard the ship. They're a private military group whose orders will undoubtedly be to protect the asset at all costs. You'll be outgunned eight to three."

"What the hell is C-Level Juliett Six?" asked Trip.

"It's an asset classification used by private security teams," Cam quickly answered. "Juliett means the asset is non-human. But more importantly, C-Level means the asset is the property of none other than the United States' Central Intelligence Agency. And Six is the value of the asset."

"On a scale of what?" questioned Trip with a hint of nervousness.

"Six."

"Perfect," mumbled the IT expert. "When does the freighter depart Peru?"

"Fourteen days," confirmed Rook. "I suggest you begin the planning phase immediately. As I've already stated, you have our complete support and we can supply any resources you need. Seven and a half million US dollars will be sent to you within twenty-four hours as a down payment."

"So that's it?" Cam barked. "An op like this will take months to prepare for. You're sending us on a suicide mission."

"Unfortunately, we don't have the luxury of time," Rook pointed out. "We chose you for a reason. I'll be in touch shortly to coordinate everything. A full target package is awaiting each of you at this very moment. Cameron, your package is in the bottom drawer of the workbench in your garage. Michael's is in the gun safe at his D.C. apartment. And William, your package is hidden behind a painting on the wall of your office in California. Not to worry, we locked the door behind ourselves. Gentlemen, I suggest you get started."

And with that, Rook turned and made his way to the stairs where he ascended into the restaurant and disappeared into the dark Washington night. The three men sat bewildered in the wine cellar, staring at the cold cement floor at their feet.

"To the next hunt," Cam quietly mumbled.

CHAPTER EIGHT

Special Agent Rand Kershaw already looked at all the possible options. He'd scanned, digested and devoured every shred of information on over a dozen high-profile robberies and heists from the previous calendar year. From his laptop just outside Las Vegas, he'd traveled the globe searching for crimes committed by three masked men—three ghosts.

It had been a week since Rand began fantasizing about possible links to the Hamilton hack. There was already an ongoing investigation being run out of the Department of Homeland Security, and the last thing he wanted to do was go waltzing in trying to convince upper-level DHS guys that a connection existed between their case and the Wynn robbery—a very *thin* connection. He'd be laughed out of the room.

Rand couldn't afford to take another hit. His career wouldn't survive it. For a fleeting second, he tinkered with the idea of going rogue. Maybe take a short leave; Brodsky would definitely go for it. The entire Las Vegas office would likely appreciate a break from his self-destruction. It would give him an opportunity to qualify his theory in the field—off the record—without anyone monitoring his movement. If he failed, no one would ever know.

Don't be stupid, Rand.

He leaned back in his chair and rolled his head toward a photo hanging across the hall. It was him, from earlier in his career. The photo had been ceremoniously hung in the hallway, lined with headshots of all the other agents who'd also been given the FBI Medal for Meritorious Achievement. He sighed heavily. The past seemed to weigh on him now.

The cluster of paperwork strewn across his desk seemed disorganized and random. But there was a method to his madness. The three documents in the center of his mess highlighted the few cases that he felt could be linked to his ghosts. And, as expected, the Hamilton hack rested firmly at the top of that pile. The rest of the paperwork lining the edges of his workspace were copies of donation receipts that had been tracked down from various charities around the globe—all with potential links to the cyberattack.

To his surprise, there were very few anonymous donations that exceeded $250,000—well short of the number he was searching for. His theory dictated that the donation would have to have been ninety percent of the total heist. The Hamilton hack resulted in a loss of six million—a lot of money, even for the world's largest entertainment corporation. Hamilton owned theme parks, movie studios and countless publishing entities. They were a household name.

According to his ninety percent rule, Rand was looking for an anonymous donation in the amount of almost five and a half million dollars—one that lined up in the months following the hack. The only problem was, it didn't exist. There was nothing remotely close to that number buried in the paperwork in front of him.

It seemed Rand Kershaw's biggest fear was becoming reality—that if the ghosts indeed committed a previous robbery and gave most of it to charity, they had broken it up and disseminated the funds to multiple humanitarian organizations, which would make it impossible for anyone to piece together. And if that's what happened, Rand's case was dead in its tracks.

The donation receipts he'd originally plucked were no more than dead ends; $150,000 anonymously given to the Wounded Warriors Foundation, $80,000 donated to the Red Cross for Louisiana Flood Relief, and dozens of other nameless donations that simply didn't fit his profile.

As Rand let his mind wander through chronological timelines and mathematical calculations, he zeroed in on a rather strange donation buried in the mess. One that he had immediately written off days before.

Four months after the Hamilton hack, one and a half million water filtration systems were shipped to an organization called Charity Water—a non-profit humanitarian effort to bring clean water to villages in Africa. It was yet another media feeding frenzy that Rand remembered seeing in the news. Much like the St. Jude mystery, the anonymous donors were championed as heroes by the press. To complicate matters, there had been no dollar value attached to the items. With none of the other receipts fitting into his formula, Rand allowed his mind to freelance.

He snatched up the donation document and read through the information. Hidden in the fine details, he located the name of the company that had manufactured the water systems—Nyofer Industries. He reached for his laptop and ran a search for the company. Within seconds, he was scouring their digital footprint.

After sifting through their website and a few related articles, Rand learned that the manufacturer was based in Burbank, California; it was the subsidiary of a large plastics company. So, he began his investigation of Nyofer Industries the same way he often began investigations—with a simple phone call.

•   •   •

Two hours later, Rand stood nervously outside Steve Brodsky's office. The door was closed, which probably meant Steve had drowned himself in vodka the night before and was sleeping through a painful day of nothingness.

Rand knocked anyway.

"Come on in."

He carefully opened the door and stepped into the office.

"Agent Kershaw, what's it going to be today?" Steve Brodsky was in the middle of doing absolutely nothing, just as Rand suspected.

"Sorry for the interruption, sir."

"Not at all. What's on your mind?" The words seemed to fight their way out of Brodsky's mouth.

"I've been checking into some other high-profile heists, as well as anonymous donations."

"Hold on, hold on," the boss interrupted. "Update me on the solar panel robbery in Furnace Creek first."

Rand was flustered by the request but quickly gathered his thoughts. "Ah, we traced the panels to a warehouse in Bakersfield, recovered by field agents," he replied, hurrying to get it over with. "Turned out to be a group of thugs from Fresno who were stupid enough to think they could unload government-issued solar panels on the black market. We also found the body of a plant employee buried in the desert half mile away, which was turned over to local homicide."

"I never saw the report," Brodsky pointed out. He was hammering Rand's armor for chinks.

"I—I submitted it last—" Rand was suddenly lost as to the location of the full report, attempting to visualize what he had done with it. "It must be on my desk," he finally confessed, clearly defeated.

Shit!

With a deep sigh, Brodsky reclined back in his chair, visibly unamused. "Alright, Rand. What the hell's going on with your Wynn case?"

Rand filled his lungs and began his pitch. "The Hamilton hack—"

Steve Brodsky raised his head in concern. "Tell me you're pulling my fuckin' dick, hombre."

"It happened roughly a year before Wynn," Rand continued. "372 days to be exact. I know it's not a strong-armed robbery, but it served the exact same purpose."

"And what's that?" entertained Brodsky.

"To steal from a large corporation and—" He was searching again.

"And what? Give it to the starving children of Biafra?"

"Actually, yes, something like that," confirmed Rand. "Remember the ten percent difference I had talked about? How the guys donate ninety percent and keep the rest for themselves?"

"Sure," Brodsky recalled.

"I just spent a week trolling through countless high-profile heists and donations." Rand's confidence was on the rise. "Six million is stolen from Hamilton, right? So, four months later, almost the exact time between the Wynn robbery and the St. Jude deal, an anonymous donation of one and a half million water filtration systems are delivered to villages in South Sudan, Ethiopia and the Congo by way of a sustainable water project called Charity Water. Sorry, Biafra was dissolved in the Seventies."

"So, what the hell's your point? Water filtration systems have to cost...what?" inquired Brodsky.

"I spoke with the CFO over the phone and asked him what he knew about the donation, which he says he's been asked a hundred times by every media outlet in the country. Of course, I put a little federal pressure on him and he says the order originated through a wholesaler. He invited me to swing by and dig through the database." Rand paused for a moment before answering Brodsky's original question. "Then I asked him what the per-unit cost of one and a half million systems would be at wholesale."

Steve Brodsky narrowed his eyes with anticipation.

"Three dollars and sixty cents per unit," stated Kershaw. "A grand total order of $5.4 million—*exactly* ninety percent of the total stolen from Hamilton Entertainment."

For the first time since either man could remember, Rand had captured Steve Brodsky's attention.

"That's pretty goddamn interesting, Rand."

"I thought so myself," added the agent, now feeling a dose of pride course through his veins.

The feeling would be short-lived.

"Keep digging," Brodsky grumbled. "You need to run this down and show me the same three assholes who stormed Wynn or you're back to square one. I'm glad your math is adding up, but you know the drill, march it backward until everything's connected."

"Yes, sir," agreed Rand. "I'm heading over to Burbank tomorrow to dig through the order information. That should lead to *something*."

"What's the name of the company again?" Brodsky asked.

"Nyofer Industries."

"Never heard of 'em. Touch base with me in the evening; let me know what you find. I'm sure Gayle can square you up on travel arrangements, stay as long as you need and don't come back until you've got something."

"You got it."

"And, Rand—"

"Yeah?"

"Good job."

CHAPTER NINE

Nyofer Industries, Burbank, California

Rand waited patiently in a large, sterile lobby. He was sure it was a power play. Every private sector executive he had ever met with seemed to enjoy making him wait. It was a show of strength to the federal agent that had come to shake them down.

Classic move, thought Rand.

After twenty minutes of sitting on a steel bench surrounded by spotless marble flooring and over-adequate natural light beaming in through wall-to-wall windows, Rand was finally greeted by CFO Timothy Battle.

"Agent Kershaw, my apologies for making you wait."

Sure you are. Rand stood to shake Mr. Battle's hand. The CFO was a tall, buttoned-up executive with a towering posture. His perfect brown hair was neatly combed back, not a follicle out of place. Battle's grip was firm and his eyes were intimidating. Clearly, the life of an upper-level plastics executive had treated him well.

"I appreciate you seeing me on short notice, Mr. Battle," Rand offered as they walked through the lobby corridor toward a set of elevators. "I'm sure you're quite busy so I'll try not to take up too much of your time."

"It's my pleasure, Agent Kershaw. More than happy to assist in any way I can."

The two exchanged more pleasantries and weather reports on the ride up to the eleventh floor, where they quickly got out and pushed through a set of broad infinity doors. Battle mumbled a passive greeting to the young, attractive receptionist at the front desk as they wove their way through the department, finally arriving at Timothy Battle's office.

The room was quite large. It offered a desk, a wet bar and what appeared to be an observation deck on the outside. Rand took his seat across from the CFO, who now sat smiling behind his German-engineered desk.

"So, you're looking for the man who ordered millions of dollars in water purification systems and anonymously donated them to Charity Water," opened Mr. Battle, framing his comment as a statement rather than a question.

"Correct," Rand coldly replied. He wanted to let his new friend do most of the up-front talking. It was a useful strategy that was meant to set the tone for the rest of the interview.

"Wonderful," Mr. Battle announced. "I took the liberty of getting my PA to pull all of the order information before your arrival, Agent Kershaw. I'm hoping it contains everything you need." Battle grabbed a folder from his desk drawer and handed it over to Rand. "I also have an electronic archive that I can access here on my computer. Again, anything to help the FBI."

"Sounds good," Rand said, as he began looking over the documents.

"I know I shouldn't ask," Battle continued, "but curiosity has gotten the better of me. We were more than happy to fulfill the order that was placed last spring. I later read in the paper that the units were given to Charity Water, a group supplying water solutions to East Africa. Needless to say, I was delighted. Yet, I find it a bit peculiar that the Federal Bureau of Investigation is interested in the donor."

"What's peculiar, Mr. Battle, is the notion that someone would spend over five million dollars on a goodwill effort and have absolutely no interest in the recognition that such a prestigious donation would bring."

Battle nodded his head in agreement as Rand continued scanning the order forms and various internal paperwork.

"So, this order was placed through one of your wholesale partners in Minnesota?" Rand asked.

"It was," Battle confirmed. "Twin Cities Water Solutions submitted the order directly with us. They're a large distributor for our northeast markets, but even they didn't have one and a half million units of inventory available. All of the filtration systems were shipped directly from our manufacturing facility in Santa Clarita."

"Shipped to where?" Rand pressed.

"By request of the buyer, the units were delivered directly to Charity Water's headquarters in New York City."

Rand flipped through a few pages of the folder until he came to the original order that had been submitted by Twin Cities Water Solutions. It stated that a deposit of three million dollars was made to the distributor, which was, in turn, sent to Nyofer to secure the order. And just below that, on the line for *Payment Method*, was a word Rand had hoped to avoid: *cash*.

"Three million in cash was laid down as a deposit? That seems strange," the agent inquired.

"*Very* strange, Agent Kershaw. As you may suspect, we never see cash payments made on this type of product. Or any of our products to be honest."

Rand continued delving into the file. In an effort to follow the money trail, he flipped to an accounting document, which revealed that the cash was placed into a secured account and cleared by the bank. The distributor received a seventeen percent commission on the order, which amounted to $918,000 that was taken from the original deposit. Rand also noticed that, when Nyofer Industries deposited the cash, it was quickly transferred overseas into a capital gains account, where it eventually garnered several thousand more dollars in interest before being reshuffled back into Nyofer's financial matrix. It suddenly dawned on Rand that Battle was nervous about the legalities of the money trail. *He thinks I'm here about the handling of funds!*

"Lots of cash flying around on this one, huh, Mr. Battle?" he finally pointed out, playing into the CFO's fears.

A fake, tight-lipped smile was all the agent got in return. Battle was well prepared for the conversation and had been advised by his legal department to deflect any questions regarding capital gains or money transfers. Clearly, he didn't want to go down that road with the FBI.

"Fine," Rand finally said, breaking the awkward silence. "I'm not here about any of that, Mr. Battle. I'm here because I have reason to believe that this order is tied to three men who have committed serious crimes. Make no mistake, regardless of our findings your money is secure, and from all indications Nyofer Industries simply and legally fulfilled an order that ultimately helped impoverished children around the world. However, my job is to identify the person or persons responsible for placing this order."

A sense of relief filled the large office. Battle's demeanor seemed to morph into a more relaxed, cooperative state. Exactly where Rand wanted him.

"That said," Rand continued, "I'll need to speak with the distributor."

"Absolutely." Battle was almost too eager to help now. He began typing into his keyboard and seconds later pulled up the profile for Twin Cities Water Solutions. "I can get them on the phone now if you'd like."

"Yes, that would be perfect."

Within minutes, Battle had the owner of Twin Cities Water Solutions on speaker phone. He introduced Special Agent Kershaw, then relayed the situation and how the distributor could be of help.

As it turns out, the owner of Twin Cities was a dedicated and helpful professional with a deep passion for distributing water solutions to developing countries across the globe. In fact, he had surrendered a bulk of his near million-dollar commission to a local organization that fought poverty in the Minneapolis area.

"Thank you for speaking to me, Mr. McCarthy," Rand began. "I just have a few questions about the order."

"Happy to help, agent," the man replied. "It didn't seem out of the ordinary at first. We work with a lot of anonymous philanthropists."

"I understand, sir. But, did the sheer volume of the order ever raise any red flags?"

"I guess," McCarthy confessed. "I mean, I was somewhat hesitant to put in the fulfillment at first. The guy called early on a Tuesday and demanded anonymity at every level. But I eventually just wrote it off as some eccentric billionaire who didn't want the publicity."

"Perfectly fine," Rand approved. "You did nothing wrong, I'm simply trying to connect some dots. But the deposit was made in cash. Did that not further your suspicions?"

The man hesitated again with remorse. "Special Agent Kershaw, you have to understand that this order was for millions of water systems going to a charity to support children living in the harshest conditions imaginable."

Rand felt like an asshole now. "Again, Mr. McCarthy, I completely understand. You did the right thing. But, do you have any other information regarding the payments?"

"The second and final payment was made via a bank transfer. I have the account number here in front of me."

"Could you read that off to me?" asked the agent.

Mr. McCarthy gave him the number and Rand jotted it down in a small notepad. Their call ended abruptly with Rand promising to be in touch if he had any more questions.

He left Burbank with a sense of accomplishment. Since day one, there had never been a solid lead of any kind in the Wynn case, and while it seemed a stretch to think that a donation of water purifiers was the result of a separate crime by the same criminals, it only stressed the importance of small details. He now had a casino robbery, two large donations and a potential connection to the Hamilton hack. Rand Kershaw could smell victory inching closer.

CHAPTER TEN

The timeline seemed painfully impossible.

The freighter would leave Peru in a week, embarking on an eleven-day voyage up the Pacific coast. The team's plan was to intercept the ship on the final day of its journey. This timeline, however, left just eighteen days until go-time.

Cam checked his digital wristwatch and picked up the pace. What started as a relaxing jog through the park turned out to be the exact opposite. His mind raced through the most minute of details. He'd learned early in his career as a soldier that success ultimately depended on preparedness and the ability to adapt. It was natural for him to overanalyze and dissect—to pick apart each piece of an operation beforehand. Every challenge, every solution, every possible outcome. And after an hour of spinning his wheels, the odds of success hadn't gotten any better.

As the former SEAL reached the trailhead, a blanket of clouds began to roll in. He walked to his truck and checked his pulse.

What the hell have we gotten ourselves into?

Cam sighed with frustration and fired up the engine. He threw it into gear and slowly pulled out of the lot, then drifted up the winding road toward Providence. It had been a long week and all Cam wanted to do was spend time with the girls. He couldn't get home fast enough.

The father of two arrived just in time for lunch with Hannah and the kids. Afterwards, he volunteered to take Abigail to her dance lesson, where he gossiped with other parents while she practiced her twirls. He loved every minute of it, embracing these menial moments that served as an escape from his stressful life. When Abigail was all danced out, he took her for ice cream, then back to the house where the family shared details about their day over pork chops and baked potatoes before retiring to the living room for a movie.

The last bursts of energy were spent devouring popcorn, and eventually, the girls began to fade. Cam and Hannah sat on the couch, their children entombed in pillows on the floor at their feet.

As an animated movie stretched into its final scene, Hannah sifted through some discovery documents from her case. She could sense Cam's meandering stares and silent requests for attention, which she was happy to satisfy.

"Everything alright?" she finally asked.

"I love you," he muttered.

"Well, I love you too. So, what's got you? I know that look."

"Just trying to work out a few details."

"You haven't told me about your trip yet. I assume you boys had fun."

"We always do," he smirked.

"Have you told them yet?"

"Told them what?"

"Cam, you know what I'm talking about," she pressed. "That this is your last hunt."

He hesitated with guilt. "No, not yet."

Hannah pursed her lips in disappointment. Their trust in each other was without measure and it was this unwavering transparency that sealed their relationship. She was aware of the hunts—she knew the when and why, but never the how or what. Staying out of the loop on details such as targets and tactical plans afforded her plausible deniability. It was a delicate dance between concerned wife and federal prosecutor.

"You haven't changed your mind, have you?" she challenged.

"No, honey. Not at all. This is the last one."

"I've been on board with this because I know what it means to you. I support you, Cam. But three short years has taken its toll. At some point, the statistics will catch up to you guys, you can't outrun the odds forever. And I need you here, not—" she darted a glance at the girls. "Not, *somewhere else.*"

"I know, Hannah," he stubbornly implored under his breath. "We've already talked about this."

"But I need you to really hear it. You've met your objective, soldier," she teased. "You've given more to this world than the rest of us could ever dream of. But you can't keep doing it at our expense."

He knew she was right. "Last one. Promise."

She leaned over her notepad and kissed his cheek. "Good. So, what's the charity?"

"I think we're doing this one a little different," he replied with a crooked smile. "High risk, high reward."

"Cameron!" she scolded.

"It's okay, just tricky." His smile was gone now. "But since it's our last, we're just splitting it three ways, each choosing how to give back. No mass team donation this time."

The look on her face didn't seem to agree with the words coming out of his mouth.

"But *my* charity of choice," he continued, "is going to be the one we start for us, for the girls."

As her mind quickly pieced together his insinuation, a proud grin sprouted across her face. Her arms found their way around his neck, embracing him with every ounce of her being.

Cam pulled back and stared deep into her eyes. "I want to build something that will always let us follow that dream. Only this way without all the...you know, stealing."

Her smooth giggle returned yet again, this time followed by a long, passionate kiss.

Moments later, Cam carried the sleeping children to their beds, one by one. He escorted Hannah to the master, where she quickly fell asleep while he was brushing his teeth. He smiled at her and crept beneath the covers.

Cam stared anxiously at the ceiling, his mind drifting to the mission and the impossible timeline. Eighteen days. He and Michael were handling all tactical and logistical elements such as location targeting and exfiltration plans. The intelligence gathering efforts, however, were being tackled by Trip, a guy whose ability to run rampant and unrestricted through the Internet was again proving to be valuable. And to fill in all the blanks, the Knights of Medina had been astonishingly capable of supplying mission-critical resources, no matter how random or unrealistic the request.

But there was still one element of the hunt that continued to chew away at Cam—the ossuary. And, unfortunately, this unsettling factor had not changed. He hated the idea of rolling the dice on a target that couldn't be valued—an artifact that didn't even exist in the eyes of scholars and historians. An artifact that was officially the property of the CIA.

For the first time since he could remember, Cam realized that the risk may very well outweigh the reward.

Chapter Eleven

The phone rang shortly after two in the morning. Still half-buzzed, Rand had only fallen asleep an hour earlier. He fumbled around before retrieving his cellphone from the nightstand. His eyes struggled to adjust, but finally allowed him to read the screen. It was Steve Brodsky.

"Steve? What's up?"

"Hey Rand, you know that intel APB you put out on three men conducting high-value robberies? We just got a hit."

Rand's eyes widened as the butterflies in his stomach churned uncontrollably.

"What kind of a hit?" He was sitting up now, his brow furrowed with intrigue.

"Analysts at Homeland intercepted some chatter from three Americans planning to hijack a freighter in open water. There was a chain of encrypted emails intercepted a week ago. It took the boys in Washington a while to decrypt the contents, but it could be your guys."

"When's it going down, do we know?" Rand excitedly asked.

"Now, actually. You need to pack for shitty weather. I want you there when the takedown happens. You'll have maybe a couple hours of interrogation before DHS totes these assholes back to American waters and their legal rights kick in."

"What do you mean American waters, shitty weather? Where am I going?" Rand asked, already pulling his pants on and using his toes to search for a pair of shoes on the messy closet floor.

"North Pacific. You're gonna catch a heli-ride with the Coast Guard from an air station in Los Angeles to the *USS Princeton*, a hundred miles out."

Rand peered down at his slacks and dress shoes—these weren't going to work.

"What's the shipment, Steve?"

"Call me on route and I'll brief you. But you're on a tight schedule so get the hell outta bed and get your ass to LA. I called in a favor to get you out there. Coast Guard is waiting. Don't fuck this up."

"Walking out the door now."

•   •   •

North Pacific Ocean, 89 nautical miles from the California coast
The sun crested above the horizon behind the MH-60 Jayhawk roaring through the air over the Pacific. Rand gazed out the side window of the Coast Guard helicopter at the passing ocean eighty feet below. He hoped the peaceful waters surrounding him were a sign of things to come. Perhaps this was the moment he'd remember when telling the story of how he'd captured his ghosts.

Minutes later, they were hovering above the *USS Princeton*, a guided missile cruiser with the Navy's Abraham Lincoln Battle Group, which had been patrolling nearby waters when Homeland Security put in a call for assistance.

Rand was ordered out of the bay door by a faceless officer as the co-pilot tossed a thick, black cord out of the helicopter. The agent hadn't fast-roped since the academy, something he'd been stressing over for most of the ride. Rand tightened his gloves, zipped up his breaker then grabbed the line and plummeted to the deck with a thud. He unclipped himself and shielded his face from the water tearing through the air from every direction as the helicopter lifted its thrust and sped away. He'd forgotten how calculated every action of the military was. *They never wasted time*, he recalled.

Meanwhile, nearly fifteen nautical miles from their starboard side, Homeland Security had already planted three operatives aboard the *Titan Missouri*, a US-flagged cargo ship steaming toward American waters. The previously intercepted emails had indicated she was the target of a small group of men intent on hijacking the ship, presumably to sell off the sensitive cargo to the highest bidder.

The DHS plan was to await word from their operatives aboard the *Titan Missouri* that the ship had been taken. From there, the missile cruiser would move in.

Rand struggled to maintain his footing as the waters became increasingly aggravated. A sailor quickly ushered him through a passage from the main deck and out of the cold, violent winds of the Pacific. He was led through a steel hallway and up a narrow staircase to another passage, then guided past the sonar room and into a makeshift command center buzzing with DHS analysts and Navy sailors. Rand removed his windbreaker and folded it in his hands.

"Special Agent Kershaw, my name's John Milliner with DHS, I'm in command of this operation." Milliner was a six-foot-three grinder with all the charisma of a high school football coach.

"Thanks for the invite," replied Rand, extending his arm for a handshake that was quickly returned.

"Your boys at the Bureau tell me these guys fit your profile. Kind of a big leap from casinos to cargo ships, don't ya think?"

"Sure." Rand didn't appreciate the subtle jab.

"Have a seat there," barked Milliner, pointing to a metal fold-down chair in the back of the room. "Our Hawkeye just spotted the pirates approaching in a fast-boat a mile out. I'll bring you with us when it's time to board the Titan Missouri. You get an hour, maybe two with 'em. That's it. Off the record."

Rand nodded and made his way to a tiny corner of the room. Several analysts were monitoring their laptop screens, which appeared to show body-camera footage of the DHS agents planted on the *Titan Missouri*.

Moments later, the clamoring voices and background chatter collectively stopped—a sure indication that things were about to get under way.

"Fast boat inbound." The word crackled over the radio from one of the undercovers on the nearby freighter. The fast boat was now closing in—right on schedule.

The next few seconds felt like minutes. Finally, another transmission. "We have contact. Three tangos now boarding."

Prior to the operation, the DHS operatives had prepared for a potential hostage situation by securing the real crew of the *Titan Missouri* in a cabin below deck. With two Navy SEAL snipers in position aboard the *USS Princeton*, any hostage situation would be quickly resolved. In the event that the captain of the *Missouri* or any of the undercover agents were put in danger, the SEALs had shoot-to-kill orders.

For the next three minutes, the only communication from the cargo ship was random, distant yelling and shaky footage from the operatives' body cams. The anticipation was eating Rand alive. *What the hell is going on?*

Finally, from the bridge above, the captain of the *USS Princeton* came over a closed radio frequency. "Python closing in, over."

Milliner took a few steps toward Rand, sensing the agent's anxiety. "We're about to take 'em down. Won't be long now," he yelled over the background noise.

The Navy cruiser sped toward the *Missouri* with purpose. After a daunting, seven-minute charge, Rand could now hear the loudspeakers from the outside deck instructing the pirates to put their weapons down and prepare to be boarded.

Milliner turned to Rand and waved his index finger, giving the sign for *one minute out*.

Seconds later, one of the undercovers gave an update over the radio. "Python, we've got two tangos surrendered on the deck and one still armed, approaching the bridge, over."

Milliner spoke to the snipers through his headset. "Cobra Team, do you have target locks?"

"Confirmed. Cobra Team has visual lock on all three targets," came the reply.

Milliner searched the room for the Naval lieutenant, who rushed to his side.

"Lieutenant, I need warning shots fired above the bridge of the *Titan Missouri*. How far are we?"

"Seven hundred meters and closing, sir," replied the lieutenant. "Shall I notify the captain?"

"Yes." Milliner was now monitoring the screens in front of him. "Guys, let's take this to the deck. I want live eyes on the situation."

With that, Milliner and three of his men gathered themselves at the exit of the command center to head for daylight. He waved for Rand to follow.

As they broke through the steel doors leading to the cruiser's deck, the giant hull of the *Titan Missouri* closed in on them. The deafening blasts of a 140mm broadside gun tore through the air. Rand shuddered as the rapid explosions echoed in his ears, yanking him into an unwelcome reality. He looked up just in time to see a half-dozen tracers scream through the air above the freighter's bridge.

Milliner stood firmly on the deck and pulled up his binoculars. The rounds had clearly startled the pirates, who were now yelling at each other in a collage of frightened expletives. Their heist had gone horribly wrong, and they were now at the mercy of a combat cruiser and all her battlements.

With a closer eye on the action, Milliner could see two hijackers on the *Titan Missouri*'s deck trying to convince a third to surrender. After another earth-shattering 140mm round ripped through the air above him, the third pirate dropped his assault rifle and raised his arms above his head.

"Cobra Team stand down," Milliner said into the small microphone attached to his shoulder.

He walked with the fearless stride of a battle-hardened general to the bow of the cruiser and posted up with his hands on his hips. He was George Washington crossing the Delaware.

The *USS Princeton* was now inching closer to the cargo ship, slowing its rudders to gently slide up to the freighter's port side. One of the DHS undercovers aboard the *Titan Missouri* tossed a netted ladder over the rail.

After an agonizing climb up the woven ladder, a tired Rand Kershaw finally put eyes on the three men he'd been chasing for so long—his three ghosts.

They had all been detained without further resistance and were now on their knees, lined up with their hands zip-tied behind their backs. Armed Naval personnel and a few DHS operatives circled the prisoners like vultures. Rand was fixated, he could barely restrain himself. He began a sudden lunge toward the detainees, but, before he could break into his first step, Milliner slid in and stopped the agent dead in his tracks.

"Not so fast, Kershaw. We've got protocol to follow. These are international waters and we need to do this right, you understand?"

Rand offered a hesitant confirmation.

"Give us forty minutes to photograph, fingerprint and clean up," Milliner said. "After that, you've got until we reach American waters."

Rand inhaled deeply and glanced across the deck at his prize.

CHAPTER TWELVE

Rand paced the deck of the *Titan Missouri* for a little over an hour, spitefully ignoring the high winds and crashing waves. His ghosts had been taken to the ship's galley where they were being put through DHS's documentation process and first passes at interrogation. The *Titan Missouri* was now moving toward the California coast at twenty-two knots by the escort of the *USS Princeton*. The hijackers would be held aboard the freighter until the ships reached American waters where they would officially be taken into custody by the US Navy.

With every passing moment, Rand's window of opportunity tightened. He couldn't possibly wait several weeks for the criminals to be pushed through the channels of the US justice system. He needed access to them now.

Milliner finally emerged from the galley and onto the deck.

"John!" Rand yelled through battering winds.

Milliner addressed Rand with a wave of his hand, squinting through the light rain. "They're all yours, agent."

Rand returned a nod and shielded his face from the wind. "Thank you, sir. Well done, by the way."

"Appreciate it. Listen, they're not talking. You've got maybe an hour. Give my best to Brodsky." Milliner walked away and disappeared through the rain.

Rand hurried across the deck to a narrow passageway leading into the ship. He marched up the hallway and barged through the second door on the right. The ocean-soaked agent pulled his rainproof hood down to his shoulders and scanned the room. Rand was now standing face-to-face with three men handcuffed to utility hooks mounted on the wall, their hands bound above their heads.

"You boys are a long way from home, don't ya think?" he began.

But there was no response—just defeated blank stares.

"Your prints are being run through DOD, DOS and nationwide law enforcement databases, as we speak. Hell, even Interpol is running you down. It's only a matter of time, so I really don't give a shit if you talk to me right now or not. We'll have *years* to get to know each other. You idiots just hijacked an American freighter and are about to spend the rest of your fucking lives getting your asses stretched out in a federal prison!"

Rand's tactics were by meticulous design: to storm in with authority, to dive into an introductory tirade, then observe the body language of his ghosts. The pirates were mid-thirties and in pretty good shape, he noted. After a moment, Rand profiled the three with uncanny accuracy. He knew who the leader was, which one had the brains, and which one was most likely a smartass. Rand had always been naturally intuitive to the human condition—a skill that came in handy as a federal agent.

"Let me guess," he pressed on, motioning to the guy with military tattoos spilling onto his biceps from beneath a black t-shirt. "You're the hotshot, right? The leader of this pathetic band of morons." He gazed into the man's eyes, waiting for the next tell. "You have military experience; it's literally written all over you. What about your girlfriends? You ladies former military, too?"

None of Rand's questions were meant to elicit an answer. They were meant to condition the captives. *I am in control.* That's all the prisoners needed to know.

"I'm curious as to what you boys have been up to over the years," Rand echoed through the galley. "Who's the hacker? You?" he pretended to guess, darting his eyes at the softer of the three men dangling from the wall.

The supposed hacker expelled a deep breath in boredom, followed by a roll of his green eyes.

"Here's the deal, DHS is gonna grind the shit out of you guys once you're on US soil." Rand looked down at his wristwatch for effect. "That starts in about an hour. Show me some fuckin' intelligence before that happens and we might be able to work something out."

"Work something out?" the leader finally asked. "You gonna pull your panties down for us or something?"

So much for that, thought Rand.

The quick wit wasn't lost on the guy's accomplices, who engaged in a bit of snickering.

Just then, a random DHS officer entered the galley and handed Rand a mobile tablet, which was quickly examined by the agent. It held the identities and profiles of the three ghosts on display in front of him, courtesy of the Department of State.

As he scanned through the files, Rand caught himself blinking excessively, revealing his confusion.

The three hijackers were former collegiate athletes, one of them a former Marine with combat experience. Rand swiped through the bios as a heavy, sinking rock plummeted to the bottom of his stomach. The other two men had done hard time at the Oregon State Penitentiary for armed robbery. The crime certainly fit the profile, but it was the timeline of incarceration that struck down upon Rand like a ten-pound hammer. The two convicts had been released a mere one to three months ago, respectively. Only one of the men had *not* been in prison at the time of the Wynn and Hamilton heists, as well as the donations.

Fuck!

His chances of success today were a long shot, but he'd convinced himself these were his guys. The deflated agent looked up at the blank faces staring back at him. They were no more than amateurs—former athletes and soldiers that had seen too many movies and met too many criminals.

"Goddammit!" he screamed, his outburst reverberating against the steel walls of the galley. "You two pricks were locked up in Oregon for the last five years?" he shouted.

The convicts hung their heads in disgust.

"Best of luck to you," the agent mumbled as he stormed back up to the deck.

He inhaled the salty air and stared angrily at the rolling sea below. Rand was faced with a startling realization.

His ghosts were still out there.

Chapter Thirteen

Archaeological discoveries at the Port of Arica in southern Peru suggested that the harbor had been inhabited and used as a maritime mecca since 8,000 BC. It was now a nondescript South American industrial port serving Peru, Bolivia and Chile.

Eleven days ago, the *Maersk Burgundy* had pulled out of port against the backdrop of a melting sun over the cliffs of El Morro at the southern end of Arica. Now moving up the Mexican Peninsula, the freighter barreled ahead at twenty-four knots, northbound through the Pacific to its destination—San Diego, California—a mere twenty miles away.

As the *Maersk Burgundy* plunged through six-foot swells, a Coast Guard Cutter sprinted toward it from a distance.

"Captain, we have a vessel approaching from the north at twenty-five knots. Radar signal indicates United States Coast Guard," the watch officer called out from across the bridge.

Seconds later, the captain received a crackling transmission from the approaching boat.

"Maersk Burgundy, this is United States Coast Guard Vessel UN17A. Do you copy?"

"Copy that, UN17A, this is Maersk Burgundy responding. Over."

"Top of the morning, Maersk Burgundy, we are on approach and request permission to board. Over."

The captain was taken aback. *Board for what?* he thought to himself.

"Copy, UN17A," he finally responded. "Do we have cause...or reason for that request? Over."

"Routine check, we've got suspicious activity in the area," the cold voice of the Coast Guard officer confirmed.

Irritated, the captain of the freighter sat idly in his bridge.

"No more than a formality," the Coast Guard officer added. "Title 14 United States Code, Section 89. Just doing our job. Over."

"Copy that," the captain replied.

Familiar with the maritime law which allowed the US Coast Guard to board any vessel without cause, he hastily switched the communications channel to *ALL*, then made an announcement to his crew over the loudspeaker.

"Prepare to be boarded. Clean deck, clean crew," he called into the microphone before hanging it up next to him. "Here we go," the aging sailor growled to himself.

Prior to departing Peru, the captain had gotten a gut feeling that this was never going to be a typical transport. His manifest included hundreds of perfectly normal cargo containers, but also listed several "priority" items. He'd been captain of the *Maersk Burgundy* for many years and understood the complex relationship that existed between the CIA and the Maersk Group—one that allowed the US intelligence agency to use the freighter for transporting sensitive materials through the shipping lanes of the Pacific.

The last thing he wanted was to get tangled up in the middle of an armed confrontation between a bunch of undisciplined thugs hired by the CIA and the Coast Guard's finest sailors. At this stage of his career, the captain wasn't cut out for it.

Moments later, the red-and-white military cutter approached the *Maersk Burgundy*, slicing through the mild waters of the open ocean. The captain watched intently from the safety of his bridge, perched eighty-five feet above the deck.

The cutter bore down its engines as it prepared to dock alongside the large freighter, which had been brought to a crawling four knots. A Maersk crewmember quickly lowered the hydraulic gangway on the portside to just above water level, allowing the USCG servicemen to easily board.

Armed with machine guns, three Coast Guard personnel made their way up the gangway and over the railing to the ship's deck. They were awkwardly greeted by five Danika PMC operators—also armed. Two of the Coast Guard soldiers instinctively raised their M4 rifles as the officer in charge stood between them.

"I am Petty Officer First Class McKenzie. Weapons on the ground, now. I will *not* ask you again," commanded the Coast Guard officer.

"Sir, we are private military contractors hired by the US—"

"Perhaps you were not briefed, son," interrupted McKenzie, "on maritime laws in US waters. Guns! Now!"

Cameron Lyle's face was stone cold beneath his Coast Guard issued blue ball cap. Michael stood at his side, staring down the barrel of a shiny new M4 rifle, as Cam dressed down the Danika PMC contractors.

The five mercenaries, wrapped in cargo pants, jackets and scarves, exchanged glances before slowly removing their rifles from their shoulders and placing them on the ground.

"Now let's see some identification and paperwork," Officer McKenzie barked.

As the five men began pulling their ID badges and other CIA-approved documents, Michael, Cam and Trip silently noted that three Danika PMC contractors were unaccounted for, surely lurking somewhere within the ship.

Containment of all eight contractors was mission-critical. And the clock was ticking.

"Call the rest of your unit to the deck," McKenzie ordered.

The obvious leader of the private security team—a tall, battle-hardened soldier with most of his facial features hidden beneath a thick beard—handed over a stack of folded papers and reached for his radio.

"All operators to the main deck. Over," he commanded.

"And while we're at it, have the captain bring all crewmembers up as well," Michael added.

The bearded contractor responded with a hesitant nod. "Captain," he said into his radio, "we'll need to get your crew on deck. Coast Guard needs to check all personnel, over."

"Roger that," the voice on the other end replied.

Cam was pleased with the cooperation. He took a moment to read through the government-issued documents as Michael and Trip fanned out and began patrolling the top deck, rifles still at the ready. Cam, meanwhile, was digging for specific paperwork—cargo descriptions, locations and names—any piece of intel would do. As he made his way through several pages, he noted something strange—the document listed eight assignments for Danika PMC members and one assignment for a CIA field operative. The words temporarily froze him. Their plan had not accounted for a CIA agent. He frantically turned the page, his mind trying to catch up to the reality at hand.

The three remaining Danika PMC operators made their way to the deck, where they were politely disarmed by Michael and Trip, then ushered across the ship to join their friends. Over the next couple of minutes, a dozen of the ship's crew also emerged, many of which now lingered on the deck smoking cigarettes.

"Alright, fellas, here's the deal," Cam screamed into the now gusting winds at the PMC soldiers gathered in front of him. "We have intelligence reports that there is an ongoing human trafficking operation aboard a freighter running this corridor." He waved up and down the ocean for effect. "This is a routine check, our third of the day to be exact. Obviously, you boys being here on the merit of the US government makes this a bit tricky, but just bear with us. We're going to run a quick sweep of the vessel and send you on your way. Understood?"

Disgruntled and frustrated, the Danika PMC team nodded their heads in agreement.

Beneath his gruff and confident exterior, Cam grew more concerned as the minutes passed. He had eight private soldiers contained, but, somewhere aboard the ship, a CIA operative was hiding in the shadows. After a long, deep breath, he decided to take a gamble.

"The CIA field agent from this order," he said firmly to the men, waving the document in the air. "I'd like to speak with him."

The PMC soldiers remained stone-faced. They didn't so much as blink. Finally, the bearded leader raised his eyebrows and simply shook his head.

"Officer Sheldon!" Cam finally yelled over his shoulder. "Go to the bridge and have the captain call for his CIA contact to join us on the deck. At the request of the United States Coast Guard."

"You got it, sir," Michael replied. He broke into a light jog toward the metal framing of the staircase leading to the bridge above.

The captain of the ship watched intently. "Great," he muttered to himself.

Meanwhile, Trip had already slipped below deck. After successfully gaining access to the interior of the ship, he was now creeping through the aft cargo corridor and making his way to the second platform beneath Hold #2—he and Michael's pre-determined rendezvous point. He could feel the pressure of time pounding against his chest. Every second had to be perfectly accounted for.

Still holding the Danika PMC team on the main deck, Cam knew Trip was potentially walking into a CIA trap that could turn this entire operation upside-down. Beneath a reserved face and nerves of steel, Cameron Lyle was sweating bullets.

After reaching the bridge, Michael stepped in and found the captain and the officer of the watch standing in confusion.

"Captain," he calmly announced, "my name is Petty Officer Brian Sheldon. Apologies for the inconvenience, but I have orders for you to contact your passenger from the Central Intelligence Agency. We didn't see him on your manifest, but the security documents issued by the US government list a single CIA field officer aboard this ship. We just need to get an official confirmation that your armed security contractors have the authority to be here."

The captain gazed stubbornly back at Michael. "Officer Sheldon, as the captain of this ship, I have the legal bandwidth to confirm all passengers, military and civilian, that are authorized to be on my ship. With all due respect, sir, check the vessel all you want. But, with the exception of myself, you have no authority to interview any other ship personnel without cause, not to mention a warrant."

The captain was right. Michael realized his overreach.

He shook it off and tried to stay in character. "I understand, captain, we just thought it would be helpful to qualify these guys from a direct source." Michael was backpedaling now.

"The CIA officer you're referring to never made the trip," confessed the captain. "That's why I left him off the final manifest. Last-minute reassignment or something. But I can tell you he's not aboard this freighter."

With a scowl, Michael accepted the captain's answer. He wanted to believe the man, but his instincts sensed a deviation from the plan—a plan they had spent weeks preparing. And it was driving him nuts.

"Thanks for your time, captain. Give us a few more minutes and we'll wrap it up," Michael said with resolve.

And with that, he exited the bridge.

"Jesus Christ!" he cursed to himself while hurrying down the metal staircase.

Michael hated surprises, and the more he spoke and interacted with crewmembers, the more likely he appeared to be full of shit. He needed to get off this ship as soon as possible.

Back in the bridge, the watch officer turned to his captain. "Well done, just sit here until they're gone," he commanded.

"What have you guys gotten me into this time?" the captain asked with a hint of disdain.

"None of your concern." The watch officer's eyes narrowed as he peered down at the deck below, and the Coast Guard officers threatening his operation.

CHAPTER FOURTEEN

Trip had made his way through Hold #2 and slipped through a door into Hold #3, continuing to move toward the middle of the ship. At the end of the corridor, he descended a ramp that reached the second platform holding area—his rendezvous point. Breathing heavily, he checked his watch and waited for Michael. Radio transmissions were out of the question, because good private military contractors, such as Danika PMC, were known to carry portable interception devices. The Huntsmen were determined to pull this off without leaving a trail of any kind—no radio comms, no material evidence and no fingerprints. This mission was to be a sterile and untraceable visit.

Trip knelt between two crates, patiently staring down the holding bay. A few seconds later, a figure appeared at the top of the long platform, thirty yards from his position. He raised his 9mm and held his breath, trying to focus on the shadowy target. It was Michael, dressed in his Coast Guard uniform with a rifle at his side. Relieved, Trip motioned to a large metal case in the back corner of the hold.

Without a word, the two crept up and began examining the giant steel framework. It had a digital locking system with a high-tech display screen.

Trip instinctively reached into the cargo pocket of his pants and pulled out a flat, handheld decryption device with wires dangling from its side. It was time for the genius to work his magic.

He connected the thin, flat tips of the wires to the appropriate ports located on the safe's display module. The row of lights on his handheld device flickered green for a moment before finally syncing up. Deep within the safe, Michael and Trip could hear the locks disengaging as they exchanged boyish grins.

The door sprung open. Inside they found a cargo crate with the letters "SDFO" spray-painted on the side—*San Diego Field Office.* Trip stepped into the vault and examined the green transport ticket that had been taped to the wooden crate. After confirming its data, he turned to Michael with a thumbs-up. They had located their target—exactly where Rook said it would be. It was now time to get their prize off the ship unnoticed.

The crate inside was heavy, but freighters like this held an endless supply of pulleys, hooks and, more importantly, cargo carts. Michael wheeled the nearest one over to the safe and the two men swiftly removed the crate and lunged it onto the escape vehicle. They rolled it twenty yards to the exit door and out onto an exterior platform that overlooked the ocean from the back of the ship.

While Michael and Trip began pushing the heavy box onto the platform, Cam nervously waited above deck. At some point, he knew, the Danika PMC soldiers would get nervous about their cargo. The mercenaries' obvious orders were to shoot and kill anyone attempting to steal it. Coupled with the potential of an unaccounted-for CIA agent, Cam took little comfort in their current situation. With every passing second, their success rate plummeted.

Below deck, Michael and Trip stood on the back platform of the ship, carefully wrapping their target with large straps, which were then attached to the steel loading hook above their heads. Once it was secured, Michael reached over and activated a cargo winch that gently lifted the crate from the small platform deck. The violent waters of the Pacific raged beneath them. Their hearts pounded with adrenaline.

Finally, Trip and Michael shoved the crate out over the ocean and away from the platform. From a small control module, they lowered it down to the crashing waters below, halting it a mere three feet above the billowing swells.

As their target dangled safely from the back side of the *Maersk Burgundy*, Michael and Trip sprinted back through the interior cargo holds and up to the deck of the ship.

After six minutes—the longest six minutes of Cam's life—Michael appeared in the distance, briskly walking between stacks of containers across the main deck. When his brother approached, Cam threw his right hand in the air and waved it in a swirling motion, the international sign for *let's get the hell out of here.*

Trip emerged seconds later and made his way across the deck toward the gangway.

"Ship's clear, sir," he called out to Cam.

Officer McKenzie grinned through the bill of his cap, then turned to the Danika PMC soldiers and handed their credentials back.

"Sorry for the delay, boys. I appreciate your cooperation," he said. "We'll have a report of our engagement submitted to the base and available for your superiors by tomorrow morning. You guys are all set. Have a safe ride to San Diego."

He turned and made his way back to the gangway to join Michael and Trip.

Still aboard the Coast Guard cutter below was one of Rook's operators, on loan from the Knights of Medina. He waited anxiously at the helm before finally catching a glimpse of the Huntsmen, descending the gangway. They hurried aboard the cutter and the engines began grinding into reverse. There was one last maneuver to pull off before this phase of the mission was complete.

"Back platform," Cam whispered to the captain.

By now, the Danika PMC guys had gathered at the edge of the ship and peered down at the Coast Guard boat as it backed away from the *Maersk Burgundy*'s hull.

Something was off.

"Morris, Glendale—check our cargo immediately," the bearded leader ordered over his shoulder.

Two men—Morris and Glendale—grabbed their assault rifles and ran across the deck to a metal door that led to the large holds in the belly of the ship. Meanwhile, the Coast Guard cutter slowly pulled around to the back of the freighter and out of site.

It was a race now. Cam could hear the engines of the *Maersk Burgundy* as they began roaring to life. Their window was quickly closing. The team had anticipated that once they disembarked the freighter, it would only take a trained soldier thirty seconds to run from the deck to the cargo hold and confirm that the asset was gone.

That was their window—thirty seconds.

To Cam's relief, the cutter pulled around the portside corner of the ship and began maneuvering itself toward their target, still dangling against the hull. Cam looked at his watch. *Twenty seconds.*

As the cutter moved into position, Trip reached out to get a hand on it. Michael and Cam jumped in to help as the Knight gently guided the cutter in reverse. They frantically unharnessed the crate and pulled it onto the small deck, where it landed with a thud.

"Go! Go! Go!" Cam yelled as the boat bore down into the rolling ocean, leaving a trail of sea foam in its wake.

Below the deck of the freighter, Morris and Glendale arrived at a large metal safe in the second platform hold.

"It's gone," Morris announced into his shoulder mic.

From the bridge, the watch officer listened to the transmission with exasperation and fury. He removed his officer's cap and placed it on the control dash, then stood up and glared at the Coast Guard cutter pulling away from behind the ship.

"The goddamn comms are out!" the captain suddenly complained. "I think they're scrambling our transmissions, and they've turned off their GPS transmitter. I can't even track them."

The watch officer didn't react. He cut his gaze through the window at Cameron Lyle as the cutter broke free and bounced away from the *Maersk Burgundy.* For a fleeting moment of intensity, the two men locked eyes.

The Huntsmen were now putting as much of the Pacific between themselves and the freighter as possible. As the sun reflected over miles of rolling ocean beside him, Cam focused on the crate that now sat at his feet. He clung to a metal rail as they rushed through choppy waters, wondering what the hell he had just risked his life for.

Back on the *Maersk Burgundy*, the captain was visibly shaken, standing dumbfounded in the bridge. He felt like he had missed something—something very bad that had just occurred under his watch, but he wasn't exactly sure what.

"Shouldn't you call somebody?" he eventually asked.

"They're blocking our satellite communications with a scrambling device," the watch officer calmly stated. "And if it's long-range, they can shut us down for up to thirty miles. By then they'll be long gone."

The watch officer unbuttoned his white jacket and removed it, exposing a beige t-shirt and a sidearm. He reached for the handheld mic that was channeled for the ship's loudspeakers—his only line of on-site communication.

"Quentin, report to the bridge," he said in a firm, authoritative tone.

The Danika PMC team leader hurried from the deck to the bridge, where the officer waited impatiently.

"We have just been robbed by the United States Coast Guard. I'll be initiating the Octagon Protocol as soon as our comms are back."

"Roger that, sir. I'll inform my men."

While he didn't know the exact details, Quentin knew the *Octagon Protocol* meant his team was being deactivated, and that this operation was now solely in the hands of the CIA.

CHAPTER FIFTEEN

Cameron Lyle glanced down at his USCG-issued wristwatch as the cutter began closing in on the Coronado Islands. It had been exactly ten minutes since they pulled away from the *Maersk Burgundy* and the team's success was dependent on the preciseness of timing. They had disarmed the freighter's satellite communications with a sophisticated scrambler—personally chosen by Trip for its ability to scramble from long range. And, so far, it was working.

But, as the *Maersk Burgundy* sped toward San Diego, the giant freighter would eventually escape the range of Trip's device. They had calculated that timeframe to be twenty-three minutes.

Thirteen of those now remained.

And as soon as the freighter's comms returned, a distress call would be sent out to the CIA and it wouldn't take long for fast boats and helicopters to descend on the Pacific in search of the pirates.

The Coast Guard cutter pulled into a small bay on the northern tip of North Coronado Island. It was a deserted, tropical oasis carefully chosen due to its proximity to their point of intercept. Given the direction they had sped away in, it wouldn't take long for authorities to determine their destination. It was imperative for them to stay ahead of any search efforts.

The engines shut down and the cutter drifted in the direction of an old, dilapidated dock. The guys shed their uniforms, gathered their packs and hustled to the portside. With an outstretched arm, Cam grabbed hold of the old weathered post.

"Let's move!" he yelled, leaping onto the dock.

Cam tied off the boat as the crate was lifted to the edge of the cutter, over the railing and onto the dock. Michael and Trip quickly disembarked and huddled around the large box.

With the help of their hired Knight, the crate was again hoisted into the air and moved from the dock to dry land. There, at the end of the wood platform, was a black, four-wheel ATV with a small trailer locked into the back hitch.

The guys maneuvered the crate onto the trailer and strapped it in. With their prize now secured, Cam jumped on the ATV and tore off down a narrow trail into the nearby jungle. Hidden in the tree line up the beach were two more ATVs. Trip and Michael sprinted over and jumped onto the Yamaha Raptors that had been planted days before.

Prior to speeding off, Trip shot a quick smile to the nameless Knight who'd driven the cutter. He received a humble nod in return as the mysterious operative pulled a denim jacket over his back and jogged into the trees. Half a mile away, a twenty-two-foot yacht awaited him.

Trip and Michael bolted into the tree line and caught up with Cam. The three now sped through the jungle toward their next rendezvous point. The ATVs broke single file through a seam in the trees and emptied into a clearing. It had now been seventeen minutes since they left the *Maersk Burgundy*, and an estimated six minutes remained until the CIA's air and sea cavalry would launch a manhunt. Six short minutes until the hunters became the hunted.

There in the clearing, rotating violently above the jungle floor, were the long, outstretched rotors of an unmarked Huey UH-1. The helicopter was yet another layer of exfiltration that the team had meticulously prepared and organized.

Cam wasted no time pulling his ATV—with trailer in tow—next to the waiting helicopter in the middle of forest clearing. The team jumped off their vehicles and lifted the crate onto the open cargo deck of the chopper.

Cam stepped to the skid and jumped into the cargo bay, then turned and reached for his comrades, pulling them aboard one by one. Within seconds, the Huey raised off the ground and into the air, turning briskly to the east as it accelerated over the treetops.

"Four minutes!" Michael announced over the blasting rotors of the UH-1. He rolled his neck backward and smiled. "Four fuckin' minutes!"

Through aching muscles and adrenaline-filled eyes, a series of victorious grins spread across the men's faces. With the Huey now darting across the water toward Puerto Nuevo, Mexico—their final destination of the day—the bay erupted with cheers and high fives.

"Holy shit!" Cam finally said with a chuckle.

There was a release that suddenly tore through his veins. It was the feeling he lived for—the feeling he needed.

Minutes later, after passing over the Mexican coastline, the Huey touched down in the back field of a small farm beyond the hills of Puerto Nuevo and unloaded the three men and their cargo. The helicopter and its pilot shot upward and disappeared into the clouds.

CHAPTER SIXTEEN

Rook waited patiently in the cool night air blowing over his balcony. His withered hands danced along the thick, cement rail. He knew the mission was under way, and that shortly he would receive word that the ossuary was safely in the hands of his American counterparts. It couldn't come soon enough.

The lights of Bruges decorated the cityscape before him. Rook's tuxedo had been slowly broken down, he now stood with his shirt unbuttoned and a bow tie hanging from his collar.

It occurred to him that the Scotch was wearing off.

Just then, a servant appeared with a satellite phone, carefully placed on a silver serving tray. Rook was traditional in that way—the servants, the silver trays, the white gloves, the whole bit.

He grabbed the phone and waved off the help. "Yes?"

"The asset is secure, sir. We'll be coordinating the handoff shortly."

Rook hung up the phone without replying. His gaze once again turned to the welcoming lights of Bruges. With a devious smile, he poured a glass and raised it to the skyline. The Scotch had never tasted so good.

•   •   •

The Knights of Medina were originally founded in a subterranean cave system beneath Hyères, France, in 1292 AD. Within deep caverns, guided by wooden torches, a group of engineers, soldiers and academics came together and dedicated their lives to preserving the human knowledge that had been lost from the Ancient Library at Alexandria. The cultural archive had been destroyed little by little over the previous millennia: drowned by the Persians, buried by the Arabs and burned by the Romans. By the time the Knights of Medina were born, little, if any, of the original texts remained.

If any group had invested themselves more into archiving, documenting and searching for the lost scrolls of the most technologically advanced civilization to ever walk the earth, it was the Knights of Medina.

Over the centuries, the order blossomed, as did their archive of teachings and philosophies. By 1495, the Knights' membership had grown to thousands—national dignitaries, statesmen, judges, astrologers, warriors and philosophers. In 1496, King Charles VIII of France hired the Knights of Medina—by Royal Appointment—to secure the Crown of Thorns worn by Jesus Christ.

The Knights succeeded in their objective and were paid handsomely in return. Their prominence swelled over the next two hundred years. The brotherhood was not just tasked with protecting the lost knowledge of Alexandria, but also hunted down ancient technologies that would eventually lead to some of the greatest discoveries in modern times. The irony, the Knights understood, was that each discovery—from the harnessing of energy to human flight—had been realized by civilizations thousands of years prior.

Today, the Knights consisted mostly of fringe scientists, astrophysicists and billionaire philanthropists. While their existence was rarely recognized, the mystery surrounding them had been debated by historians and conspiracy theorists for centuries.

Rook, after a lifetime of service, often questioned the amount of power and influence his knighthood still held. He'd reached the highest rank possible for someone not born into the order, and as a result his life had become a clouded memory, blurred by time and space.

He entered the sitting room from the balcony and slowly pulled the bowtie from his collar. Rook sat down and lost himself in a red leather chair. Relaxed, he allowed the weight of the ossuary to lift from his shoulders.

The old man would sleep well tonight, knowing that his prize would never make it to San Diego, and that it now rested in a Mexican safe house under the protection of three American cowboys. His trophy may have been thousands of miles away, but tonight it felt so much closer.

CHAPTER SEVENTEEN

Puerto Nuevo, Baja California, Mexico

It was just before dawn, and with the exception of some short-lived naps, no one slept during the night. Trip sat quietly, hovering over his laptop, which had been linked to the Internet through a Chinese satellite passing overhead. The location of the drop was to be established through a random online chatroom within hours of the heist.

Trip scrolled down the page through layers of random posts. He continued scrolling until something finally caught his attention.

Hatshepsut_1507. It was Rook's handle.

Trip knew exactly what to look for—numbers. He examined the post, which was timestamped twenty-three minutes ago.

Hatshepsut_1507: 0401230146110915

It was simple really. Trip was looking for coordinates and a meet time. The message was an order of numbers: the location coordinates in reverse followed by a timestamp. He quickly noted that the meet time—the last four digits of the code—was 9:15 AM, a mere three hours away.

Cam entered the small, wood-paneled room, just as Trip punched the coordinates into a satellite map on his screen. He quickly zoomed in on a small town forty miles away. *San Jose de la Zorra.*

"Looks like we're headed inland, for the hills," Cam observed, pointing to the rendezvous point, then back to their current location. "If this is our SP, we need to leave in an hour."

"The ossuary?" Trip asked.

"Let's get it out of the crate before we load it up. It's too bulky packed up like that, we need to be as nimble as possible."

"Roger that."

Trip holstered a 9mm into his black fatigues as Cam slipped out of the room and into the main quarters of the small, damp *palapa*, where he found Michael ducked beneath a window, scanning their surroundings through the night vision scope of his rifle.

"Hey bro, three hours," Cam whispered. "Sixty clicks out, small town called San Jose de la Zorra. We hit the road at oh-seven-hundred."

Michael checked his watch and responded with a thumbs-up. Cam pushed through an exit and marched briskly around the thatched hut to the outbuilding behind it. There, he pulled back a dirty tarp to reveal a baby blue, rusted-out, 1964 Chevy C10 with bald, whitewall tires. The pickup truck had to have a million miles on it, he thought.

Inside the house, Michael and Trip began the process of breaking down the crate. Once finished, they buried the planks beneath the dirt outside. The ossuary, however, was carried to the old Chevy as the sun rose above the hills to the east.

"Is she running?" Michael asked his brother.

"She is!" Cam shouted from behind the steering wheel.

With a turn of the key and a press of the pedal, the old truck growled to life.

Michael and Trip wrapped the limestone ossuary within a tarp and strapped it to the truck bed. Satisfied, they went back inside to search for hats and jackets—anything to hide their black fatigues and gringo faces.

Cam quickly donned a brown leather jacket and beige gaucho hat. He checked his weapons and stood by the door. As Trip and his brother looked on, they noted how ridiculous he looked, and feared for their own mischievous costumes. Michael dug through a small closet, producing a similar coat and large-brimmed hat that hid his face. He then tossed Trip a colorful poncho.

After a thorough check of their GPS coordinates, the aging Chevy rumbled its way off the property and south onto the coastal roadway known as México 1D. With a cloud of orange dust in their wake, the Huntsmen were on the home stretch.

A thirty-minute drive took them to the small village of Primo Tapia. Trip huddled up in the truck bed, his back against the cab with his knees folded up to his chest. A submachine gun rested in his carriage, hidden by the green and blue wool poncho. He bowed his face beneath a large straw hat. It quickly dawned on him why Rook had chosen broad daylight for the handoff; the small towns and villages between point A and B were buzzing with similar pickup trucks, each loaded down with some sort of large cargo or equipment, and most carrying a passenger or two in the truck bed. They blended in perfectly.

The pickup darted through town, the dirt road pulling them deeper into the Baja Peninsula. From the passenger seat, Cam held out five fingers as Michael pushed the Chevy into its final climb up the mountain range west of San Jose de la Zorra. The metallic clicks of gun safeties disengaging and rounds being chambered put a sudden exclamation point on the moment.

There was no specific landmark or road name that had been transmitted to them—just coordinates, which the Chevy was now approaching as it struggled up steep hurdles and deep potholes that had been left over from the rainy season. Trip bounced around in the back, prepping himself for what lay ahead. Now out of sight from the main village below, he stood up and removed his hat to scan the passing mountain terrain.

Cam finally signaled Michael to stop the truck. The forest around them glistened in the sunlight as a soft rain began to fall.

The truck pulled off the trail beneath a canopy of a banana palms as Trip took up position in the back, resting his short-barrel submachine gun on the roof of the cab. He peered with focused intent into the deep thick of the mountainside terrain, searching for any movement.

Cam exited the passenger side and stepped out onto the soft ground. He removed his costume jacket, then grabbed a green Kevlar vest and pulled it over his head, strapping it around his chest. Michael and Trip followed his lead and slipped into their armor.

"This is it," Cam confirmed.

"We're five minutes early," Michael noted from the other side of the truck. He shouldered his M4 rifle and squinted down the scope into the weaving mountain trail they had just climbed. All was quiet.

"I feel exposed out here," complained Cam. "Trip, how you feelin'?"

"I'm good," Trip replied from the top of the truck, still scanning the jungle around them.

Cam's only weapon was a 9mm pistol holstered on his right thigh. His job was to run point, with Michael and Trip acting as security. They were meeting with Rook's gang, the Knights of Medina who, so far, had treated them well. But nonetheless, this was the handoff of a priceless artifact to an organization that had promised them millions of dollars. It was a volatile moment that could easily go sideways. The guys had prepared for all possibilities, good and bad.

A black Range Rover finally appeared over the horizon in front of them, only thirty yards up the trail. With a sense of relief, Michael and Trip lowered their rifles and Cam made his way to the front of the pickup truck. The ossuary, however, sat undisturbed beneath a dirty tarp in the back of the old Chevy.

Two large, muscle-bound men emerged from the front of the Range Rover, both clad in combat boots, cargo pants and baseball caps. M16 machine guns hung from their shoulders. The rear doors swung open next and two more men exited the SUV. It was clear now who the leader of Rook's team was—a slender middle-aged man in khakis and a white, button-down dress shirt. His shoes seemed overly expensive for a trip to the jungle.

He approached Cam in the middle of the wet, soupy trail.

"Cameron Lyle?" he asked.

Cam nodded.

"I believe you have something for us."

"I need confirmation of payment," Cam sternly requested.

Michael stood beside the truck, protecting their cargo and locking eyes with one of the meatheads across the road. Trip remained hovering above the cab, his eyes fixated on the tree line to his right. The mountain was surreal and for a brief moment he reveled in its pristine beauty.

One of the Medina thugs marched onto the trail with a digital tablet and handed it to his boss. The man in the white shirt swiped the screen and spun the tablet to Cam, confirming the final payment had been made.

Cam turned to his brother and motioned to the ossuary. Michael retreated to the truck bed and pulled the wooden gate from its slots, tossing it to the side of the road. As Trip was about to step down and help unload, he caught a sudden movement in the forest. Then a sharp noise.

"Close in. Now," he calmly called out.

Michael backpedaled to the front of the truck with his M4 raised and ready.

The Medina strongmen, clearly spooked, began pacing backward toward their vehicle. Just as Cam reached for his 9mm, shots rang out from the perimeter. All hell broke loose as everyone scattered for cover.

"Ambush!" Michael yelled from the side of the truck.

He quickly returned fire into the tree line and shielded himself behind the truck, where several rounds pinged off the side of the old Chevy.

Cam dove beneath the vehicle and blindly returned fire into the jungle. His pistol seemed overwhelmed by the opposing automatics. There was an extra M4 hidden behind the driver's seat, but he couldn't risk making a move for it. Up the trail, he could see Rook's team return fire into the green canopies to the south.

And just as quickly as the attack began, it all stopped. The guys held their fire and caught their breath. Their focused remained on the endless mirage of green in front of them. An enemy was only yards away.

"Anyone hit?" Cam yelled from beneath the truck.

"I'm good," Michael shouted.

Trip echoed the response.

Then, without warning, the opposite tree line exploded with gunfire. Their attackers had them in a deadly crossfire. The entire mountain raged with the sound of battle. Michael, completely exposed now, rolled to his left and dashed around the truck to the other side, where Trip was unloading his APC-9 in a sweeping barrage of laser-focused return fire.

Cam, pinned down under the pickup, shifted his eyes up the road and saw all four of the Knights lying dead in the road.

The incoming fire continued without mercy. Just then, Michael made a fast break from behind the truck to the base of a thick tree across the road. He was doing exactly what his brother had trained him to do—advance on his enemy.

"Michael, get back here!" Cam yelled from beneath the pickup.

The younger brother continued to make small advancements into the trees—inch by inch, yard by yard, under heavy fire. He could hear the high-pitch whistle of rounds slipping past him.

Cam rolled out from under the truck and jumped to his feet. He raised his 9mm over the hood and tried to place strategic shots into the thick mosaic that hid the small army.

"We gotta go, Cam!" Trip yelled from the rear of the truck. "Michael!"

It was pure chaos.

Michael Lyle peered back at his team. He was now elevated on an embankment above the road, crouching wild-eyed behind a tree. With a thumbs-up, he laid down one last blanket of gunfire into the forest. He was fighting brilliantly but couldn't tell if the enemy was being eliminated or simply moving quickly from position to position. He had no idea how many there were. *Maybe ten, twenty, thirty?*

The attack had begun from one side of the road and then switched to the other. Cam, Michael and Trip appeared to be surrounded.

Somewhere out there, Cam knew, in addition to the army attacking from the north, was a death squad lying in wait down the trail. *Surely, our escape route's been cut off,* he thought.

Michael continued squeezing the trigger until he ran out of ammo. From the cover of a tree, he slung the M4 over his shoulder and anxiously bounced from his knees as he zeroed in on the pickup truck, now riddled with bullet holes, behind him.

Cam sensed his brother's next move. He ducked his head and reached for the driver-side door handle. Pulling it open, Cam grabbed the hidden M4 from behind the seat and smoothly pulled it to his shoulder. The hardened soldier, now properly armed, stepped out in front of the truck and released a crushing wave of gunfire into the jungle.

Aided by Cam's momentary rain of cover, Michael sprang to his feet and sprinted through the leaves. As he closed in on the truck, he dove into the bed, slamming his back against the base of the ossuary. It knocked the wind out of him, but he was alive.

Cam was now fully exposed in the road and continued to exchange fire with the tree line. As he bore down the barrel of the rifle, he could see glimpses of men in camouflage. It was his first visual contact. He noted their textbook movements; these were pros. The soldier kept his aim five feet above the jungle floor to ensure kill shots. Then, in a sharp flash, he was slammed to the ground. It felt like a sledgehammer had swung into his chest. The former SEAL couldn't breathe, or move.

"Cam!" Trip yelled from nearby. "Cameron's hit!"

Michael, still laying against the metal bed, scurried his way around the ossuary to the backside of the truck, where he slithered out onto the muddy trail. He ran to the front of the truck, where Cam lay in the road only feet away.

"I need cover!" he yelled to Trip, who quickly responded with a litany of .45 caliber rounds.

Mud spit up around Cam as bullets burrowed themselves into the nearby ground. Michael grabbed his brother's collar and pulled all 225 pounds of him to the safety of the Chevy.

Cam forced himself into a sitting position against the wheel and yanked the vest from his stomach. No blood. He grabbed the Kevlar and noticed a bullet fragment embedded in the front, still smoking.

"You okay?" Michael yelled above the sound of continuous gunfire.

"Yeah. Yeah. Let's go." Cam was fighting for a breath, unable to find it.

"Trip! Let's do this!" Michael yelled over his shoulder. "Trip!" he screamed again.

"I'm okay," he finally shouted back. Trip was leaning up against the back bumper, holding his neck.

Michael peeled off and joined his teammate. He quickly noticed the blood escaping between Trip's fingers.

"You hit?"

"Just a graze." The hacker pulled his hand away and revealed a deep gash across the side of his neck.

Cam was now on his feet, slightly crouching for cover. He checked the clip of his M4 and chambered another round. He realized now that the Chevy had been murdered. There must've been three dozen rounds buried in the engine. It was clear they wouldn't be getting off the mountain the same way they arrived. Cam glanced up the road and set his sights on the Range Rover.

The gunfire paused—an unexpected break in the fight.

"You and Trip stay here," commanded Cam. "I'm going for the Range Rover. When I get down here, jump in and we're gone. Got it?"

"The ossuary!" Michael blurted.

"Fuck the ossuary! Are you good?"

Michael replied with a steely nod. *We're good.*

Cam found a deep breath and prepared for a long sprint to the Range Rover. Michael laid down another barrage of cover fire, allowing his brother to break for the open trail. The small army responded with a fury of their own. As bullets chased Cam up the road, he came to a sudden halt, the mud in front of him exploded angrily. His eyes widened with the familiar fear of death.

Down the trail, Trip mustered everything he had and rose to his feet. He lifted his machine gun and marched unafraid onto the dirt road, flashing a hail of rounds into the trees. He paced further toward his enemy.

Under the protection of Trip's assault, Cam surged onward up the trail. He jumped in the Range Rover and threw it in drive, his foot dropping on the gas pedal as the SUV fishtailed through a flurry of bullets, finally coming to a slide in front of the old Chevy. He stared out at the insanity around him as rounds shattered against the glass windows. *They're bulletproof,* he thought with a grin.

"Trip, let's go!" Michael yelled.

No response.

"Trip!"

Nothing. Michael peered over the hood and saw Trip stretched out in the mud. He catapulted around the truck and dropped to his knees, then began a quick check of his teammate. As more gunfire pounded their position, he grabbed Trip's arm and yanked the limp body up and around his shoulder, then dumped him into the back seat of the waiting Range Rover.

Michael hurried back to the ossuary and lifted it from the pickup to the SUV and dropped in into the back hatch. He leapt into the Range Rover as Cam hit the gas. They sped down the trail with adrenaline coursing through their bodies, the ping of bullets ricocheting off the back window. Seconds later, the Range Rover turned a corner and disappeared into the thick forest.

"Is he okay?" Cam yelled over his shoulder.

"I don't know," his brother quietly replied, wrestling to get a look.

"Is he okay?"

"I said I don't know!"

Michael rolled Trip onto his back as the Range Rover careened around another sharp corner. The SUV raced downhill through the slippery trail, rallying to get as far away from the ambush as possible. Blood ran from Trip's nostrils and mouth, all the way down to his neck. His teeth were stained in it.

"Trip, stay with me," Michael begged.

"I can't feel my legs," Trip finally replied, struggling to speak.

"You're gonna be okay."

"Tell Elena I'm sorry," he attempted through labored breaths.

"You can tell her yourself." Michael ripped the poncho and Kevlar vest off his friend, then tore through the black shirt.

Blood sprang up from two holes in Trip's neck. Putting pressure on the carotid artery, Michael reached for the other side with his left hand. There was an exit hole and a light pulse.

"I need you to relax your breathing, buddy. We're gonna get you to a hospital."

Trip stared blankly into the air, surrendering to the pain. "I wanna go home."

Michael gripped his friend's hand tightly. "Cam, What do I do? I don't know what to do!" he cried.

"You know what to do, Michael. Put pressure on the wound."

"I'm trying...it's...it's too much. We need to help him!"

"He's dying," Cam whispered from the front.

Then, following a few painful seconds, Trip's pulse stopped. Michael sat in a state of momentary shock—numb to the reality around him.

"He's dead. Trip's dead," he coldly announced.

Cam clenched his teeth and closed his eyes tightly. With a heavy sigh, he worked the steering wheel through the winding turns and rugged terrain of the trail.

Michael forced himself back into combat mode. He gathered a couple rifles from the floorboard and began reloading them with fresh clips. He placed the poncho over Trip's face and climbed over the back seat to get into shooting position.

Cam blazed the Range Rover down the mountain with ferocity. There were no words to utter, no emotions to feel. The mission was still in progress and they couldn't afford to be distracted from their objective—surviving San Jose de la Zorra.

CHAPTER EIGHTEEN

The Range Rover slowed to a crawl. The gunfire had stopped and they were now a mile from the ambush site.

"The first strike team," Cam said with a heavy breath. "They hit us from the south, then disappeared when the second team attacked from the north. Those were two different teams."

"Yeah," Michael agreed. "So where are they now?"

Cam tried to think, searching for a logical answer that would give him insight into his enemy's next move.

"The first team that hit us from the south, they've slid down the mountain to cut off our escape route. This trail is the only way out."

"Great, so we're driving into a trap," Michael replied.

Cam peered over his shoulder at the poncho laid across Trip's face. In the heat of battle, there hadn't been time to take it all in—to wrap his mind around the fact that his friend had just been killed. He'd been trained to dig in and keep fighting, to turn everything else off. For the sake of the mission.

But that moment had passed. Post-traumatic stress now coursed through his veins.

This isn't happening.

He brought the SUV to a stop in the middle of the narrow road. Tree limbs and vines hung over the trail ahead of them. To his left was a small creek running along the road. It was only a foot deep, littered with river rocks and debris. Cam slowly crept the Range Rover off the trail and down a small ditch into the creek. The tires climbed each rock as it made its way through the shallow water.

"That first attack team is down the trail somewhere," Cam repeated. "Looks like this creek veers off, maybe it'll take us to the bottom of the mountain unnoticed."

"Who the hell were those guys?" his brother asked.

"I have no idea."

"Rook's guys are dead. Trip's dead. And all we have to show for it is some goddamn ancient box. We don't even know what it is!" Michael was losing it now.

"Keep it together," snapped Cam. "We still got work to do."

"Oh, Jesus Christ, Trip," Michael said through a deep exhale. "I'm so sorry. I'm so sorry." He placed his hand on the poncho over his friend's face and began to cry.

"C'mon, Michael. Stay with me. Don't lose your shit, man."

The SUV steamed through the creek bed, sliding further and further down the mountain, and more importantly, away from the main trail. Soon, they were completely engulfed by thick, lush forest.

A few miles away, at the trailhead of the mountain, a heavily-armed platoon waited patiently for their prey. The crackle of a radio brought the strike force to life.

"Alpha Two, they should be to you by now. What's your status?" a voice snapped through the handheld radio in one of the soldiers' hand.

"I got nothing," the man replied.

CIA Agent Brent Carson stood further north, at the top of the mountain in front of a shot-up Chevy pickup. He tightened his jaw in frustration and raised the radio back to his mouth.

"We're about to work our way down the trail, they should've reached you by now. Get your team back into the village and secure all exit routes out of town. We're hunting a black Range Rover and they're being slowed down with a dead body. The two survivors are *not* to exfil with our asset, do you understand?"

"Copy that," Alpha Two called back into the radio.

Few at the CIA knew Carson's real identity. It was buried deep within the archives of the Black Budget Committee. He'd seen every corner of the world through a thirty-five-year service to his country. Carson had helped overthrow governments, pioneered countless paramilitary ops, and tortured and killed jihadists, diplomats and foreign spies. He began his CIA career on the battlefields of Afghanistan during the Soviet invasion, helping the Mujahedeen covertly move Stinger missiles through the country. And after all that, he'd failed to move one little box from Peru to San Diego.

The three cowboys were proving to be more skilled than he'd given them credit for. Their evasion here today warranted respect, even from a polished veteran like Carson.

He stood in the road and peered through his deep brown eyes at the footprints next to the Chevy C10. The ground was riddled with shell casings. The smell of gunpowder and gasoline hung in the air. With the sweltering sun high above him, Carson reached down at the fresh blood dripping from the bumper of the pickup truck. He rubbed it between his fingers and smelled the iron within its cells. He noticed a dark puddle in the dirt at his feet and a trail of blood that led through the muddy terrain to the point where Trip's body had been pulled into the Range Rover.

"Get a sample of this," he said, gesturing to the bloody steel bumper of the C10.

One of his operatives immediately produced a small plastic bag and a cotton swab to gather a blood sample. Carson walked to the middle of the road and glared down the trail into the wilderness. *I'm going to take pleasure in hunting these animals*, he thought.

•　　　•　　　•

The sun was now directly over them. It had taken nearly an hour to inch their way down the mountain creek. The black Range Rover, now covered in mud and dust, came to a stop just before a small, wooden bridge that crossed the water. The density of the trees ended just ahead and in the clearing, Cam could make out a small farm surrounded by a picket fence.

"Stay here," he insisted as he cut the engine.

"We need to get Trip out of the car," Michael said.

"We'll take care of him. I promise," Cam assured as he got out and snuck forward through the shrubbery, methodically making his way toward the tree line.

He retrieved a scope from his thigh pocket and slowly panned across the property—into the windows of a small, ill-conceived farmhouse sixty yards away. The place was abandoned. Considering the amount of traffic in the main village earlier that day, Cam suspected the owners had gone into town for supplies. He turned back to the SUV and motioned to his brother with two fingers.

Michael exited the Range Rover and pulled Trip's body from the seat. He threw his friend over his shoulder and maneuvered his way to Cam. The brothers continued down the dense tree line and into the open meadow. Once they reached the farmhouse, Cam entered first and began a room-to-room check.

"Clear!" he yelled moments later from the back of the farmhouse.

Michael barged in and laid Trip's body down on the kitchen table. The men pulled off their gear. The metallic clanking of guns, ammunition, scopes and knives slammed against the counters, echoing through the house. While being placed on the table, Trip's face had been slightly exposed. Bloodied, dirty and bruised, he looked like most KIAs Cam had seen on the battlefield.

"How the fuck did this happen?" Michael asked.

"I have no idea," admitted Cam. "They either traced us from North Coronado or we were sold out."

"Sold out by who?"

"I don't know, maybe the old spooky bastard who *wasn't* here today," Cam implied.

"Rook! You think Rook double-crossed us?"

Cam thought through the logistics of a double-cross. "Probably not," he determined. "I don't think he'd just kill his own guys like that. All four of those Knights are dead."

"Then who, Cam?"

"I said I don't fucking know!" the older brother yelled. "We *did* steal this thing from the CIA, remember?" Cam took a sharp breath and ran his hands over the back of his head. "We went too far this time."

"You think?" Michael snapped back sarcastically. "Our best friend is lying dead on a table in the middle of nowhere!"

"He's not the first."

"No! You're right, he's not! But this whole thing was for a cause. We don't do this shit to get killed. We do it for—"

"I know *exactly* why we do this, Michael!" Cam fired back. "Don't ever think you have to remind me! But we all knew the risks involved, now get it together!"

"Fine, but what are going to do with him? We can't drag his body back to the states."

"Trip is coming home with us," Cam firmly stated. "We don't leave our brothers behind. End of story."

"How the fuck are we going to get him back across the border unnoticed? Are you out of your mind?"

Cam lunged at his brother and gripped his collar with intensity. "This kid has no family, Michael! We're all he had, and we're *not* leaving him here!"

The two brothers exchanged dead stares before Cam finally let go and backed away. A long silence filled the room, tensions ran high.

"We're only thirty miles from the US border," Cam finally pointed out. "We'll bury Trip once we cross. I can get somebody out here to pick us up."

"How long?"

"Three, four hours, tops. But we need to put the call in."

"It's Mexico," Michael reminded him. "Landlines everywhere."

"Sounds about right. You need to dump the Range Rover outside of town. I'll meet you back here in two hours and we'll hike Trip's body and the ossuary to our extraction point and wait for our ride."

"And who's our ride?"

"An old friend—a contractor taking time off in LA. I'm sure he can exfil us before sundown."

"Can we trust him?" Michael asked.

"We don't have a choice."

CHAPTER NINETEEN

Carson sat idly in the back of a nondescript, gray van parked outside the only bank within eighty miles. The van served as his mobile communications post and was equipped with radio systems, a satellite feed and four monitors. On his left-most screen, Carson stared at grainy, hours-old satellite footage of the Range Rover descending the mountain, escaping his team's chokehold.

Three and a half minutes into the footage, the SUV drifted off the trail and disappeared beneath a canopy of trees. Carson pulled a printed map from the floor and quickly identified the small creek that ran along the road. His finger traced it all the way to the base of the mountain.

A voice ripped over the radio: "Alpha One, this is Alpha Two. We just found the Range Rover abandoned on a bluff just west of town. Over."

Carson reached for his handheld radio. "Copy that. Any sign of the asset?"

"Negative, sir."

Carson closed his eyes, searching for serenity. "Burn the vehicle. And get the drones airborne. Run alternating sweeps up Route 3. They've slipped through the net, they're running."

"Roger that. Alpha Two out."

An old delivery van rumbled across the hilltop and eventually came to a grinding halt at a run-down vegetable stand, just north of San Jose de la Zorra. The sun was now setting over the Baja Peninsula. The driver leaned over the steering wheel and squinted into its glare. There was no sign of life for miles.

A quick check over his shoulder revealed a small outcropping of trees, nestled like an island in the barren wasteland of the Sierra de Juárez foothills. The stout American gently pulled the box truck off the dirt road and around the vegetable stand. It came to a stop near a small patch of pine trees.

Hours earlier, Cam had made his way to the village to call for help while Michael ditched the Range Rover. They met back at the farmhouse and, in separate treks, hiked both Michael's body and the ossuary more than three miles each way to their current position—a total of thirteen miles on foot through the rugged landscape of northern Mexico.

Cam's distress call had gone out to Brad Mitchell, a former SEAL who served with him in Afghanistan. The two had been in bar brawls, combat patrols and firefights together. A trusted friend was coming to the aid of his former teammate.

As the truck came to a stop, the tall, muscle-bound soldier lunged out onto the dusty terrain. Cam emerged from the brush to greet him.

"This your idea of fun?" Brad Mitchell quipped, hoping to lighten the mood.

It didn't work.

Cam waved him back to their hide, revealing what was clearly a body draped in burlap. Brad's heart sank.

"Jesus, Cam," he whispered. "What the hell happened?"

"We need to get him in the truck and roll outta here," Cam replied.

Together, the three of them hoisted Trip's body from the ground to the bay of the delivery van. They went back for the ossuary and secured it next to the body. Michael climbed into the passenger side as Cam checked his pistol and crouched in the back next to their cargo.

The engine started with a jolt and the old truck careened around the vegetable stand back onto the dirt road. They wove through the mountains to Route 3, then fled north.

Following a short ride, the delivery truck arrived at a border crossing just outside Tecate, Mexico.

The vehicle gently rolled up to the gatehouse, its headlights illuminating the dusty night air that hovered over the ground. A Mexican border agent held out his hand, signaling the truck to halt. With a machine gun hanging from his shoulder, the guard approached.

Brad struggled to roll down the window and greeted the soldier. "Hola, amigo." His Spanish was excellent for a Gringo.

"A dondé vas?" the guard sharply asked.

Brad handed him a fake passport. "Phoenix," he replied.

The border agent examined it closely. "Que hay en el camión?"

"Nada," replied Brad. "Equipo."

"You are American?" the agent finally asked.

"Sí. I had a delivery in Tecate. My paperwork was checked on my way in."

The border agent seemed agitated now. He motioned to the back of the truck. "Abre la puerta," he demanded.

Brad reluctantly stepped out and led the agent to the rear of the van. He peered over his shoulder, scanning the area with concern. There were four more guards gathered in the next gatehouse over. If things went sideways, the team would be outgunned.

Hearing the footsteps approach the back door, Cam braced for the worst. He tucked himself against the back wall with his pistol at the ready. The door latches began to shudder. He trained his weapon and released a long, calming breath.

Brad fumbled with the lock as the border agent impatiently crossed his arms. The doors finally unlocked and slung open with dramatic flair.

"See? Tools," muttered Brad.

The border agent narrowed his eyes and stared deeply at the contents of the metal shelving within the bay. Hidden behind it in the shadows, Cam gripped his pistol with bated breath.

The border agent's flashlight danced throughout the cargo hold until the crackle of a radio broke his attention. The agent snatched a small device clipped to his shoulder and began arguing with another agent in Spanish.

He quickly motioned for Brad to close the truck, then waved him through the checkpoint.

Brad shut the bay doors and meandered back to the driver's seat, offering a casual wave to the border agent.

Pushing the truck through the checkpoint and past the gate, he exhaled into the windshield and exchanged looks of relief with Michael. When Brad Mitchell got up that morning, he never thought he'd be smuggling two soldiers and a dead body through the Mexican border.

The rusted blue truck continued north on Highway 88, then west on 94 until they reached the small town of Dulzura, California. Brad pulled the tank-like vehicle into the garage of an abandoned body shop on the outskirts of town and killed the lights. The garage had been secured ahead of the mission, a safety net in the event something like this happened.

Michael jumped out and pulled down the large garage door, then helped Brad remove the faux shelving from the back of the truck and unloaded the ossuary.

"Who is he?" Brad finally asked, gazing at the mysterious body wrapped in burlap. The soldier knew better than to ask questions, but he had just taken a huge risk to help the Lyles escape Mexico.

"It's Mark Montgomery's little brother," Cam confessed.

Brad Mitchell threw his hands atop his head. "You gotta be kidding me."

"I wish I was," replied Cam. "We can't thank you enough, Brad."

"No worries, man. Glad I was close by."

The two came together for a quick hug and pats on the back.

"I was never here," Brad requested. "Be safe and get your ass home."

He slipped out a back door where his black Camaro awaited. The hotrod fired up with a sharp roar and sped out of the drive.

"So, what now?" Michael asked.

"We need to bury Trip."

"Where?"

"Mount Laguna. It's only an hour north of here."

Michael took pause. "That's where he proposed to Elena."

"I know. He loved it there. He and Mark used to hike that range when they were kids."

"And then what?"

"One problem at a time, bro. We bury Trip and then solve our next problem, and then the next."

A black Chevy Suburban sat in the mechanic's area beyond the old delivery truck. In the backseat was a neatly folded body bag, which Cam retrieved and carefully laid out next to his fallen comrade. They took time to clean Trip's face and wipe the blood from his body before transferring him into the bag, then loaded it into the Suburban behind the back seat.

The brothers changed into street clothes and now found themselves staring at the old ossuary. It was taunting them. They'd nearly lost their lives for it. Trip was dead because of it. Yet here it sat.

After a moment of deliberation, Cam looked around the garage and zeroed in on a crow bar strewn nearby.

"Fuck it," he said as he grasped it into his clutches and raised it above his head.

Michael watched as his brother swung with rage and struck the ossuary on its side. Then again. After another big swing, the ancient box crumbled into a dozen pieces.

Satisfied, Cam dropped the crow bar at his feet. It clanked eerily against the cement floor as he and Michael gazed in bewilderment at the mess in front of them.

"We deserve to know," Cam stated.

"What the hell is all that?"

"Whatever it is, it's not worth Trip's life."

Cam fell to his knees and examined the pile of dusty limestone shards and other random debris. He ran his hands through the rubble and began pulling items out for a closer look. His first grab was a dark stone slab decorated with strange hieroglyphs. He reached for another—a small brick of polymer-like material. Cam then wiped away the dust covering a third item—a ten-inch long piece of...*machined steel?* He grabbed it with his right hand and pulled it from the pile.

"Is that metal?" Michael asked.

"It's not just metal, it's...it's electronic...I think." Cam was stuttering in bewilderment.

"That's not right, Cam. This ossuary is supposed to be over a thousand years old. It looks like a damn lightsaber."

Cam blew the dust from the metallic wand, which indeed looked just like the handle of a Star Wars lightsaber. It revealed what appeared to be a button, along with various wires and circuitry. This wasn't some relic, it had been manufactured. It had been engineered.

As the Lyle brothers meticulously examined the device, their focus was cut short by a low hum in the distance.

"You hear that?" asked Michael.

"Yeah," Cam replied, darting his eyes to the ceiling above. "Helo. Kill that flashlight."

The guys marched through the darkness to a nearby window. The sound was getting closer now.

"Feds?"

"Probably," Cam confirmed. "They're likely to circle in eight-kilo loops, intervals of ten minutes."

"Where's that leave us?"

"In a hurry." Cam finally got a visual on the lights of a helicopter circling the night sky above. "They should finish this vector and keep moving east in a few. We'll probably have a five-minute window before another one shows up."

He grabbed a backpack from the Suburban, and then knelt down and began stuffing the artifacts in one by one. He picked up the lightsaber last, gave it a final look of disdain and slipped it in with the other items.

Cam slung the bag into the backseat and lifted the adjacent bay door. Moments later, as the large SUV crawled out of the body shop and into the shadows of southern California, Michael and Cam peered through the windshield at the black abyss overhead. The helicopter had moved on.

CHAPTER TWENTY

Mount Laguna, Southern California

The Suburban sped up the winding asphalt of Sunrise Highway. It was nearly two o'clock in the morning and fatigue was starting to set in.

Cam pushed the SUV up another hill, climbing to the summit of a sprawling peak. He pulled the vehicle over and sat solemnly behind the wheel.

Michael fidgeted in the passenger seat, nervous that someone would spot them. He was frustrated that his brother was willing to take such chances on the heels of what had just happened. He felt vulnerable.

"There's a trailhead a few miles north," Cam pointed out. "But everything along this ridge is completely untouched. We'll carry him past those cliffs, down into the valley a bit and find a spot."

Michael stared out into the vastness. The barren mountains were illuminated in the night by a waning moon. It was beautiful. He remembered hearing Trip talk about the area as if it were the most gorgeous place on earth.

They exited the Suburban, armed with a couple folding shovels, and lifted the body bag from the back. Together, Michael and Cam ventured beyond a series of bluffs and hiked down into the shallow valley, carrying the body of their closest friend.

They reached a small nook, hidden from the moonlight in the shadows of a cliff, and began digging. It was a scenic location, surely more enhanced during the daylight hours, thought Cam.

As the last throws of dirt were strewn across the grave, Cam sat on the ground and crossed his arms over his knees. He was tired and afraid—two things he could never reveal to his younger brother.

"Let's gather some rocks, build a headstone," he finally huffed.

With Michael's help, he stacked a series of hand-sized boulders at the head of the burial plot. Cam reached into his pocket and pulled out a large coin, and got lost in its inscription. A black rubber stamp covered one side, with an image of a skull and the words *Sons of Odin* inscribed on it. He leaned over and gently placed it on the mound of rocks.

"What's that?" his brother asked.

"It's a challenge coin...from a joint operation in Afghanistan. We took a lot of knocks during that deployment."

Michael knew he was talking about Mark and the operation that took his life. He found it fitting that Cam would lay it entombed with Trip, a man with no family left, who lost his own life the same way his brother had—fighting at Cam's side.

"I know we have to leave," Michael whispered. "But, do you want to say something?"

Cam listened closely to the insects, to the wind and the silence around them. Everything seemed surreal, like a strange dream. He struggled to find the words fitting of the moment.

"In this life," he slowly began. "We're faced with countless..." he searched. "Countless challenges, and decisions. Victories, losses...and sacrifices." Cam's eyes began to well.

"You don't have to do this," Michael begged. He'd never seen his brother shed a single tear.

Cam waved him off and found his voice. "Trip, you were the smartest, most stubborn... sonofabitch I ever met. You embodied everything that makes a *good* man. I know you wanted to get out of this, I *know* you did...but, I didn't listen and I'm sorry."

Cam fell to his knees and continued to weep, collapsing under a wave of guilt. "You fought hard, my friend, and I'll never forget it. We're gonna find out who did this to you, I promise."

He placed his hand on the rocks and closed his eyes.

Michael wiped the tears that now covered his own face and joined his brother on the ground. He placed a hand on Cam's shoulder, the other against the burial mound.

"I'll miss you, Trip. You deserve better than this, but you're home now...with your family."

•   •   •

The two eventually rose to their feet and marched back up the ridge through the darkness to the waiting Suburban. They drove out of Mount Laguna in a crushing silence and raced eastbound through the night and into the next afternoon, stopping only for food and gas.

Closing in on their destination, the Suburban barreled north up Interstate 25 and crossed the Colorado state line.

Cam's thoughts were now on his children. He thought of the beauty that captured their youth, the whimsical innocence with which they saw the world. He wanted to be a part of their lives forever, to sit in pride at their graduations and to walk them down the aisle. It all suddenly seemed at risk.

CHAPTER TWENTY-ONE

Hannah Lyle whisked herself out of the courtroom and into the atrium of the Federal Courthouse in Providence, Rhode Island, with a rushed sense of determination. She had been juggling her case and her home life for days while Cam was away under the charade of hosting field training sessions at Naval Station Mayport. But today he was coming home. Hannah was exhausted and couldn't wait to get some much-needed parental reinforcement.

On her way down to the parking deck to the car, her cellphone rang. It was a number she didn't recognize.

"Hello?" she answered.

"Honey, it's me."

"Cam! How are you, babe? Did you beat me home?"

"No," he hesitated. "I need you to listen to me, Hannah."

There was something in his voice that stopped her in her tracks. "What's the matter, Cam?"

"I'm okay, but...the uh...the training didn't go so well." He took a long pause, searching for his words. "The, ah...the weather—"

"Cameron?" She was suddenly worried.

"The weather in Florida is unseasonably warm. We had to clear off the base."

His wife quickly pulled her fears together and put on her game face. Cam was speaking in code, which meant something was seriously wrong. She and the girls were in danger.

"Honey, do you understand?" he finally asked, desperately seeking confirmation.

Hannah peered over both shoulders and broke into a fast walk toward her car. "I understand," she said, trying to sound strong.

"I love you, baby. It's gonna be alright, I promise."

Hannah managed a cautious smile as she unlocked the Audi and tossed her purse over to the passenger seat. "Copy that, soldier."

With that, she hung up and drove home to relieve the sitter and get Abigail and Lindsay packed for a road trip. On several prior occasions, Hannah had been given strict and detailed orders by her husband, but had lived in hope she would never actually have to execute them. It was the moment she had prayed would never come.

•   •   •

Cam placed the phone back on its jack and stepped out of the booth. The storms had calmed, but the humidity was rising. He lunged into the Suburban and leaned his head back against the seat. He was clearly wrestling with his thoughts.

"Everything alright?" Michael asked.

"Yep." Cam stared blankly at the long dirt road ahead of them.

The power lines ran all the way to the horizon and melted into the hot reflection of the sun.

"You think they've made us yet?"

"Who?" asked Cam.

"Who do you *think*?" his brother snapped. "The small army that ambushed us in Mexico. They have to know who we are by now."

Cam shook his head. "I don't know. There's a good chance they got pictures of us prior to the attack. If they're intelligence guys, they see everything." He sighed with frustration. "Christ, I don't even know where they would have picked up our scent in the first place."

"I'm telling you," Michael started in. "We were out clean. Everything was clean until we hit the rendezvous point—until we met up with Rook's guys. Maybe they were the ones being tracked and we just got caught in the crossfire."

"Who knows. *Someone* brought those thugs to the party: if it wasn't Rook's guys then it was us," Cam guessed.

"No fuckin' way! If they got a lock on us, they would have cut us down in Puerto Nuevo when they had the chance. You're the tactical genius, so tell me...if they tracked *us*, why would they wait until we drove all the way to the top of that mountain? They had a million other chances to take us out and grab the ossuary."

"I dunno," Cam replied with hesitation. "Maybe they wanted to see who we were handing it off to. Ambush us all at the drop. Two rocks, one stone."

"I'm not buying it," Michael argued. "Either this whole thing was a setup or there's a mole in Rook's little clan."

"That's another possibility," Cam agreed. "But the obvious answer is the CIA."

"So, what now?"

"At some point, we need to make contact with Rook. We'll lay low for a couple days and figure out what the hell we've stolen. And why we were paid fifteen million dollars to steal it."

Cam was frustrated. He'd broken the first rule of combat—never underestimate your enemy. It cost Trip his life, and it now threatened the well-being of his wife and children. Cam knew it was only a matter of time before the CIA traced everything back to them. And when they did, the rules would drastically change.

Defeat began to rear its head. He was now up against the largest intelligence agency on the face of the planet.

CHAPTER TWENTY-TWO

Rand stared into a large mirror beyond the bar at the defeated face looking back and judging him. He had just made a spectacle of himself in front of the Coast Guard, Homeland Security and the FBI. The last thing he wanted to do was attend tonight's event—the annual Federal Law Enforcement & Intelligence Gala. If not for Brodsky's threat to end the agent's career early, Rand would be sleeping off a drunken stupor on his couch right now.

Yet here he sat, tired and unhinged, slouched at the open bar of Bellagio's Grand Ballroom as a private party danced around him.

"Another round, sir?" the young male bartender in a black vest asked him. "I don't think I got your name?" he kindly continued with an outstretched hand.

Rand took a moment to stare awkwardly through the man. With a frustrated exhale, he simply pushed his now empty highball to the bartender and spun his stool to view the unfolding circus around him.

As the live orchestra began their set, a familiar face slid up to the bar. Rand Kershaw had known Melissa Dagan for years. She'd been his first partner—a mentor who'd shown him the ropes during his early days at the Bureau.

Each year since, they enjoyed a brief drink together at the annual gala. They had grown close in their early years working together, and there were times he missed her leadership and methodology.

Climbing into her fifties, the veteran officer looked just as good as the day they'd met.

"Rand Kershaw!" she announced with a wide grin.

"Melissa," Rand managed through a thick tongue.

The two shook hands and looked each other over.

"I was hoping to run into you," she confessed. "How's life?"

"It's a blissful combination of work and play. How's Seattle treating you?"

"The weather is miserable," she replied, motioning for a drink.

"Five years after being recruited by the CIA and you're still slumming it, huh? You should've stayed with us. We miss you around here."

"Well, isn't that sweet of you," Melissa said with a coy smile. "You were always a charmer, Rand. Still single?"

He replied with a snort and a pull of his drink.

"I'll take that as a yes. Anybody sitting here?"

"It would seem *you* are," he smirked.

Rand was happy to see an old familiar face. The two spent a few minutes sipping drinks, comparing old war stories and regaling over some former colleagues and informants that had gone off the radar—*what's he up to? Where's she live? Is this guy or that guy still alive?*

"So, after all these years," Melissa finally pointed out. "I still know you. And I know those slouched shoulders and puppy eyes. What's hurting so hard in your world?"

Rand returned a slow nod and a slick grin. "Yeah. Let's just keep talking about the old days."

Melissa laughed. "Alright, alright. I'll try guessing." She took a draught of her beer. "You either had your heart broken...or you're workin' a case that's beating you up."

Rand kept a tight poker face until finally tapping his index finger to his nose.

"Tough case. I knew it!"

"It's a career killer, Melissa," the half-drunk agent asserted.

"No, sweetie. There are no career killers. Only bad cases and screw-ups that might land you in a different field office," she reconciled.

Melissa had always taken a slightly maternal approach to Rand. He was an eager young agent when he arrived from the academy and she quickly grew to respect him.

"This one's different," Rand offered.

"How bad can it be?"

"Let me put it this way, I just got back from the middle of the goddamn North Pacific chasing pirates that were supposed to be casino robbers but turned out to be pirates."

"Ouch! Bad week at sea, apparently," noted Melissa.

"Yeah," Rand agreed. "Bad week at sea." He chugged the last drops of whiskey before blasting the highball back against the bar.

"Well, did you at least get to fast-rope?" she asked.

"I did actually," he confirmed with a light laugh. "Wait a minute. What do you mean it was a *bad week at sea?*"

Melissa didn't think twice about it. "I don't know, sounds like you weren't the only agent that experienced bad luck in open waters. A few of our guys had a rough operation out there, too. Couple days ago, just off the Mexican Peninsula."

"No shit," Rand replied.

"Yeah, I guess the San Diego office lost some kind of *off the books, high-profile* asset to a few, as you say, pirates."

Rand perked up again. "How many pirates?"

"Three or four...I think. The only reason I remember is because the guys were posing as Coast Guard officers. The intel was shared with all the Pacific coast teams. We had a good laugh."

"What was the asset?" Rand inquired. "Anything valuable?"

"It sure sounded like it," she confirmed. "I kept hearing the word 'priceless' but I have no clue what it actually was. Why do you care so much?"

"Just curious, I guess. Been up to my damn ears in shipping lanes, cargo freighters and pirates lately. Guess I'm starting to take an interest in the topic."

"You think there's a connection, don't you?" Melissa finally asked out of pity. "You know, when you're desperate it's easy to see connections that don't exist."

She had always been the voice of reason.

"Well, I just happen to be looking for three highly-skilled adrenaline junkies with a knack for grand theft felonies. A coincidence, I'm sure," concluded Rand. "I'm fine, really. I just can't keep my mind straight, ya know. This one's got me bogged down."

"Listen, if there's anything I can do to help just let me know." The CIA agent stood and handed Rand her card.

"You know damn well I have all your information," he responded. "It was great running into you. Let's not wait so long next time."

"Call me if you're ever in Seattle, I'll buy you a drink. Take care of yourself, Rand."

The two embraced in a genuine hug.

"Hey," Rand snapped over the music. "Did you guys capture the pirates?"

"Nope. Still at large," she confirmed with a wink. "I got your email address, I'll send you everything I have."

They shared one last smile before Melissa's red dress melted into the sea of suits and cocktail gowns.

Rand raised a fresh glass of whiskey to the face staring back at him in the mirror.

"To the greatest crime that ruined your career," he toasted sardonically.

CHAPTER TWENTY-THREE

The following Monday, Rand arrived early at his desk and noticed a large manila envelope perched against the filing cabinet. The return label just happened to be from Minneapolis—Twin Cities Water Solutions. Rand hesitated for a moment, fully expecting another lead to fall apart. Nonetheless, he ripped open the seal and thumbed through the pages. His heart raced with excitement when he realized it contained order documents for the water purifiers: payments, logistics, shipping dates, receiving signatures and international customs filings.

He paused to peel back the lid of his gas station coffee and blew over the top of it. He took an exaggerated slurp and checked over his shoulder for any nosey co-workers.

As he dove through the payment documents, Rand noticed a familiar name he hadn't seen in a while, and it caught his waning attention: *Atlantic International Bank*—a financial institution in Belize with a reputation for protecting expats from tax indictments—and right there in black and white was the twelve-digit account number for the final payment to Twin Cities Water Solutions. The wily agent's eyes zeroed-in on the numbers.

He fumbled for his laptop. Kershaw had dealt with this bank before. He had a guy on the inside—Jorge Salvatori. The bank clerk had shared valuable intel with the FBI during an investigation into an Arkansas drug smuggler who happened to be hiding money in Belize.

Must've been six years ago, Rand reminisced. He found Jorge's contact information. *What are the chances this guy still works there?*

He pulled his cellphone from his jacket pocket and punched in the international number. *C'mon, c'mon!*

A female voice answered. "Atlantic International Bank, you've reached investment specialist Jorge Salvatori's office, how may I help you?"

A vigorous fist pump. "Yes, may I speak with Jorge?"

"Who's calling?" she asked.

"This is Special Agent Rand Kershaw with the FBI." Rand cringed.

"Hold please."

Several minutes passed before the line beeped, then went silent.

"Jorge Salvatori," the familiar voice said.

"Jorge, this is Agent Kershaw," Rand greeted with a sigh of relief.

"Agent Kershaw, I don't recall offering you any additional favors but if you're in town I'd be happy to buy you lunch."

Rand smiled. "I'd like that. But, unfortunately, I'm calling long distance."

"I see. Las Vegas, is it?"

"Yeah. Vegas."

"So, what can I do for you, Agent Kershaw?"

"Well, first and foremost, congratulations on your new position. Investment specialist—it has a nice ring to it." Rand was priming him now.

Jorge replied with a deep laugh, and another inquiry into the purpose of Rand's call.

"I have a rather large money wire originating from an account at your bank, Jorge. I just need anything you can give me that might point me in the right direction."

"Agent Kershaw, you know I cannot give you any information that would incriminate our customers. Even if that customer is an expat of yours."

"That's the thing, Jorge. I can say with near certainty that the owner of this account has never stepped foot in Belize," Rand assured him. "In fact, we currently have the individual in custody here on American soil." He was rolling the dice now. Totally winging it. "But I need your help. We can only hold this guy for so long without evidence. Bureaucratic red tape, ya know. If I can't tie him to this transaction, he's gonna walk out the front door, a free man. Of course, he'll more than likely head south and turn up on your doorstep looking to empty his account. This guy brings bad juju wherever he goes, and I promise the last thing you want is him waltzing into your bank."

Jorge Salvatori thought about that for a moment. He didn't like it. "What's the account number?"

Another fist pump. Rand read a twelve-digit number to his old friend and patiently waited. After a few minutes, he could hear Jorge breathing back into the phone.

"Okay, Agent Kershaw," the banker began. "All I can legally give you is the corporation named on the account and a phone number."

Rand grimaced in disappointment. "C'mon, Jorge. I know you guys. For Christ's sake, our programmers built your Internet security and tracking software. Give me an IP address," he begged. "I know you have it. It's staring you in the face as we speak."

Kershaw was right. Jorge was staring at the data on his computer screen, which held the IP address of the last secure login to the account through Atlantic International's online customer portal. The investment banker closed his eyes and shook his head.

"C'mon Jorge. What do you want? Anything," Rand offered.

"I want you to never call me again."

"Fine. I can do that."

After a moment of contemplation, Jorge dictated the IP address from the file.

"And the company name?" the agent finally asked.

"Boro Industries," Salvatori reluctantly answered.

Holy shit! Boro Industries paid for the water purifiers! The name raced through Rand's head. It was the same dummy corporation that made the donation to St. Jude, which he had, in theory, already connected to the Wynn heist.

Special Agent Rand Kershaw now had the very first actual breakthrough—one that tied the two separate donations together, and quite possibly the Wynn heist and Hamilton hack. He couldn't believe it.

"I can't thank you enough, Jorge."

"It was nice knowing you, Agent Kershaw."

"Likewise!"

The line went dead.

Within seconds, Rand was running a reverse-IP lookup through the Intel Group's database from Washington. His search kicked back an exact location—it was a physical address on the outskirts of San Francisco.

He anxiously pulled up his web browser and his fingers couldn't type the address fast enough.

Bingo! Spartan Cyber Security. Silicon Valley.

Rand lost himself in the computer screen, gazing into each pixel that made up the map pinpointing Spartan Security. A boyish grin spread across his face like wildfire. The world seemed to stand still as he reflected on every misstep he had taken along this journey. But none of it mattered now. He had broken through the rabbit hole and finally held something of substance—something he could track and hunt.

CHAPTER TWENTY-FOUR

Rand had secured a jump seat on the next available flight out of Las Vegas—often given to federal agents and required no more than a simple request to the airline. Four hours later, a Boeing 727 touched down at San Francisco International Airport. United 1837 was thirteen minutes off schedule and the landing jolted Rand from his laptop in the tiny jump seat.

Outside, a local FBI agent sat parked on the curb in a gray sedan with tinted windows. Rand exited the airport and thrust himself into the open air and trotted over to the car through a gauntlet of travelers. He still had an hour to reach Silicon Valley before the close of business.

The agents exchanged a quick nod through the windshield before Rand jumped in the passenger side and tossed his bag in the floorboard.

"Welcome to San Francisco," the local agent greeted.

He was a short, stocky guy with dirty blonde hair. Rand pegged him as the fraternity type, disheveled and unorthodox.

"Thanks for picking me up."

"I'm Special Agent Chris Reynolds, look forward to working with you."

"Rand Kershaw, Las Vegas office."

The sedan sped away and bolted toward the on-ramp to the 101. Once they reached the freeway and blasted into the fast lane, Agent Reynolds hit the lights, which flashed angrily from the top of the windshield. Traffic parted in front of them and the sedan easily opened up to 100 mph.

"We're looking for Spartan Cyber Security, Bradford Drive," Rand said.

"Yeah, I got the message earlier," Reynolds confirmed. "Already got it in the GPS. We'll be there in thirty-three minutes."

Rand checked his wristwatch. "That should work."

"Surprise attack?"

"Yeah, sort of. Chasing down an IP address, might be better if we show up unannounced so let's kill the lights once we get off the freeway."

"You got it." Agent Reynolds took a breath and glanced out the window. "The Wynn case, right?"

Rand clenched his jaw in frustration. "Yep."

Clearly his reputation had carried all the way to San Francisco. A cloud of awkwardness filled the sedan. Rand couldn't get to his destination fast enough. Thirty minutes later, they pulled into the parking lot of Spartan Security. Rand tore off his jacket and rolled up the sleeves of his light blue dress shirt. He tightened his tie and checked his 9mm pistol, then slipped it into his side holster.

The sedan attacked the front of the large beige building and came to a screeching halt at the foot of the marble steps. The front doors of the sedan blew open and two intimidating agents leapt out and charged up the stairs toward the front entrance.

As they rushed inside, Rand raised his badge in the air. The security officer sitting at the atrium desk rose to his feet.

"Special Agents Kershaw and Reynolds, FBI," Rand shouted. "I need to speak with your CIO immediately. No one enters this building, and no one leaves."

His sense of urgency was viral—the guard reached for his desk phone and frantically dialed. After a moment of hard whispers and attempts at an explanation, he placed the phone down and told the agents that one of the executives would be down in five minutes.

"We don't have five minutes," demanded Agent Kershaw. "You need to take us upstairs now."

The overweight guard seemed eager to help. "Where do you guys want to go?"

"CIO—head of IT," Rand answered without hesitation.

The man led both agents to a nearby corridor, where an open elevator awaited and brought them swiftly to the fourth floor. They stepped out and walked past a startled receptionist, then zigzagged through the halls before finally arriving at the door of Martin Hanley, Chief Information Officer.

The guard raised his hand to knock but was intercepted by Rand, who reached in and forced the door open to find Martin Hanley sitting with two younger executives.

"Mr. Hanley, I'm Special Agent Rand Kershaw with the FBI. My partner and I need to speak with you. It's quite urgent."

"You can't just come barging in here—"

"I tried to tell them you'd be right down, sir," the guard offered, attempting to cover his own ass.

Hanley waved off the large man, who hung his head and pushed through the doorway, back to his post downstairs.

The CIO then sent his executives packing as well, whom Reynolds eyed with a smirk.

"What the hell is this all about?" barked Hanley.

He was a slick sixty-something with a solid build and an expensive suit. The C-Level officer leaned back in his brown leather chair with his arms crossed, waiting for an answer.

"Mr. Hanley, we're conducting a federal investigation and have evidence that leads us back to this building. In fact, I have an IP address I'd like you to locate on your internal servers. We need a name."

Hanley narrowed his eyes in thought, then gently picked up the phone on his desk.

"Get legal over here. Now!" he demanded to the poor soul on the other end of the line.

"Our apologies for the surprise visit," Rand interjected. "But this information is extremely time sensitive."

"Do you have a warrant?" Hanley asked.

"No. But I can assure you one is being drafted as we speak. I guess we could keep you around for another four to five hours while we wait for it to be executed."

Hanley considered the meddling threat for a moment. He had a poker game lined up with his pals in a couple hours and could almost taste the forty-year-old Scotch. He wasn't about to miss it.

"Fine. I'll give you a name, but that's it. Our work here is extremely sensitive to the security of our clients and I'm not about to put any of it at risk. That said, most of our departments use private networks, but we have specific IPs assigned to management personnel. The lower level employees—interns, assistants, junior programmers—they all share IPs with their respective departments."

"Well, in that case, this should be a snap," replied Rand.

A gray-haired corporate attorney entered the office with a soft knock. "Marty, everything okay in here?"

"Yeah, Walt. I think we're fine."

The lawyer took a moment to measure up the room. These were clearly federal agents.

"I want to see some identification, gentlemen," the attorney finally said.

Agents Kershaw and Reynolds flashed their ID badges at the lawyer, who took another look at the agents before giving a nod to Hanley. The look of disgust on his face was unmistakable as he walked out of the office.

"Give me the IP address and I'll tell you who it's assigned to and you can get the fuck out of my office," Hanley growled through his pearly white teeth.

Rand proceeded to read off the numbers as the CIO punched them into his database. Within seconds, it highlighted one name from a list of dozens—William Montgomery. The executive turned his laptop around to face the agents.

They focused on it with anxious intensity.

"Trip Montgomery," Hanley offered. "Director of our Critical Infrastructure Division."

Rand peered up from the laptop. "So, he's a hacker?"

"This isn't some collective of revolutionaries launching sloppy attacks from their parents' basements, Agent Kershaw. Our team is made up of the most professionally skilled cyber security analysts and engineers in the world."

The pieces were falling quickly into place.

"So, he's a hacker," repeated Rand.

The executive shook his head in frustration. "Look, I have no idea what Mr. Montgomery does in his free time. At Spartan Cyber Security, he is the Director of Critical Infrastructure. His office is down the hall, but he hasn't been here in weeks."

"Did he take vacation time or something?"

"Well, sort of. He took the last two weeks off but was supposed to be back yesterday."

Rand looked up in disbelief. "He hasn't returned?"

"No."

"Is it odd that he wouldn't be back yet? Maybe he extended his vacation?" Reynolds wondered aloud.

"No, it doesn't work like that around here," Hanley corrected. "It's *very* odd that he hasn't checked in. Listen, agents, Trip is a stand-up guy. A brilliant programmer, a hard-worker who's well-respected around the building."

"Can we see his office?" Rand abruptly requested.

Martin Hanley just wanted it all to be over. In the hopes he'd be shuffling a deck of cards and sipping Scotch soon, he took the agents down the hall to the office of William Montgomery.

They barged in to find the walls adorned with an old battle flag and several framed photos. But, surprisingly, his desk had been cleared off.

"Does he have a computer?" Rand asked.

"All our staff are given laptops and most of the time they take them home at night. Trip apparently left with his."

Kershaw and Reynolds scanned the office and locked in on the photos hanging from the wall.

"Who's this?" Rand quizzed.

"That was his older brother, Mark. He was a Navy SEAL."

"Was?"

"Yeah, he was killed in Afghanistan, I believe."

"When?"

"Had to be five or six years ago," Hanley guessed.

The agents exchanged knowing looks.

"Does Trip have any other military acquaintances, friends of Mark's maybe?" Rand pressed.

"I have no idea, he doesn't talk much about his personal life."

"Thanks for your assistance, Mr. Hanley. I'll be in touch if we need anything else," Rand abruptly promised. "Please keep this office locked for now, I'll be sending a team over to collect these file cabinets and belongings, with a warrant, of course. We'll show ourselves out."

Relieved, Hanley ushered them out of the office and through the hallway.

The agents made their way to the elevator and down to the lobby. They brushed past the guard and darted to the gray sedan outside, which still sat haphazardly at the bottom of the marble steps.

"What the hell was that?" Reynolds asked, as he climbed behind the wheel and checked over his shoulder. "I mean, it can't be a coincidence that the guy you're looking for hasn't shown back up for work. You think he's on the run? Or dead?"

Rand thought about that for a moment and was suddenly able to see things from a broader viewpoint—with remarkable clarity.

"I don't know," he replied. "But it makes absolute sense that he's nowhere to be found. He's either faked his own death, started a new life, or he's actually been killed." Rand Kershaw's mind raced.

"Which would all indicate he's pulled off another job," Reynolds surmised.

"Exactly," chimed Rand. It all masterfully came together. "Holy shit...they just pulled off a goddamn job! I just had the wrong one. I had the wrong one!" A giant grin spilled across Rand's face as he threw his head back and laughed.

"They told me you were crazy, Kershaw, but you're freaking me out."

"Yeah, I hear that a lot."

"Then where to now?"

"Take me to your field office, I need to set up an ops center. I don't have time to get back to Vegas."

"An ops center at the San Fran office?"

Without answering, Rand pulled his cellphone from his pocket and punched in a few numbers before bringing it to his ear.

"This is Special Agent Rand Kershaw from the Las Vegas Armed Robbery Division, I need a temporary ops center ready in thirty minutes. I could use a digital forensics analyst and any other agents who can lend a hand. We've got a time-sensitive mark on a high-value target. William 'Trip' Montgomery."

After a confirmation, he hung up the phone and shoved it back into his pocket.

"You're starting to piece this together, aren't you?" Reynolds asked with an optimistic giddiness.

"Trip Montgomery is one of my three suspects," Rand confirmed. "Something's happened to him. He was pulling a job somewhere, I just know it. We need to follow this kid's trail and it'll lead me right to all three of them."

"So your thieves have pulled off another heist, huh?"

"Yep. And I think I know which one."

Chapter Twenty-Five

Rook paced slowly toward the steps of an old brick building. He grabbed hold of an iron handrail and began climbing the cobblestone steps. It was there he noticed the dark, ashy mark left on one of the columns. It had been marked within the last hour—a signal he'd hoped to never see. Rook halted his climb and took a moment to contemplate—his life flashed vividly in front him.

After a brief pause, he continued to the top of the steps, then turned around and gazed at the quiet street behind him. Above, the orange clouds reflected the setting sun, beautifully clashing with a purple sky to form a collage over the streets of Bruges. The cold Belgian air filled his lungs. The aging millionaire pulled his coat collar tightly against his neck and reached for the large wooden door of his home.

Christopher hurried to the foyer with outstretched hands, where he reached for Rook's overcoat, then gently placed it over his forearm. Rook glanced around the well-decorated lobby before finally making eye contact with his trusted butler.

"They're waiting for you in the library, sir."

Rook checked over his shoulder and noticed blood drops on the marble floor. His eyes followed them to a wide hallway that led to the administrative wing. He could see now—down the hall where the shadows opened to an adjacent room—a body lying on the floor in a dark pool of blood. It was one of his private security guards; he suspected the rest of them were dead as well. Rook looked again to Christopher who stood like a statue.

"Were you able to hit the alarm?" Rook asked under his breath.

"I was. They should arrive at any moment."

"And the Huntsmen?"

Christopher hung his head. "No, sir. There wasn't time."

"Quite alright, my friend."

"It has been an honor to serve you, my lord," the butler said in a low, soft British accent.

"The honor has been all mine, Christopher. Your family will be well taken care of. You've done very well, old chap."

"Thank you, my lord."

And with that, the butler turned and disappeared down a hallway. Rook peered into the foyer mirror and tugged at his suit, then tightened his tie. He appeared as respectable as he could for such an important moment. The studious Knight took one last look at himself: his face was old; his hair gray. The man staring back at him was tired and weary.

Rook stood tall and marched up the main hallway to the atrium where another member of his security detail was slumped dead over a chair against the wall.

The library sat tucked in the northeast corner of the building, just beyond the solid gold statue of Zeus set in a flowing fountain. After a brief hesitation, Rook continued his walk to the library, counting his footsteps for reasons he couldn't explain.

The door was slightly ajar. He stood for a moment before opening it, then swept in with the last bit of energy he had left and made his way to his favorite chair—an antique from the Victorian period, decorated with purple and gold silk accents. The prideful Brit unbuttoned his jacket and sat down.

"I've been expecting you," the American stranger uttered from the shadows of the opposite corner of the room.

"And I, you," Rook quickly replied.

"My name is Carson."

Rook looked up at his guest for the first time. "US Intelligence, I presume?"

"It doesn't really matter," the middle-aged spook assured. "You took something from me and I want it back." His words were sharp and annunciated.

"Save your breath, Mr. Carson. If you think for one bloody moment that I'm going to squeal and squirm like the measly foot soldiers you pick up and torture in the desert, you are sorely mistaken. We can either bury this row here and now, or you can—*go fuck yourself* as you Americans like to say."

Carson chuckled under his breath. He liked the ferocity of the old man.

"I don't have it, and you know damn well I don't," Rook continued after an awkward silence.

"Yes, we're aware of that. In fact, I'm almost certain your little thieves have disappeared. Even from you," Carson pointed out. "Which means you're really no good to me in terms of tracking the asset down. But you will tell me the identities of your American henchmen."

"You have no idea who we are, do you, Mr. Carson?"

"Yeah, yeah. The grand and illustrious Knights of Medina," Carson acknowledged with flare. "I know all about your little club, it's how we found Dr. Diaz. Outlawed by most governors, not even the crown acknowledges your existence. You're no more than a bunch of delusional old men trying to grasp at the pages of history with tales of glory and honor. Spare me the bullshit. This is the real world, and what I'm about to do to you will make you wish you never swore an allegiance to this goddamn knighthood."

Rook was snapped from the moment by a loud crash outside. It was abruptly followed by more commotion and sporadic gunfire in the distance. His reinforcements had arrived. But with the rattle of more gunfire and unintelligible yelling, he knew they would never reach him.

"That's the sound of defeat, Rook. The jackals aren't at the door, they're sitting comfortably in your library. Now give me the names of your three cowboys and I'll end this honorably—quickly and humanely—for every one of your men. You just have to give me the names."

Rook knew the protocol. He had helped write it. "My father raised sheep when I was a boy," he slowly began. "And one day a few men snuck onto our property during the night and stole some of his sheep. They came again the next night. And the next. My father stood at his window each morning before sunrise, watching a handful of his sheep being marched away. Then one day, it just stopped. The men didn't come to take his sheep anymore. My mother—"

Rook paused to loosen his tie. A playful grin washed over his face as he regaled his childhood. "My mother asked him, 'Why are they not stealing our sheep anymore?' And my father, a quiet man with little initiative, replied, 'I slaughtered the sheep. I would rather go without than give to those who don't deserve.'"

He wasn't going to tell the agent anything. That much was clear.

"Great story," Carson responded. He pulled a pistol from his waistband and placed it against Rook's forehead. "I'm not asking again, you senile, old bastard!"

The Knight sat breathless in his favorite chair. Carson lowered his aim.

The first shot went through the top of Rook's knee. He flinched softly, biting into his lip. The second shot tore through his forearm, shattering every bone below the elbow. The old man grunted through the pain, but still didn't move.

Through growing frustration, Carson felt a little respect for the old dog. The agent stepped back and looked over the prisoner, who sat proudly with his hands on the armrests.

Rook quivered in pain and began to fade in and out of consciousness.

The third and final shot was placed directly into the Knight's forehead. His neck snapped lifelessly against the chair as his arms slid into his lap.

Seconds after the last gunshot, another agent entered the library. "Everything good, sir?"

"Yeah," replied Carson as he examined Rook's lifeless body. "Grab every document and device you can. We have three minutes."

"Roger that," the young agent replied before bolting out of the room.

Carson checked his watch and holstered his pistol. He took one last look at the great Intimate Secretary of the Knights of Medina. The agent knew enough about the knighthood to know they were a threat. With the swipe of his smartphone, he ordered the execution of all known members. They would all—with the exception of two—be dead within the hour. The two highest ranking members, Seneschal and Grand Master, had both managed to remain anonymous to the CIA. Carson was hopeful that an analysis of the data being taken from Rook's estate would yield him that information.

Minutes later, a commercial van packed with books, ledgers, hard-drives, and a single laptop computer, pulled away from the scene. Bruges police arrived shortly after. There were no witnesses, no distinguishable fingerprints, and no clues of any kind. Just fifteen dead bodies scattered throughout the building.

CHAPTER TWENTY-SIX

Just outside Westcliffe, Colorado

The brothers found themselves hidden among the vivid landscapes of Colorado, in a grungy motel room.

Cam burst in and flopped into a chair near the front window. Michael sat on the bed, flipping through static channels on an old television.

Nestled off a two-way interstate in the middle of nowhere, the motel held strategic value with plenty of tactical advantages. For starters, they could see for miles in almost every direction. In the backdrop, as if protruding from thin air, stood the Sangre de Cristo Mountains—offering a quick escape to a familiar fighting environment. But, more importantly, there was a working payphone out front.

"Were you able to reach anyone?" Michael asked.

"No."

"I can't believe they hung us out to dry. I don't understand; you'd think these assholes would want their expensive toys back."

"You'd think so," Cam sighed through a chug of beer.

"What if they're all dead?"

"They're not."

"But everyone from the mountain is dead," Michael pleaded. "Trip's dead. Hell, we buried him in the side of a mountain, Cam!"

"Don't do this."

"We didn't even tell Elena!"

"Calm down, Michael. We can't even consider notifying anyone that he's dead."

"We've become monsters."

"Stop whatever it is you're doing, bro." Cam had heard enough. "We will let Elena know as soon as this is over. I promise. But what do you think she'll do if we just call her out of the blue and tell her Trip's dead?"

Michael didn't have an answer.

"She'll do what any girlfriend or spouse would do," implored Cam. "She'll call the police. And tell them how her fiancé died mysteriously with his two best friends."

"She's going to call the police anyways. He was supposed to be home by now."

Cam grumbled with exhaustion. "As unfortunate and callous as it sounds, we are better off with Trip being reported as a missing person right now than we are if they launch an investigation into his death. We have to think rational," he explained, "we'll cross that bridge when we get to it."

"Fine," Michael agreed. "But she needs to know."

The two shared a silent nod and returned to their beers.

"She'll be the first one we call once we get out of this," promised Cam. "Now, any luck with the symbols?"

"Nothing. Like, nothing even remotely close."

The contents of the ossuary had left them with more questions than answers. They had spent the last couple days researching the symbols carved into the mysterious stone slab.

"It's got to be some sort of code or lost language," Michael guessed.

Cam picked up the slab and frowned at it, begging for the damn thing to reveal its secrets.

"As far as the polymer blocks go," Michael continued. "I've never seen anything like it. I mean, there's either photos inside or just images ghosted into this...synthetic resin or whatever."

There were seven of them; each roughly measured eight inches wide, four inches high and two inches thick. The polymer resin blurred any further details of what lay beneath.

"Fuck it. Let's crack these things open," Cam finally said.

"I don't know," Michael questioned. "I mean, how the hell do seven photographs and an electronic device wind up in an ancient tomb? This doesn't make any sense."

"That's why we need to know what's in those blocks."

In a shared moment of reluctance, they waited for a sign—for the spirits of history to guide them toward the right decision.

"Listen to me," Cam began. "The handoff went south, we're on our own here."

"Even if Rook sends help, they'll never know where to find us," Michael added.

"We're going to rip open these polymer blocks, then find a symbologist or something to decipher the stone." Cam took a moment to breathe before the lightbulb went off. "Dr. Diaz! We need to find Diaz."

Michael jumped off the bed to a nearby table, where he pegged the keyboard with a few strokes and produced an online search result for Dr. Ricardo Diaz. There, at the top of the list was an article dated one week ago.

Cam peered over his brother's shoulder at the monitor. The headline read, *Scientist Found Dead in Peru*. The article detailed the horrific circumstances in which Diaz and his wife had been brutally tortured and murdered.

"Jesus Christ." Cam rubbed his eyes in disbelief.

"Rook's probably dead, too," Michael guessed.

Cam shuffled over to his bag and pulled out a hunting knife, then randomly snatched one of the polymer blocks from the bed.

The first strike went right into the center of the clear block and stuck. Cam pried at it until the entire thing snapped. Shards of polymer broke off and littered the bed.

He turned and placed what was left of the block on the table and began pulling more chunks away, one by one. Finally, after a little wiping, he held a black-and-white photo in his hand.

Michael leaned in for a better look. "What the hell?"

"There's no way," Cam whispered. He held the photo into the air. After a moment of close examination, he placed it on the table. "Give me another one."

As they made their way through the strange blocks, the first one lay eerily on the table, breathing oxygen for the first time in almost a thousand years. The grainy, sepia pixels captured one of America's greatest political figures. It was Dwight Eisenhower sitting at the Resolute desk, surrounded by his peers.

Moments later, another photo fell onto the table. This one, a rather bleached-out image taken in poor sunlight, showed what appeared to be ethnic slave laborers pulling large stone blocks on sleds. Next to the slaves were three men in midcentury-style suits and hats and in the background stood a half-built pyramid in the desert.

A third image fell—tribal men in war paint and headdresses, standing in the jungle with a group of white men in sweat-stained dress shirts. A fourth—starving soldiers wading through a river with muskets raised above their heads. A fifth—more indigenous tribesmen. And photos six and seven showed small groups of white men in slacks and shirts at remote outposts around the world. It was a bizarre collection of historical photos.

"This has to be a hoax," Michael presumed. "These could just as easily have been taken at a Hollywood studio. Either that or someone went out and bought an old Polaroid and a time machine, traveled to the distant past and snapped a few shots, then buried all of this crap in Bolivia."

"A thousand years ago?" Cam questioned.

"I think Diaz was batshit crazy and all of this is one big joke," chided Michael.

"Maybe. But who the hell would pay fifteen million dollars just to retrieve a bunch of fake photos, a stone slab and a lightsaber?"

"I say we throw it all in the trash and never look back. Our money's already in the bank and there's a perfectly normal life waiting for me back home."

"There's nothing waiting for you back home except a bullet in the head," Cam reminded his brother.

"No, I'm not buying it. The CIA has no idea who we are. We covered all our tracks in Mexico. They'll never put it together."

Cam was already busily typing away on the laptop. "Never underestimate the CIA, my friend. They *will* follow this thing back to us. We have to be careful."

"What are you doing?" Michael asked.

"Digging through the National Archives."

"For what?"

"For this." Cam spun the laptop back to his brother. It was a picture of Dwight Eisenhower sitting at the same desk as in the photo plucked from polymer, with the same group of men standing around him. The image was from a slightly different angle and had been digitally enhanced, but it was, without a doubt, from the same day, by the same photographer.

"Where'd you find that?"

"A simple search of 'Dwight Eisenhower' in the Archives database. Almost too easy."

"So...what?"

"Snap copies of all these photos with the burner phone," ordered Cam. "And the tablet, too."

"For what?"

"We're sending them to James."

The words sent a shiver down Michael's spine. Their oldest brother, James Lyle, was a professor of English Studies at Wilmington University in Delaware. He still lived in Hockessin, a stone's throw from the house they grew up in. Neither Cam nor Michael had spoken to him in months.

James Lyle was a scholar with immense professional reserve. His relationship with his two younger brothers had always been one of distant closeness. He was loyal, faithful and trustworthy. Just the type of ally they needed.

"I don't know about this, Cam. We should really think this through."

"Listen, he's smarter than both of us combined, and he knows more about this kind of shit than we do."

The men hastily snapped pictures of the seven photos and the tablet, then connected the burner phone to the laptop and uploaded them.

"His email isn't secure, Cam. This is a huge mistake," Michael argued.

"We don't have time for every security measure in the book. And we can't sit here forever, so, if we don't have a game plan by sundown, we're just sitting ducks."

Cam clicked the *Send* button.

Sensing Michael's anxiety, he grabbed his brother by the arm. "I think you could use some fresh air. Go outside, take a walk and relax."

Through a scowl, Michael complied with the suggestion and left the room for a stroll around the property. Cam took a seat at the edge of the bed and held the small phone in both hands. He hung his head and tried his best to collect his thoughts.

He dialed James' cell number by memory and held the phone to his ear.

"James? It's me, Cam."

"Hey, great to hear from you! I didn't recognize the number."

"Yeah, I—I had to get a new number. Work stuff, you know."

"Gotcha. So, to what do I owe the pleasure, everything going well?"

"Yeah, yeah. Listen, did you get the email I just sent by chance? I'm working on something pretty time sensitive and I've hit a roadblock. Could really use some help."

"No, I haven't checked yet. What can I do?"

"I'm not sure exactly," Cam nervously chuckled. "Are you in front of your computer?"

"I can be." James was pillaging around his office looking for curriculum notes when Cam had called. He now turned his attention to his laptop, sitting discarded on a cluttered wooden desk. "Alright, what am I looking for?"

"I just sent an email from a random address. Check out the attached files, especially the last one."

"Okay."

Cam could hear his brother clicking through the files.

"Interesting," James finally responded.

"Ever seen those symbols before?"

"Never," the professor said. "Looks like—I dunno, it almost looks Babylonian. Or maybe even South American—Incan or Mayan perhaps. I really have no idea, I'm an English professor, not an archaeologist. Where'd you get this anyways?"

"A friend," Cam coldly replied.

"*Sure* you did. Wish I could be more help. Have you talked to mom and dad lately?"

"Maybe six weeks ago."

"I'm sensing something's up, Cam. You're not with Michael, are you?"

Cam rolled his eyes. "No. He's at a travel seminar in Arizona I think."

James could tell when his brothers were lying, especially Cam. It was an instinct of shared blood. He looked up from his desk, then stood to close his office door.

"What the hell are you guys up to?" he whispered into the phone. "Are you in trouble?"

Cam took a deep breath and rubbed his brow. "Yeah, we're in a bit of a jam. I can't tell you any more than that. If someone comes around asking about me, you just have to... just tell them you haven't talked to me since Christmas."

"I *haven't* talked to you since Christmas."

"Exactly. Listen, James, I just need to try and find out what all this stuff is. I didn't know where else to go."

James was examining the images closer now. "What the hell am I looking at, Cam?"

"Download those to a thumb drive and keep it somewhere safe. Then erase the email. Make sure you empty your deleted folder as well. You're gonna have to ask your IT department to wipe your computer. I'm really sorry, James, just tell them one of the students mistakenly put a virus on it."

"This doesn't sound good." James was uncomfortable now. "Where can I contact you?"

"By this time tomorrow, this number won't be any good. Just see what you can make of the photos without sharing them with anyone and I'll be in touch soon, okay?"

"Listen Cam, I can't make any promises. And to be totally straight with you, I don't think I'm going to be able to help. But there's a symbols and linguistics expert our History department uses quite a bit. His name's Corin Baker—Dublin, Ireland. Best in the world."

"I can't thank you enough, James. I'm sorry I called."

"Give me a week or so and I'll see if anything else turns up." James exhaled in disappointment. "Goodbye, Cam."

Minutes later, Michael returned to the room.

"What's the deal?" he asked, slamming the door behind him.

"You're going to Ireland."

CHAPTER TWENTY-SEVEN

FBI Field Office, San Francisco, California

Rand Kershaw stared deep into the matrix of information in front of him. A young female intelligence analyst sat quietly nearby, waiting for a response from her new lead agent.

"William Montgomery the third," Rand finally announced. "Twenty-nine years of age from Lodi, Texas. A programmer, correct?"

"Yes, sir," she said without hesitation. "Born on a family farm. Both parents deceased. He had one sibling—a brother, also deceased. A programmer and analyst by trade, a hacker in his free time. He spent eighteen months in federal prison for a cyber security attack on the DOS. He currently works as a programmer with a firm in Silicon Valley—Spartan Security."

"Personal relationships? Love interests?" Rand asked.

The analyst read deeper. "He was recently engaged to a one Elena Getty."

There were a dozen dossiers on the table in front of them—each daring to be pieced together.

"We interviewed local PD," she went on. "No reports of missing persons. Scoured every John Doe within a hundred miles. Nothing."

"Wonderful," Rand grumbled. "And the fiancé?"

"No contact yet, but we've got a team headed to her last known address now."

"Okay." Rand took a moment to think. "Let's move on to known acquaintances."

"Well, there are some interesting connections." The attractive young analyst was on her feet now, pulling folders from the table. "Of the inmates he was closest to in prison, most are still incarcerated, some have since passed away and a few have been released and accounted for. There's nothing of interest from any friends he made there."

"What about other hackers he used to run with?" Rand pressed.

"Are you kidding?" she teased. "They're all shadows. Non-existent."

The agent pursed his lips. *Of course they are.* "Talk to me about his older brother. The dead SEAL."

"Mark Montgomery," the analyst read aloud. "Joined the Navy at eighteen, high marks from his commanding officers and scored well above average on his ASVAB. After a couple years abroad, he made it through BUD/S, fast-tracked Green and was drafted by Echo platoon, SEAL Team 8. Served six years, active duty. KIA five years ago when the Taliban attacked an outpost in the Korengal Valley."

Rand was silent, waiting for his other two ghosts to emerge. He could feel them. They were close.

"A Navy SEAL would have more than enough talent to knock over a casino," he pointed out. "And Trip has all the tools to carry out a cyberattack on Hamilton. Are there any military contacts that Trip might have made through his brother?"

"This man here," she immediately replied, pulling a dossier from the stack. "Another former SEAL that we've connected to Trip. His name's Cameron Lyle."

"What's the relation?" asked Rand.

A devious grin swept across her face. "I thought you'd never ask. Cameron Lyle served with Trip's brother Mark on Team 8. They pulled off some of the most dangerous missions JSOC has ever executed in the Middle East. He was with Trip's brother when the outpost was attacked, probably watched him die. Cameron went on to be a BUD/S training officer at the

Naval Special Warfare Center in San Diego. He now works as a tactical weapons and training consultant for not only the US Navy, but our Army and Marine special ops units as well. Not to mention a litany of private military companies."

"Background?"

"Grew up in Hockessin, Delaware. Both parents still alive, they never moved away. He has an older brother, James, who's a professor, and a younger brother, Michael, who—I dunno," the analyst stumbled as she read through the folder. "Looks like he owns an extreme travel agency or something in D.C."

Rand hesitated. "Did you get any info regarding freighter heists off the coast of Mexico?"

"No," she reluctantly replied. "There were no reports from Mexican authorities or US Coast Guard. And for good measure we checked with all freighter companies working those waters and came up empty."

"CIA?"

"They didn't have anything remotely matching our criteria."

Rand flared his nostrils in contempt. "Fine. Do we have eyes on Cameron Lyle?"

"Not at the moment, sir."

"Reynolds!" Rand yelled out to the bullpen. "Can you join us?"

A moment later, Agent Reynolds shuffled into the large conference room.

"Alright," Rand announced. "I need eyes on Cameron Lyle as soon as possible. Track credit cards, email addresses, home address, clients, family, everything. This guy fits our profile perfectly, but we need to locate him. Grab his cellphone records and find the last tower it pinged. Start there and work your way out."

With that, the analyst dove back into her laptop and began plundering the nation's communications databases for anything that would help locate Cameron Lyle.

Reynolds and Kershaw dipped out of the conference room and lingered in the hallway.

"So this is suspect number two?" Reynolds asked.

"I can't say for certain. But he's a perfect match on paper."

"What about this younger brother, Michael? Could be our number three?"

"Well shit, Reynolds, that sure would tie this up nicely, wouldn't it?"

The two spilled out into the bullpen and dispersed in separate directions—Reynolds to his desk and Rand to a makeshift office he'd set up in the back corner of the ballistics lab.

An hour later, the team regrouped again in the conference room.

"What do we got?" Rand anxiously asked.

"We can put Cameron Lyle at a National Defense conference in New Orleans a little over a month ago," Reynolds began. "After that, his credit card receipts keep him in Providence, except for a week where all internet and financial activity goes dark. We've also got a list of phone calls made over the last year, looks like he stayed in regular contact with Trip."

"Immediate family?"

"Lyle's married, two daughters," the female analyst informed him. "We have eyes on the residence. Unfortunately, the wife and kids haven't been there for a few days and they haven't shown up on any flight lists. They've disappeared."

"And let me guess," Rand predicted. "Cameron Lyle hasn't been back on the grid since?"

"Nope," replied Reynolds. "Just like Trip Montgomery, he hasn't made a phone call, swiped a credit card, visited an ATM, or even sent an email in over a week."

"These are our guys. I can feel it," professed Rand. "We need to locate Trip Montgomery and the Lyle brothers. Get a team on the oldest brother, James, in addition to Trip's fiancé. And find me Cameron's wife and kids."

CHAPTER TWENTY-EIGHT

Michael Lyle sat inconspicuously among the travelers at Gate 9 of Denver International Airport. He clutched his ticket and fake passport as he checked his watch. It was twelve minutes until Aer Lingus Flight 8918 to Dublin began boarding.

After digging into the contents of the ossuary the day before, he was now on a mission to track down a symbologist in Ireland. It had been a tight window, but Michael was able to make the drive to Denver in time for one of the first international flights departing that day. He was exhausted.

Shortly after boarding, Michael took a rough head count, checked his exits and made mental note of any suspicious passengers. It was an instinctual habit—one of the many marks left on him from years of training with his older brother. Comfortable with his surroundings, he lost himself in his headphones and was well into a deep sleep by the time the plane left the runway.

It was an eleven-hour flight, following a brief layover in Washington. After his plane landed safely in Dublin, Michael made his way through the terminal and out to the rental lot. It was just before dawn when he crept behind the wheel of a blue, four-cylinder rental car and swiftly pulled out onto a small highway.

An hour's drive south put him in Dalkey—a posh part of town that overlooked the Dublin Bay. The small rental car came to a stop and parallel parked along the curb across from a non-descript row of shops, including a café that his target often checked in to through social media.

An hour into the stakeout, a familiar face finally emerged from the sidewalk and briskly entered the café. Michael, feeling almost too lucky, double-checked the photo from his cellphone.

"Bingo."

He slipped out of the car and checked both directions before crossing the busy street. Landing at the front door of the café, Michael casually entered and scanned the small building. His target sat alone against the wall with a black coffee and chocolate scone. The twenty-something Irishman appeared to be lost in his smartphone. With the air of a half-asleep university student, Corin Baker yawned and sipped his coffee.

Michael ordered a cappuccino and sat quietly at a nearby table. After a painfully slow, twenty-minute lull, his target finally got up and exited the café. A lengthy stroll along Cunningham Road and a few blocks up Hillside took them to a row of residential buildings.

The young symbologist hadn't noticed Michael following him at first, but after arriving at the entrance door, he caught the reflection of a man standing behind him. It was the lost American from the café.

Corin slowly turned around.

"Corin Baker?" the American growled.

"Who's asking?"

"I am. Let's go inside," Michael demanded.

"I don't have any money," Corin lashed back with a typical Northside Dublin flare. "And my place is a shithole. There's nothing to steal."

"I'm not here to rob you. I need your help."

"Piss off," Corin replied. He pulled the entrance door open and slipped into the lobby.

Michael caught the door and quickly followed.

"Listen, you dolt," the symbologist threatened. "I really don't have time for this. I'm remarkably busy and—"

"I came a long way to find you, Mr. Baker. Please."

Corin fumbled with his keys as he walked past the stairway to a brown door at the end of the hall. As a last resort, Michael pulled a torn piece of paper from his pocket and flashed it at the young man.

"Have you ever seen this before?" he asked.

Corin stopped. "Who the fuck *are* you?"

"I'm either your best friend or your worst enemy," assured Michael. "Your choice but either way we need to talk."

Corin snatched the piece of paper and turned to enter his loft, leaving the door open and heading straight for a tiny living room. He stared at the crinkled paper, examining it with deep interest.

Michael followed him inside and closed the door behind them. "My name is David Trevin," he lied, "and I'm trying to decipher that tablet. I was told you're the best symbologist in the world."

Corin scoffed. "Hold your breath, man. 'Symbologist' isn't even a real thing. The proper term is 'philologist.' I study ancient languages, hieroglyphs and semiotics. Symbols are for gobshites."

He took another sip of his coffee and tossed the printout onto the pass-through bar between a cramped kitchenette and the living room.

"So, have you ever seen anything like that before?" Michael pressed.

"Leave your number on the bar and I'll get back to you. I'm really wrecked right now, and I certainly don't appreciate being followed home. Christ, man, I'm going to have to find a new place to get breakfast."

Michael could sense this was going to be a difficult task.

As the bulky American turned away and placed his hand on the doorknob, Corin got comfortable in the recliner, silently hoping the man would just go away. But, instead of leaving, Michael reached up and deadbolted the door.

"Damnit," Corin cried. "Please just leave me the fuck alone or I'll call the guards!"

Michael angrily marched over to Corin, grabbed him by the collar and ripped the young scholar into the air and onto his feet.

"Listen to me, you little shit. I just buried one of my best friends and there's an entire army out there trying to kill me. And for some stupid reason, this stone might be the only way to get myself out of the position I'm in. Do you understand me now?"

The sudden change in tone frightened the skinny Irishman.

"So, you're going to stop playing video games and pause whatever linguistics projects you're working on and help me out!" Michael was growing more agitated by the second. He grabbed the paper and held it to Corin's face. "Deciphering this tablet is the *only* fucking priority in your life right now!" he yelled.

"Well you don't have to be such an asshole about it."

Corin grabbed the paper from Michael's outstretched hand and studied it further. The philologist paced the room before finally sitting back in his recliner.

"I already told you, I've never seen these before," he nervously stated.

"How long is this going to take?" Michael asked.

"It could take months, I just don't have the—"

"You don't have months. You don't even have that many days."

Corin's fear escalated. The room started to spin. "Where did you get this?" he finally asked, trying to focus on his own survival.

"It was discovered in Bolivia. I stole it from some very bad people. And now I just want to send it back to wherever the hell it belongs," Michael confessed.

"When it was dug up, was it with any other items?"

The question seemed peculiar. Michael hadn't told him it was dug up.

Corin could sense the American's skepticism. "I—I only ask because it would give me more context, perhaps indicate what civilization it's from," he mumbled.

Michael continued to stare a hole in his new friend. Corin's mind raced, searching for an escape route, a way to get this crazy man out of his flat.

"Listen, I'm not going to be able to crack this." Corin was almost begging now. "I have to be straight with you. The resources simply don't exist to decipher something like this. It would take an entire team—"

"You've seen it before," Michael sharply interrupted.

Corin took a long, deep breath and carefully considered his next answer. Unfortunately, the fear had frozen him. He opened his mouth, but nothing came out.

After a long silence, he gathered his senses. "Fine," Corin revealed under his breath.

The jig was up. He wasn't cut out for this kind of charade.

"I was contacted a couple weeks ago by someone named Diaz. He was acting real dodgy, like, about the whole thing. He sent me a snap of the same tablet and asked me to start looking into it."

"And?"

"That's it, I swear. He was supposed to contact me again a few days later and I never heard from him."

"That's because he's dead, Corin."

The young Irishman paused. "I'm in danger, aren't I? Are you going to kill me?" His eyes began to well.

"No. I'm not going to kill you," Michael promised with a sense of relief in his voice. "How far did you get?"

"Not far, like. I thought it was just a hoax at first, you know, Loch Ness Monster type filth. I didn't pay it much attention. But the more I examined the damn thing, it has all the hallmarks of a lost language. The best I could tell it derived from a pre-Incan civilization. There were definite similarities, you know."

"Corin, I need you to be honest with me," Michael pleaded. "Can you or can you not tell me what is written on that stone?"

"A couple of days maybe, but I have a life—"

"For the next couple of days, *this* is your life."

"Fine," Corin agreed. "How do I reach you?"

"You don't have to worry about that," assured Michael. "I'll be staying right here until you figure it out."

Corin grimaced with disappointment and locked his hands above his head. He had always dreamed of a life of adventure. Unfortunately, this wasn't what he had in mind.

CHAPTER TWENTY-NINE

A black Cadillac Escalade pulled away from LAX and headed southbound onto Highway 1. A cellphone rang in the backseat.

"Carson," he answered.

"It's Kevin. How was Belgium?"

"Overpriced chocolates and a lot of rain. What do you have?"

"Blood samples came back. William Montgomery: hacker-turned-security expert from Silicon Valley."

"Dead?"

"Affirmative. The other two obviously slipped through, so we need to get boots on the ground. Fast."

"Fine. You know the drill. I'll be there in thirty minutes."

Carson abruptly ended the call and leaned his head back against the gray leather. The vigorous agent had a nonstop battery, but the past week had taken its toll. He hadn't slept in over thirty hours, and was in desperate need of a recharge.

Upon his arrival at the CIA black site just south of Los Angeles, he gazed out the window at the abandoned three-story factory. It was blanketed by rusted metal siding and steel framing. Many of the original pulley systems and hardware were still mounted in various places inside; the rest had been completely gutted over the years.

A decades-old industrial elevator brought Carson to the third floor, where his team had assembled a small command center. He wiped the sweat from his brow and approached the cluster of computers and servers. Agent Kevin Bailey met his boss at the first row of monitors, where several analysts typed away on their keyboards.

A glass wall had been erected in the center of the mess, somehow jammed between rows of desks and endless cables running along the floor. Taped to the glass were headshots of seven males, one in particular was taped above the others. It was marked 'William "Trip" Montgomery.'

"What's the score, Kevin?"

"Alright, KIA at the top. William Montgomery the third. His friends called him 'Trip.' The others are known associates."

Kevin's beady eyes scanned the faces on the wall as he spoke. "These are the six males that had the most contact with him over the last three years."

"I'm listening," Carson blasted.

"Three of the six are former hackers—one dead, two unaccounted for. None of which match our profile," Kevin assessed as he struck through the headshots with a red marker. "This other guy is David Grainger, a software engineer with a specialty in satellite communications systems, worked with our boy Trip at Spartan Security. No training or military background, no prior arrests."

Kevin marked through his face as well.

Two headshots remained on the board, staring back at the agents.

"And these jokers?" Carson pried.

"We've traced all credit card purchases, emails and phone calls for these last two, both of whom have gone dark. Cameron and Michael Lyle— brothers. They've been in the wind since the day before the Burgundy heist."

Carson suddenly perked up. The agent was wide awake now.

"Cameron, the older of the two, served with Trip's brother, Mark, in Afghanistan," Kevin confirmed.

"What branch?"

"Navy. They were both frogmen, fought together during the height of our ops in Kunduz and Korengal."

"Jesus, they were in the thick. Nothing but firefights and roast beef. What about the younger brother, Michael?"

"He's been a little tougher to crack," Kevin admitted. "We learned more from his Instagram account than any of the databases. He was a good student, an athlete. Spent some time abroad after high school. He's now an extreme travel guide. Takes rich folks all over the world on crazy expeditions—summit climbs to Kilimanjaro, rafting the Amazon, you name it. He's an expert mountaineer, survivalist, and, from what we saw in Mexico, very skilled in combat."

"Where the hell did he get that type of combat training, his brother?" Carson wondered aloud.

"I would imagine Cameron buttoned Trip and Michael up pretty nicely. It's what he does for a living."

The young agent pulled the photos marked with red from the wall—leaving only Trip, Cameron and Michael. "These are our boys."

"One down, two to go," Carson sighed.

"Yes, sir. We're still pulling at some strings, something'll shake out."

"They're too smart to go to their old networks, so they're in the wild—alone," Carson pondered.

"They'll screw up somewhere, sir."

"No, they're perfectly at ease in this situation. They're immune to fear, used to being hunted, and experts at evasion. They might actually drag this out several hours or more," the veteran added with a sense of sarcasm.

The two agents examined the board, both deep in thought.

"Next move?" the younger asked.

"Activate the entire North American network."

"That's sixty-three operatives, sir."

"I know what it is, Kevin. Make it happen. I want everyone pulled off whatever the hell they're working on. Now."

Just then, one of a dozen senior analysts appeared from behind the massive server at the edge of the command center.

"We've got something," the analyst announced. "There's an older Lyle brother, James. Teaches English in Delaware. Agents are on route now, sir."

"Good," Carson responded. "Eyes only. No contact."

"You got it. Anything else?"

"Yes. I want facial recognition run on every video from every gate, at every terminal, in every airport within two hundred miles of the Mexican border. Go back seventy-two hours."

"Yes, sir. We'll start pulling it now."

And as swiftly as the analyst had appeared, he was gone.

●　　　　●　　　　●

Cameron Lyle took short breaths, gazing at the city lights that hovered beyond the dashboard. A sudden movement in his right peripheral snapped him from a temporary daydream. It was just another random businessman walking past his car and melting into the darkness. The black Honda sat undetected on the curb, neatly blending in with a line of parked cars that stretched for blocks.

With Michael in Ireland, Cam knew better than to visit any friends or family. He realized at some point the CIA would put his name and face to the shootout in Mexico, then cast a net over everyone he knew. Yet, here he sat, parked across the street from Wilmington University in Delaware on a stake-out for his older brother. Cam rubbed his hands together to keep the cold at bay and focused his eyes on the Dorothy M. Peoples Library Building.

It was a simple tactic. Cam knew that if he or Michael had been identified by the CIA, the agency would send a team to monitor James— standard operating procedure.

So, Cam was essentially using James as bait—a dangerous attempt to lure any potential CIA teams out into the open, and, more importantly, to lay eyes on the men who'd murdered his friend. It was a pre-emptive strategy that Cam had carefully plotted. In the two hours since he pulled into town, nothing had caught his attention. But he was aware that his counter-surveillance skills couldn't match the CIA's best field agents. His only advantage would come in the form of operational combat tactics. And he was poised to use them.

CHAPTER THIRTY

Carson was finally getting some sleep at a nearby safe house when his phone rang. In a pre-programmed, robot-like response, he sat up from the bed.

"Yeah."

"We've got a hit on Cameron Lyle, sir." It was Kevin from the ops center.

"Where?"

"The team we put on the older brother in Hockessin just checked in."

"Cameron's with the older brother?" *He's dumber than we gave him credit for,* thought Carson.

"Not exactly. Our recon team actually identified him in a perimeter sweep. Cameron Lyle is apparently staked out in a black, late-model Honda."

"What do you mean 'staked out?'"

"For some reason, he's monitoring James."

Carson was slightly perplexed. "Keep our guys back, but don't lose sight of him."

"You don't want to pick him up?"

"Not yet. Our target is the ossuary, not the Lyles. Figure out what the hell Cameron's up to, and nobody move until either Michael pops his head out, or we have a visual on the target."

"Copy that."

．　　　　　．　　　　　．

Hours later, after following James back to his residence from campus, Cam pulled the black Honda out of the neighborhood and onto a backroad that took him to a Super 8 Motel in nearby New Castle. He had kept a safe distance between himself and James during the drive home and didn't notice any suspicious followers. It seemed strange. Surely there was a CIA team somewhere out there.

It was only a matter of time, he thought.

．　　　　　．　　　　　．

Meanwhile, the sun was setting on the west coast. Rand returned to his hotel with a bottle of whiskey. It had been a long day of hits and misses at the San Francisco field office.

Settled in his room, the agent pulled the bottle from a brown paper bag and lifted it to his lips. Before he could get a taste, his moment of relaxation was interrupted by a phone call.

"Hello?"

"Rand, it's Agent Reynolds."

"Hey, what's up?"

"We got something here."

"You're not at the office still, are you?"

"Yeah, we were getting a few surveillance teams in place," Reynolds explained. "I wanted to wait until everyone checked in. Get this shit—I just heard from the team assigned to James Lyle in Delaware. And guess what they picked up?"

"What?"

"There's another surveillance team on him."

"Another team?" Rand set the bottle of whiskey on the nightstand and paced over to the window. "What *other* team?"

"Definitely not ours. NSA or CIA, maybe."

"And they're tailing James Lyle?" Rand echoed.

"That's the funny thing," replied Reynolds. "Our guys had only been on him for an hour before they noticed the tail. But whoever the hell they are, they were following James back to his house, then peeled off."

"*Peeled off?* So where are they now?"

"They're staked out at a jewelry store parking lot across from a motel in New Castle."

"So, you think they were tailing James Lyle, but now they're in New Castle? Reynolds, please don't tell me our team has pulled off their target just to chase some random assholes who *might* be tailing our guy," dared Rand.

"Listen, I completely understand," Reynolds agreed. "But our guys had to make a split-second decision. They're keeping tabs on everything. I promise."

"Fine. I'm on the next flight out. Have a car ready for me in Philly."

"You got it, man. Have a safe trip," Reynolds offered before hanging up.

Rand placed the phone on the dresser and began packing. He hadn't checked in with Brodsky in over forty-eight hours and made a mental note to do so when he got to the airport. The Special Agent in Charge would surely be upset with a cross-country manhunt, but Rand was confident all the pieces were falling into place.

Then it hit him—if the Lyles had indeed stolen a CIA asset from a cargo ship in the Pacific, the tail on James was most certainly theirs. And it wasn't a surveillance detail—it was a hit team. He scrambled for his phone and scrolled through his contacts until he found Melissa Dagan, then made the call.

"Hello?"

"Melissa, this is Rand." He tried his best to sound calm.

"Hey, stranger! Great to hear your voice. You in town?"

"No, I'm in San Fran, believe it or not."

"Oh okay. Well, I'm about to leave the office, what's up?" Melissa asked.

"That heist at sea you were telling me about—"

"Listen, Rand. That's all off-the-record, I'm not sure—"

"No, I get it. I do," pleaded Kershaw. "And this is going to sound crazy, but I think I have your pirates wrapped up in my case. And we just made one of your surveillance details on a next of kin."

"Really?" Melissa's interest level shot up. "What's the name?"

"James Lyle. His brother, Cameron, is our suspect."

Rand could hear her working a keyboard.

"I got nothing," she replied. "None of our current surveillance ops are assigned to a James Lyle."

"Black ops maybe?"

"We're not going there, my friend."

"Fine." Rand was losing patience. "You know what I think? I think those are *your* guys out there, and the second my suspect shows up they're going to put a bullet in his head and effectively ruin my career." He took a deep breath. "You gotta help me out, Melissa. Please."

"Look, I really don't have anything earth shattering for you. I've got the report pulled up from the freighter heist, but most of this stuff is redacted. There's one file here, and a bunch more that are classified. I don't have that kind of clearance."

"What's in the unclassified file?"

"Um, it's just that field report our San Diego team filed from the cargo ship, *Maersk Burgundy*. Agent's name is blacked out. Not a lot here except what I've already told you—three male suspects posing as Coast Guard personnel. They pretended to run a routine check of the ship, then stole the asset."

"That's it?"

"Well, wait a minute. There's one more report attached to it." Melissa waited for the file to download. "Okay...this is weird."

"What is it?"

"It's a Pentagon document dated April 17, 1962." Melissa spoke slowly, paraphrasing the report as she read it. "USS Oklahoma City, on her way back from training exercises off Japan, picks up four castaways from an unknown island in the middle of the Pacific. Says they carried with them a 'strange device of some kind.' The castaways were brought aboard the Oklahoma City and taken to Pearl Harbor for eventual transport back to the mainland."

"Anything else?" Rand asked, clearly perplexed.

"That's it. Make heads or tails of it, but that's all I can give you. The rest is above my pay grade."

"Wait a sec—" Rand fumbled. "What *strange device* are they talking about?"

"I have no idea."

He took a moment to let it all sink in. "I can't thank you enough, Melissa. I promise I won't bug you with this again."

"My pleasure. But listen closely, Rand," she was whispering now, "if we get your boy in our sights and he's the one from the Burgundy, he won't last long. You want these guys? Better take your chance as soon as you get it."

"Understood."

CHAPTER THIRTY-ONE

New Castle, Delaware

It was shortly after four in the morning when a Chevy Tahoe pulled off the exit ramp. His local team had already confirmed that the presumed CIA spooks were still camped out across from the Super 8. Rand Kershaw struggled to keep his eyes open as he navigated his way through a matrix of one-way streets and finicky traffic lights.

He needed to get eyes on the situation and somehow course-correct the mission. Soon, the town would awaken, and a new game of cat-and-mouse would commence.

The dark blue Tahoe pulled into a convenience store where two agents sat idly in a black sedan next to a dumpster. Rand parked in a space out front and exited the vehicle. He walked to the front entrance and briefly locked eyes with his agents sitting in the sedan. With a nod, contact was established.

He spent no more than a minute inside the small, run-down store before returning to the Tahoe, where he then placed a small microphone into his right ear. Rand pulled out of the space and exited the small lot. The black sedan followed.

"Talk to me," Rand said, checking his rearview.

"Special Agent Kershaw, this is Briggs and Vacano. Thanks for joining us."

"My pleasure, gentlemen. Do we know if our mystery boys have a second-layer perimeter in place, or are they alone?"

"Can't confirm that, sir. We were a little light on resources, but haven't caught any additional teams in our net. Just two guys in an old Mercury."

"Are you both absolutely certain these men were on James Lyle, or are we about to crash another agency's investigation over a coincidence?"

"Yes sir, they were definitely tracking James Lyle back to his house last night. All of their movements were classic tradecraft."

"Copy that. I'm circling around to the west, gonna try and sneak in a little closer."

"Sounds good. Keep your head down," Briggs warned from the sedan.

Rand pushed several blocks north before hanging a left at a major intersection and wrapping around to the opposite side of the jewelry store. He inched the Tahoe one more block and into one of the many motels lining the street. It gave him a safe vantage point of both the jewelry store and the Super 8.

After a prolonged scan of the area, he made them. It was the early model Ford Mercury with a faded dark green finish. *A real piece of shit*, Rand thought. *Perfect cover for the neighborhood.*

He jumped out of the SUV and slung his messenger bag over his shoulder, then marched to the motel entrance where a young Indian man rested behind the counter.

"FBI," Rand sharply announced, as he flashed his federal badge. "I need a room facing the street. This is a federal investigation so don't bother typing anything into the computer. Just a key. Now."

The kid fumbled for a room key and handed it over the counter. Rand exited the rear of the motel and hustled up a flight of stairs to the second-floor walkway, where he checked his room key and broke right down the catwalk. Barging into room 6C, he pulled a set of binoculars from his messenger bag. He now had eyes on the two men sitting in the Ford Mercury.

"What the hell are you guys up to?" Rand whispered to himself.

He patiently sat on the bed, raising and lowering his binoculars every few minutes until the sun began cresting over the skyline to the east. Once the sun rose above New Castle, he moved to the floor, countering any reflection from his binoculars.

Ten minutes later, as he crouched in front of a full-length sliding glass door, he noticed some movement inside the Ford.

Rand again pulled the binoculars to his eyes. Two hundred yards away, in the green car, a man peered intently over the steering wheel while another rustled with something in the passenger seat—it looked like a camera. The men were suddenly fixated on the front of the Super 8 across the street.

Rand swept his binoculars to the right. He squinted deeply into the lenses and adjusted the focus. A man emerged from a first-floor room and began walking to a nearby car. As everything came into focus, he saw it.

It was Cameron Lyle. Rand held his breath in disbelief. In a hushed tone, he spoke into the earpiece. "We've got eyes on Cameron Lyle. Repeat, I've got Cameron Lyle."

"Copy that," Briggs confirmed from several blocks away.

•　　　　•　　　　•

Cam reached for the door of his car when he first felt it—the eyes watching. His finely tuned instincts assured him. He opened the door and sat in the car for a moment before moving a muscle. His mind raced, but he had been trained for this type of scenario. At the very least, he knew his cover was blown. His next move would determine his fate.

He put the car in reverse and glanced into the rearview mirror. *There they are*, he thought when he spotted an older green car; he could make out the silhouette of two adult males inside. He jerked the Accord back into drive and hastily pulled out of the parking lot. Surely, the spooks would follow. He decided to continue as planned and headed straight for Hockessin to pick up James' tail again. Any variance from his previous behaviors would tip off his new CIA friends. He needed to appear completely oblivious to their presence.

Cam drove several miles and checked the rearview again. The green car was nowhere to be seen, but that's exactly how it was supposed to be. He made his way to James' Hockessin neighborhood, where he saw his brother leaving for work. *Right on schedule*, he thought.

Cam followed from a distance. It was now time to make his move.

His plan was to lure the CIA team to a place that gave him a strategic advantage—a bridge underpass, an empty building, anywhere he could hunker down and win a gunfight.

Meanwhile, Rand had hustled from the room to his vehicle in pursuit of his ghost. He now crept the SUV along a side street to keep up, all while trying to remain undetected by the CIA agents lurking in the area. Cam's black Honda Accord had just u-turned a half-mile from Rand's position and was about to cross in front of him as the agent rested at an intersection. Seconds later, the Accord passed by.

"He's headed north on Burlings. All units stay back. I repeat, stay back. There's too much commotion as it is, I don't want to give ourselves away just yet."

Rand hit his blinker and carefully pulled out behind his target and stayed several cars away. The mystery men were still nowhere to be found. He knew for certain they were CIA—*who else would be chasing Cameron Lyle?* And according to Melissa Dagan, his target wasn't going to last long. He needed to get Cameron off the street as quickly and quietly as possible.

CHAPTER THIRTY-TWO

James Lyle parked his car and walked through the brisk morning air to campus hall. Wilmington University was quieter than usual. It was a Friday and Spring Break was only a week away.

As the professor disappeared from sight, Cam pulled away from the campus and kept his attention in the rearview mirror. They were out there—somewhere.

On his drive into town the day before, he'd taken note of a small abandoned service station off a quiet street. The building's longer-than-usual driveway and overall position fit perfectly into his new strategy.

Several blocks from campus, he hung a right and went straight for the service station. Cam pulled the Honda Accord up its long driveway. The building had been abandoned long ago; its faded white brick exterior relayed a long history of forgone mechanics, customers, drug dealers and loiterers. Several of the window panes were smashed and tags had been spray-painted onto the walls by local gang members. It was a perfect hunting ground.

He parked the car around the back, leaving it just noticeable enough to be seen by anyone passing by—anyone who happened to be looking for it. Cam dug through his backpack and quickly found a knife, which he clipped to his belt. He checked his 9mm pistol and tucked it into his waistline.

The former SEAL slipped into the building through a broken window and took up position. Knelt behind a row of old metal stock shelves, he had the perfect vantage point down the long driveway leading up to the service station. Now, he waited.

Thirty minutes went by before any movement stirred outside. Just as he'd hoped, the old Ford Mercury slowly turned in and crept its way up the gravel drive toward his position. The trap was set.

With a few preparatory breaths, Cam trained his 9mm on the front door as the sedan came to a stop just outside. Suddenly, from the shadows behind him, he heard the unmistakable click of a pistol. He'd been out-flanked—they'd gotten the jump on him. Cameron braced for a quick death.

"Drop your weapon," the voice demanded in a low, soft tone.

Why isn't he screaming at me? Why am I not dead?

Cam calmly surrendered his 9mm to the air and was very careful to avoid any sudden movements. He glanced at the CIA agents standing outside observing their surroundings, seemingly unaware of what was happening inside.

They're not from the same team, Cam noted with startling confusion.

"Special Agent Kershaw, FBI," the voice warned.

FBI? Cam could hear the man's footsteps draw closer.

"We don't have a lot of time," the agent said, as he snatched the pistol from Cam's hand. "That's a CIA hit team outside with a dozen more on the way. You need to come with me now. I'm your only way out alive."

CHAPTER THIRTY-THREE

They emerged from the woods in a full sprint and spilled out into a back lot behind a shopping center. With his gun still fixed on Cam, Agent Kershaw motioned his prisoner to the car.

"Let's go," Kershaw ordered.

Without argument, Cam jumped into the passenger seat. The SUV pulled away and tore around the building and east onto Ridgeland Boulevard.

"Suspect in custody," the agent called out, gasping for breath. "I repeat, I have Cameron Lyle in custody."

"I don't get it, what is this?" Cam asked. "How do you know that was a hit team?"

Rand chuckled sarcastically at his captive's lack of situational awareness. "Because, whatever the hell you stole from them, they plan on killing you for it."

Cam was stunned. *How did the FBI know about the heist? Did we not hide our tracks at all?*

"I, on the other hand, am not here to kill you," Rand assured him.

The Tahoe careened around another corner. Rand punched the gas, still anxiously gripping his pistol in his hand. The SUV now darted toward the interstate.

"So, what the hell does the FBI want with me?"

Rand smiled. He'd waited for this moment for so long. "The Wynn job. Hamilton. We put it all together. You guys are *good*!"

"I don't know what the hell you're talking about. You're with the Knights of Medina, aren't you?" Cam guessed. "Let me outta this fucking car right now!"

"Knights of who? You're not going anywhere, sweetheart."

Rand yanked the wheel and slammed the brakes as the Tahoe dug into a sharp turn and came to a sudden stop. He jumped out and walked around to the passenger side.

The adrenaline-rushed agent opened the door and yanked his prisoner out at gunpoint. Rand forced his captive's hands behind his back and the moment he reached for a set of zip ties, Cam thrust his weight down and slid to the right. The maneuver was executed within the blink of an eye and after a slippery tussle, Cam grasped Rand's wrist, trying to loosen the FBI agent's grip on the pistol.

Rand was strong and well-trained. Instinct immediately guided the bottom of his right foot to Cam's chest, where it made direct contact—a seamless counter-assault on his adversary. The former Navy SEAL gasped and fell backward. Rand's gun was again trained on Cam.

"On the ground, asshole!" the agent yelled.

"You're making a huge mistake—"

"I said on the ground!"

Cam's eyes wandered above the agent's shoulder—just in time to catch a dusty sedan turn in their direction from the adjacent intersection.

"Shit," Cam blurted out.

Rand wasn't biting. But that all changed seconds later when Cam's reaction was supported by the sound of screeching tires behind him. The agent quickly spun and pinched his weapon toward the oncoming dark green Ford Mercury.

As Rand peered down the barrel of his FBI-issued .40 caliber Glock, he saw that the car wasn't slowing but gaining momentum toward him. His training told him to squeeze four immediate rounds into the windshield. But there was something holding him back—these were CIA agents.

Screw it.

Rand released the air in his lungs and began pulling the trigger. Everything was in slow motion now. Silence blanketed the street as three cloudy bursts appeared in the car's windshield. And in one fluid motion, Rand released a fourth round before diving for cover behind his SUV.

The Ford swept to his left and spun out in the small parking lot just off the main street. Within seconds, two men leapt from the Mercury as their shots echoed in the morning air, pinging off the opposite side of the Tahoe.

"FBI, hold your fire!" Rand yelled, his back now pressed against the passenger door.

To his surprise, the command was returned with more gunfire. He could hear two sets of footsteps against the pavement—one approaching him slowly, the other flanking him from the side. Both attackers continued with sporadic, well-placed rounds of fire.

Rand quickly checked over his shoulder. *Shit!* Cameron Lyle was gone.

"Shots fired! Shots fired! Target is on the move!" he yelled over the channel, hoping Briggs and Vacano were coming to his aid.

He was about to be in the crossfire of two shooters and needed to quickly find another position. He rolled right and unleashed a flurry of rounds, then darted into the open toward a small liquor store.

After a full sprint, he found cover along the outside wall of the building. Sixty feet away, a CIA agent grunted in pain as a .40 caliber round bore through his shoulder. There was now one injured and one still on the attack.

Where the hell is my backup?

Rand popped his head around to check the area and spotted the injured shooter squirming behind a large trash can. The second shooter, however, was suddenly unaccounted for. Everything was happening too fast.

The abbreviated silence was interrupted by a powerful blast of semi-automatic rifle fire. Rand crouched in defense as sparks of hot shrapnel lit up around him. The rapid bursts blanketed his position. He began inching his way against the concrete building, blindly returning fire at the CIA agent closing in on him from thirty yards.

His heart sank when he turned the corner of the building. The metal fencing behind the liquor store guaranteed there would be no escape route here. Rand was outgunned and pinned down, trapped like an animal.

His plight was elevated by the popping of secondary gunfire—a pistol. At first, Rand assumed the previously injured attacker had gotten back into the fight, only increasing the odds he would die. Seconds later, he realized the 9mm was *returning* fire, not supporting it.

Now pinned between a dumpster and the wall, Rand could see the advancing CIA operative was being driven back by something—or *someone*. To his shock, the bullet-riddled Chevy Tahoe peeled around the building in reverse between he and the shooter. There in the driver's seat was Cameron Lyle—completely unhinged, firing from the window as the Tahoe screeched to a stop.

"Get in!"

Rand unleashed his last four rounds and leapt into the backseat. With a sudden jerk of acceleration, the Tahoe roared through the front lot and disappeared from sight as a few desperate shots from an assault rifle ricocheted against the rear doors.

CHAPTER THIRTY-FOUR

Rand reached for his right ear with concern, then patted both of his pockets.

"My earpiece!"

"We just survived a firefight and you're looking for an earpiece?" Cam shouted.

Rand's eyes shifted to Cam, then to the floorboard. He'd lost the upper hand and desperately needed to regain it. With breakneck precision, he snapped his Glock to Cam's face, only to be matched with equal speed. The two pistols hung ominously in the air.

The Tahoe sprinted down the four-lane city street and, without taking his eyes off the FBI agent, Cam accelerated with purpose: 80...90...100. The Chevy was nearly floating now.

"You pull that trigger and we're both dead," he threatened.

110...115.

Rand found himself again in an unwinnable situation. After a brief gut check, he reluctantly lowered his weapon. But Cameron wasn't reciprocating—his 9mm still frozen in the air like a death wish.

"I'll lower this as soon as you throw your cellphone out the window," Cam demanded. "Do it. Now!"

"I need to—"

"You need to throw that goddamn phone out before they track our location. Don't make me cancel you, man. I just risked my damn life back there."

"I'm turning it off, Cameron. Completely off—untraceable," Rand said, doing his best to hold on to his only line to the outside world.

"Fine. Turn it off and give it to me!"

Rand dug into his pocket and pulled the cellphone out. He shut the power down and handed it to the wild-eyed man behind the wheel.

The Tahoe's speed leveled off and a slight calm began to fill the cab.

To the agent's relief, Cam finally lowered his gun and veered onto a side street. Both men were completely turned around now, with absolutely no idea where they were.

After a moment of pause, Cam zeroed in on a pharmacy he remembered from his childhood. Having grown up in neighboring Hockessin, it was a familiar landmark in an otherwise unfamiliar part of town.

●   ●   ●

CIA Black Site, just outside Los Angeles, California
"You lost them?" Carson screamed into the phone. "You're supposed to be the best goddamn surveillance team in the world, and you lose one retired SEAL and an FBI field agent? You're pathetic!"

He slammed the phone down in frustration and reached for his bottled water. Cameron Lyle had slipped his noose twice in the last week—something no man had ever accomplished before.

Seconds later, his assistant appeared from the shadows and joined the rest of the ops team, who were now scattered among the abandoned third floor. The place buzzed with energy. Something was up.

Carson sat frustrated as Kevin approached. "What is it?"

"We've got Michael Lyle on the grid, sir."

The enraged vet jumped from his seat. *Thank God for small favors.*

"We're still working Cameron and the FBI agent," Kevin continued. "But facial recognition got a hit on Michael at Denver International forty-nine hours ago."

"Where was he headed?" Carson was eager for a victory that would end this madness once and for all.

"We don't know exactly, but he was at the international terminal when security cams caught him getting off an escalator. There were only three flights that left the terminal within an hour of the video."

"Locations?"

Kevin shuffled through some paperwork. "One flight to Dublin, another to Amsterdam, and a third to Barcelona with a stop at JFK. We checked the New York footage—nothing there, which leaves Dublin and Amsterdam."

"Perfect. Activate our agents in those two cities. I want teams on the ground within the hour."

"Recon or assault?"

"Both."

●   ●   ●

Dalkey District, Dublin, Ireland

Michael Lyle waited patiently for his food delivery of chicken cordon with a side of egg noodles ordered from a quaint little restaurant down the street.

It was his third day in Dublin and the low-budget bottle of Irish whiskey was almost dry. Time was drifting painfully slow.

Michael was snapped from his wandering thoughts by Corin, who peeled around the corner from his cluttered office. The look on his face said it all.

"I think I've done it," the young Irishman proclaimed.

"Don't mess with me," Michael threatened, as he sat up from the couch. "I swear to God—"

"No, seriously. I mean, it's not really earth-shattering, but I think I cracked it."

Corin pulled up next to Michael on the couch. The stout American could see the excitement in the young man's eyes. The philologist was truly passionate about his work.

"Okay, I composed a formulaic process that breaks down basic syntax and—"

"Speak English. What the hell does it say?"

"It reads like instructions of some sort," Corin explained, placing a photocopy of the tablet on the coffee table. "It says, 'Release the valve and blood shall flow.'" Corin's finger traced the tablet photo as he read. "Then, 'Push, or *move*, toward the face of Medina.'" Corin paused for effect. "And finally, there's this last part, 'Activate the Sun, and the stars shall open.'"

"What the hell?" Michael tried to wrap his head around the words. "Release the valve," he repeated. "Push toward the face and activate the sun."

"Yeah, pretty much," confirmed Corin.

The deciphered message played repeatedly in Michael's head as he tried to visualize the strange elements of the device. It slowly began to make sense. *These are instructions on how to turn the damn thing on!*

The bigger question, however, was what would happen once the device was activated?

"I need a computer," Michael demanded.

"Yeah, sure."

They made their way down the hall and into the office—a poorly lit sanctuary of pin-up posters and action figures. Several expensive monitors lined the wall.

"This is a closed network, right?" Michael asked.

"Of course, only the best."

Michael typed away until he landed on a peculiar Internet forum—the same message board they had previously been contacting Rook through. He and Cam were now using it for their own cryptic communications.

Michael logged in and posted a short message.

LibertyBell_12: we crossed the positive with negative.

It was a message Cam would understand. And now that it had been posted, Michael needed to move.

"Corin, this has been a real pleasure," he began. "But I'm afraid it's time for me to go."

After copying the translation onto a small piece of paper, Michael grabbed an extra pair of jeans from the floor and a set of keys off the coffee table, shoving both into his backpack and dashing to the front door.

"That's it?" Corin asked with confusion.

"That's it. I owe you one, me auld flower—to use the Dublin vernacular for friend."

"But what about your food?"

"It's all yours!"

And with that, Michael left the apartment, exited the building and began walking westward to the nearby DART station. His work in Dublin was complete.

He paced up the footpath along Ardeevin Road, then ducked into a pharmacy. He used cash to purchase an envelope and a few stamps, then quickly left. Michael continued up Ardeevin to the station and slid a few Euros into a ticket kiosk outside. With a push through the turnstiles, he descended a set of stairs to the platform below.

Michael checked his surroundings and shoved the notebook paper into the envelope. The finishing touch was written on the front with a black permanent marker.

P.O. BOX 2499

PHILADEPLHIA, PA 19130

He checked his watch—it was nine minutes until the next train would arrive. Michael marched to the end of the platform where a postal kiosk sat in a corner behind two vending machines. He stuck three Priority stamps on the outside and slid the envelope into a small mail shoot. While it would take four days to arrive in the States, it was an insurance policy that assured the decrypted information would be passed on in the event something happened to him.

Chapter Thirty-Five

Cameron Lyle and Rand Kershaw sat face-to-face in the booth of a diner, located just over the Delaware River off Interstate 295 in Pennsylvania.

"So, what's our status here, Cameron? What's your play?" the agent asked.

Cam inhaled, deep in thought. "I'm not holding you hostage. It's not like that. You can walk out that door right now. But you're not taking me with you."

Rand glanced at the front door. It was time to lay his cards on the table. "I know everything," he stated.

"I don't see any crystal ball in your hands."

"I know that you and Trip Montgomery held up the Wynn in Las Vegas and that you donated most of the loot to St. Jude's. The third member of your team is your little brother, Michael."

Just then, the waitress came to refill their coffee, putting Rand's big reveal on a momentary hold.

"You can't prove anything," Cam pointed out once she was out of earshot. He was absolutely stunned that Rand knew *that* much.

A sly grin appeared on the FBI agent's face. "I can prove everything. How a year earlier Trip orchestrated a cyberattack on Hamilton, and how he used a dummy corporation—Boro Industries—to transfer the final payment of over a million water filters to suffering children in Africa."

The agent was getting too close for comfort now. Cam maintained his best poker face, but a rage began to swell within him. Rand took note of the increased pulse in Cam's neck, the reddening of his ears. *I've struck a nerve,* he thought.

"You seem to have it all figured out," Cam blankly stated.

"That's the thing," confessed Rand. "I still haven't figured out why you would board a cargo ship at open sea and steal a CIA asset." He began to chuckle at the soldier sitting across from him. "I mean, what the hell were you guys thinking?"

Cam was saved from having to answer by the arrival of their food. The waitress dropped plates of pancakes, eggs, bacon and other sides amongst the table. And just as quickly as she had brought the food, she was gone again.

"If you think I'm going to confess to you at this goddamn diner you're crazy, Agent Kershaw. Besides, what do you think is waiting for you out there?" Cam motioned toward the parking lot and the world that extended far beyond it. "After what happened today, you think the CIA is gonna let you off the hook?"

Cam covered his breakfast in syrup and began cutting away with his fork.

"I'm a federal agent, Cameron. I'm not in danger. Or is this all just part of your escape plan?"

Cam found amusement in the bluff. He leaned over his plates and spoke in a low tone. "I'm a former Navy SEAL. Hell, I trained some of the fiercest fighting machines the world has ever known. Do you really think you *have* me here? I'm one punch away from never seeing you again."

The death stare sent shivers down Rand's spine.

With that, the two adversaries continued eating their breakfast without revisiting the subject—or *any* subject for that matter. Instead, they each contemplated their next move in silence. For Cam, it was how to get rid of the pesky agent. For Rand, it was how to bring his prisoner in without getting himself killed. They were at a crossroads.

After their meal, there was a delicate standoff at the Tahoe.

"I'm driving. It's my truck," Rand finally snapped.

"Fine, but I'm still hot," Cam threatened with a tap of his waistband.

It was the first thing they'd agreed on since the shootout. Rand toiled with the idea of heading straight for the Philadelphia field office—a mere thirty minutes away—but instead chose to pull the SUV aimlessly out onto the street, with no clear destination in mind.

"I need a convenience store," demanded Cam.

"For what?"

"A phone."

"Okay, but I thought you said no phones? Mine's in your pack."

"Not *our* phones. I need a burner."

"Fair enough," replied Rand. "Ya know, at some point within the next ten minutes, I'm going to call in to my team. I can't just let you walk away from this, Cameron. There's too much at stake."

"Like what?"

"Like my entire career."

At the next red light, Rand jerked the Tahoe into a gas station and pulled into an open space. Cameron jumped out and hurried inside, silently hoping the agent would simply pull away and disappear forever.

He marched to the counter and paid cash for a prepaid flip-phone. He grabbed his change from the cashier and broke left toward the bathrooms, then slipped out the back exit. As the metal door closed behind him, Cam made his way beyond a dumpster to a narrowly wooded area.

He flipped open the phone and dialed James' number. *C'mon...c'mon!*

"Hello?"

"James!"

"Cam, where the hell are you?"

"I'm fine. I'm in Mexico," he lied. "I just wanted to—"

"They came, Cam."

"Who came?"

"Two local detectives. Except I don't think they were local detectives, if you know what I mean."

"They weren't. What did they want?"

"Exactly what you said, they asked when we had last spoke and if I had any idea where you or Michael were. I *knew* you were with Michael, you liar!"

"Listen to me, James. These men are very dangerous and—"

"Then why did you drag me into this?" James scolded.

"I didn't know where else to turn."

A brief silence followed, only to be broken by James' update. "The photos you sent. I don't know if you noticed, but there's one man in particular who's in all of them."

"No, I didn't catch that," Cam replied with concern.

"Well, he is. The link you attached to the National Archives photo, it was taken in the White House. So, I checked the visitor logs for that day, February 3rd, 1960."

"How the hell did you do that?"

"It's public record, moron. Of all the men scheduled to meet with Eisenhower that day, only one of them wasn't a cabinet member or Pentagon official."

"Who?"

"Dr. Marco Damion, an Italian physicist, worked on a lot of US government projects in his late-twenties and thirties. I looked him up, it says he's living in France now. Retired."

"James, you're a fucking genius!"

"Listen, I'm out. You can't call me again, do you understand?"

"I'm sorry, I didn't mean to—"

"Don't be sorry, bro. Just be safe. Take care of Michael and for Christ's sake do the right thing—whatever that may be."

"I will, I promise."

"Be careful, Cameron."

"Bye, James."

Cam had never intended to put James in danger and instantly regretted ever calling him in the first place.

It was time to break free from his FBI friend. As he turned to creep further into the shrubs and over to a library behind the store, he was met by

Rand—standing firmly against a tree with a .40 caliber aimed at his forehead. *Damnit, I left my bag in the truck!*

"Going somewhere?"

"Jesus Christ," Cam complained.

"This is it, Cameron. Toss the gun on the ground."

"Or what?"

"I've put a year of my life into this moment. Don't think for a second I won't put holes in your kneecaps and drag you back to Vegas. The fun's over, drop the gun."

Cam knew the agent had him. The fun was indeed over. He was out of options and maybe, just maybe, the FBI gave him a better shot at survival than anything else. He slowly reached for his 9mm, and for a split-second considered squeezing off a quick round at Rand. But his better judgment prevailed, and he dropped the pistol onto the ground at the agent's feet.

"Good," Rand said, as he leaned down to pick it up. "Hands behind your back."

Cam followed the agent's orders and allowed the zip ties to be secured around his wrists behind him. The pair made their way around the building and piled back into the Tahoe.

Rand yanked the burner phone from Cam's pocket and held it in his hand as he pulled away. He immediately dialed the Las Vegas field office— Steve Brodsky's line.

"Steve, it's Kershaw. I've got Cameron Lyle in custody."

"Jesus, Rand, what the hell is going on out there?"

"It's been crazy. I pulled Lyle from a standoff with another team, we think it was CIA. A firefight ensued and I lost all my comms. I'm heading to Philly now."

"Damn right you are!" Brodsky sounded good and pissed off. "Get your ass to the local field office immediately! And yes, that was the CIA. They've got agents swarming our offices. You are to bring Lyle in and hand him over to them. This is officially out of our jurisdiction."

"You have to be kidding me!" Rand shot back. "This is our guy, Steve!"

"Well, apparently, he's their guy, too. They've had him under surveillance for months in connection to an international gun-smuggling operation. You'll get your shot at him, but he's theirs for now. Nothing you can do."

"That's all bullshit, Steve. I'm bringing him back to Vegas and we'll get the brother, too."

"It's not happening, Rand. This is a direct order, and it's not worth me losing my job over. Take Cameron Lyle to the Philly office immediately!"

And before the frustrated agent could argue further, the line went dead.

Rand knew better. His mind spun through various options and potential next moves. Rand Kershaw the FBI agent was bringing Cameron Lyle in and handing him over to the CIA. But Rand Kershaw the human being was not about to send a decorated war veteran to his certain death. He peered over at Cameron, who sat quietly next to him, staring out the window as the world passed by. Rand had read his military files—the man had saved lives, risked everything for his country. He was a hero.

And in that moment, the Wynn and Hamilton heists meant a little less to Rand Kershaw—the human being.

CHAPTER THIRTY-SIX

Michael caught the first glimpse of his train cornering the overpass above Sorrento Drive. An anxious curiosity started to run over him. He hadn't spoken with Cam since leaving the States and did his best to assume that all was going according to plan.

He stood passively as the train's doors parted, then stepped off the ledge and onto DART #33 along with a dozen commuters. The train set out and took him along the scenic cliffs overlooking the Irish Sea. Beyond his window, Michael took note of the sparkling water, dancing beneath the hovering sun. It was his first moment of calm since arriving in Ireland.

As his mind drifted, he caught the intercom announcement for Blackrock Station, where he got off and observed the passengers who disembarked with him. The stop at Blackrock was no more than counter-surveillance tradecraft.

Michael rested on a bench and awaited the next train, which would take him to Connolly Station before a short bus ride to Dublin Airport. It was time to go home.

• • •

As the minutes passed, it was clear Rand had no destination in mind. He was frozen in his thoughts. The Tahoe wandered aimlessly through the outlying communities east of Philadelphia on the New Jersey side of the river.

"Let me guess…CIA's waiting for me in Philly?" Cam reasoned. "Your ass is on the line, and you're trying to figure out what to do with me. Am I close?"

"I'm bringing you in," Rand assured. "Why did you do it, Cameron?"

Cam grunted. "I have no idea. We were hired to steal it off the ship and return it to its rightful owner, who I now believe to be dead."

"Michael was in on it, too, wasn't he? Where is he now?"

"Someplace safe. Far away from here."

"What about Trip?"

Cam took a moment of pause. Hearing his friend's name sent shivers of guilt down his spine.

"He's dead," the soldier finally confirmed.

Rand closed his eyes with regret. "I'm sorry to hear that. Where did he die? I didn't think anyone was killed aboard the freighter."

"It wasn't the freighter," explained Cam. "He was killed when we were ambushed at the handoff."

"And the thing you stole?"

Cameron hesitated. "Well, how about before you turn me in, I show it to you? Turn left."

Rand gave him a pensive stare, then bucked the Tahoe left off Hadden Avenue and pushed north on 676 until they crossed the Delaware River again, back into Pennsylvania.

"Pull over here," Cameron directed.

Without argument, Rand banked the Chevy into a gravel parking lot. It was dusk and a painted sunset cast a glow above the Philadelphia skyline. It would be dark soon and Cam was intent on staying mobile. Surely, he was the subject of a multi-state, all-points bulletin by now. And the last thing he wanted was for Rand to receive backup.

They parked in a lot behind the Electric Factory, a standing-room music venue that was starting to fill with patrons. Rand cut the zip ties from Cam's wrists and the two men slipped out of the lot and made their way on foot down 7th Street. It was a pivotal moment for Special Agent Rand Kershaw.

He paused on the sidewalk and turned around to take one last look at the parking lot behind them. The weight of the world seemed to press down on his tired shoulders. He was taking a huge risk following Cam into the concrete jungle of Philadelphia, but he wasn't about to let his suspect slip away.

They continued their walk below the 676 interchange, southbound through Franklin Square and several blocks further until they reached Chestnut Street. From there, they broke left and marched another block before coming to a halt.

"Why here?" asked Rand.

"I just wanted to see it one more time."

The two men stood in the shadows of Independence Hall. The last of the tourists had shuffled out and were now meandering around with maps and cameras in hand. Cam stood straight with his arms at his sides, staring across the street with childish pride. The Liberty Bell glared back at him from behind her glass encasing.

She's beautiful, he thought.

For the next minute, they stood in silence. It was a moment of brevity they both sorely needed, and the great symbol of freedom and independence did not disappoint.

Rand had never seen her in person. Cam, however, had spent countless hours of his youth standing in this very spot. There was a connection he could not explain. He had been recruited at a small Navy office not far from here. He remembered it like it was yesterday—the day he signed his life away to the US government, grabbed a hot dog from a street vendor on Walnut, then walked into the Liberty Bell Center and placed his hand on her copper side. He'd returned many times in his life. But now, as he stood in her presence yet again, he wondered if it would be their last moment together.

Cam silently bid his old friend farewell and moved up the sidewalk. With Rand hot on his heels, he hailed a cab at the corner of Independence Hall East and Chestnut.

"Where to?" the young driver asked.

"The airport. International terminal," replied Cam.

"No!" Rand corrected from the sidewalk. "We're not doing this!"

"Get in, Special Agent Kershaw. I'm going to show you what all the fuss is about."

Rand reluctantly got in the backseat. "I can't let you flee the country. Please don't make me shoot you," he pleaded under his breath.

"I promise no one is getting shot. And I'm not fleeing the country." The lie felt easy to Cam.

"If you put me in danger, I'll kill you."

"Fine."

After a few passing minutes, Cam took stock of his situation and thought of his family. He needed to know if Hannah made it out with the girls. He needed to know they were okay.

"Give me the burner," he finally asked. "I need to make a call."

Rand reached into his pocket and handed over the small phone.

Cam dialed a number by heart.

"Hello?" a concerned voice answered.

Cam's eyes began to well. "Hannah, it's me."

"Cam! Oh my God! I've been so worried. Where are you, baby?"

"I'm okay—"

"No one's been up here. We're safe and sound. The girls are safe." She was crying now.

"I love you so much," he granted. "I never meant for any of this, I promise."

Cam finally broke down. He was gasping for air, doing his best to hold back the tears.

"I know, baby. It's okay," she sobbed. "We just want to see you."

Cam clenched his eyes closed. "I miss you and the girls so much. Can you put Abigail on?"

"Of course." Hannah shuffled the phone around as tiny footsteps drew closer to Cam's ear.

"Daddy?" the small voice said.

"Hey doodle-bug, it's me. Are you having fun at the cabin?"

"Yeah, but it's boring without you," she replied. "I wanna go fishing, but Mommy doesn't fish so good."

"No, she sure doesn't," he chuckled. "I'll be there soon and we'll do some real fishing."

"Okay, Daddy! Are you on your way?"

"Not yet. I need to go help Uncle Michael right now. But we'll try to get there soon, okay?"

"Uh-huh."

"Can you put your sister on the phone?"

The phone muffled yet again and seconds later the six-year-old began breathing heavily into it.

Cam's smile spoke a thousand words. "Hi Lindsay, it's Daddy."

"Hi, Daddy."

"Is everything going good up there?" he asked in a sweet, fatherly voice.

"Yes."

"Good. I miss you."

"I'm scared," she mumbled into the phone.

"I know, honey, but there's nothing to be scared of. Mommy won't let anything bad happen to you, I promise."

"Okay. I caught butterflies today. The pretty yellow ones you like."

"Oh, that sounds fun. I wish I was there to see them. I love those yellow butterflies."

"Yeah. Me too," she giggled.

"I love you so much, Lindsay."

"Love you too, Daddy. Here's Mommy." And without a goodbye, she handed the phone back to her mother.

"You girls go outside and play," Hannah was heard telling them. "Cam?"

"Yeah?"

"When can we go home?"

"I'll let you know something soon," he replied.

Hannah understood. The escape plan that took her and the children to the mountains was only to be executed in the most dangerous of situations. Surely something terrible had happened.

"Honey, is everyone okay?" she asked.

"Michael's traveling, but he's fine. We lost Trip."

Hannah closed her eyes and bit her lip. "Oh, Cameron, I'm so sorry. Am I ever going to see you again?" she whispered.

"Of course, you will. I'm Cameron freakin' Lyle."

She laughed. It was just enough to keep the tears back. "I can only assume you need to neutralize the threat first?" Hannah Lyle was in full military-wife mode now.

"Yeah, something like that. I'll be out of the country for a couple days, but I'll call you the second my feet hit the ground back home."

"Promise?"

"I promise. I love you and the girls so much, keep your heads down. You know what to look for."

She nodded silently. "I love you, too. Be careful."

"I will. Talk soon." He hung up and shoved the small phone into his pocket.

Rand watched with heartache. This criminal—this soldier—that had saved him from certain death, was displaying remarkable resolve. Cameron Lyle wasn't just a trained killer but was also a husband—a father who had just spoken to his children like any other loving parent would have.

In that moment, Rand respected Cameron more than he thought possible. He watched as the muscle-bound SEAL wiped tears from his face, bracing for what was to come next—whatever monumental hurdles the soldier would have to endure before being able to reunite with his family. It must've taken amazing strength to not drop everything and go to them—a strength that Rand didn't have or didn't understand. There was something important about what lay ahead. Something important enough that Cameron was willing to leave his family for. Rand began questioning his own resolve, and more importantly, his purpose.

The taxi pulled up on the curb at the International Terminal. Cam tossed the driver a twenty-dollar bill and grabbed his backpack.

"Where are we going, Cameron?"

"Follow me."

"No," Rand snapped. "Where the hell are we going? Do you have any idea the trouble I'm in?" he said under his breath.

"You're in more trouble than you can possibly imagine, agent. I need to get online."

"Not so fast," Rand grabbed the soldier's bicep. "You said you'd show me the asset."

"Assets—plural," Cam corrected. "And I will, but first I need to check on Michael."

"There's an internet cafe inside," assured Rand. "But we'll need to get through ticketing."

"There," Cam pointed. "American Airlines."

"Are you kidding me?"

"You're an FBI agent and this is a federal emergency," Cam envisioned. "You're carrying a prisoner to Paris. Just demand two seats on the next flight out and they'll push us right through security."

Rand hesitated.

"Look, Agent Kershaw, this place is probably already crawling with CIA operatives. We don't have time for considerations."

Cam was right. Rand needed to keep them moving. They were too exposed.

"Fine," the agent complied.

Cam pulled a blue passport from his pocket and handed it to Rand.

"Howard Groves?" the agent stated as he read the name inside. "Nice."

They made their way to the American Airlines ticketing desk. Cam pulled a ball cap from his pack and slid it onto his head. His gray cargo shorts, faded blue t-shirt and red Phillies hat provided camouflage among hundreds of other casually dressed travelers. Rand's disheveled suit, however, had all the markings of a federal agent.

After a few tense minutes at the desk, Rand was issued two tickets.

They proceeded to the first security check where Rand flashed his FBI badge at a TSA officer, who promptly escorted them around the metal detectors. As casually as possible, they rushed to the atrium and found an internet café.

In the back corner, Cam jumped behind a computer and began typing away on the keyboard. After a hurried login to a nondescript website, he scrolled through a message board until he found what he was looking for. *LibertyBell_12* had posted a message just over an hour ago.

He sat back and read the post. A sense of relief washed down his shoulders.

"What is it?" inquired Rand. He was getting more agitated as the seconds passed.

"Good news, that's what."

Cam began typing a response.

LibertyBell_75: stay where you are.

Unfortunately, there had been no pre-determined code phrase for it. Cam had to be direct and literal in his request for Michael to remain in Dublin. Now that they'd been made by the CIA, he couldn't risk his brother trying to re-enter the United States.

Rand watched with interest. "Stay where?"

Without answering, Cam stood and threw the backpack over his shoulder.

"Give that to me," demanded Rand. "The backpack."

Cam raised a disgruntled eyebrow at the agent.

"Prisoners aren't allowed a carry-on, dumbass. Besides, I need to put these guns away."

With a scowl, the soldier turned over the navy blue backpack. "Fine."

"You know we're not really flying to Paris, right?" said Rand, covertly placing both firearms in the pack.

"Yeah, sure. Follow me, I want to show you something."

They slid their way around gift shops and coffee kiosks until spotting a concierge desk outside the British Airways VIP Lounge.

"Passport," Cam insisted. "I need my passport back."

Without question, Rand handed it over. They approached the desk and flashed their IDs to the attractive young female and were immediately welcomed through the lounge and into a members only area. The two men casually turned left down a long hallway with cheap carpeting and light yellow walls. Finally, they reached the spa—a small room with several dozen lockers stacked along the right wall.

Cam retrieved a key from the backpack and shoved it into a locker at waist-level. Rand stood behind him, guarding against anyone who may have followed them in.

With a firm pull, Cam yanked a small brown duffle bag from the locker, then closed it shut.

He flashed a grin at his new friend. "You look like you could use a drink."

CHAPTER THIRTY-SEVEN

Michael Lyle got off at Connolly Station and walked hurriedly toward the *Dublin Coach* sign ahead, keeping one eye over his shoulder. An uneasy feeling fell over him as the corridor slowly emptied.

Then he saw them. His only escape was a public restroom immediately to his left. He lowered his shoulder and lunged hard, barreling through the door.

The two strangers bolted into action, pursuing their target into the bathroom, only to find a few travelers cleaning up at a row of white porcelain sinks. The men waited calmly for everyone to finish. And after the last traveler exited, one of the goons posted up outside, assuring no one else would be entering.

The second operative, a tall muscular man in street clothes, checked under the stall doors one-by-one. Nothing. As he made his way to the fourth stall, the metal door suddenly sprang open, hitting him in the face and tossing him several feet back.

Michael leapt from the stall and bore down on his assailant who swiftly countered the attack with a barrage of uppercuts. The two large men were now tangled up, tossing each other in unison against the wall, then to the sinks. A chunk of porcelain fell to the floor and shattered with a loud crash. With his hands around the man's throat, Michael swung to the left and launched him through another stall door, which snapped from its hinges and rested below the man, who now lay dazed on his back.

Just as Michael pulled a knife from his waistline, he could feel the cold steel tip of a silencer pressed against the back of his head. He'd felt it before, there was no question what it was. He slowly held the knife in the air as it was snatched from his hand.

The giant grizzly resting in the stall picked himself up and rose to his feet, grinning at his prey.

"End of the line, princess."

●   ●   ●

The foot traffic at Philadelphia International was starting to thin out. Cam and Rand sat at a small high-top inside Cibo Bistro & Wine Bar in Concourse B. They'd watched airport security, local police and federal K-9 teams pass by at a steady frequency. The walls were closing in, and Rand could only hold out on this charade for so long.

A couple gin and tonics sat in front of them.

"We were told it was excavated in South America. Supposed to be over a thousand years old," Cam explained, as he lifted the duffle bag onto the high-top and opened it up.

Rand leaned over his drink and peeked inside, unsure of what he was looking at. After a brief glance, he lifted his head nervously and leered over his shoulder, then back to the duffle bag for closer examination.

"Are those photographs?" he whispered.

"Yeah."

"Is that a goddamn lightsaber?"

Cam rolled his eyes. "Yeah."

"You're totally fucking with me, right?" Rand's voice began to rise.

"No. I'm not fucking with you," replied Cam as he sat back in his chair and took a pull from his glass. "People are dead."

Rand finally pulled his head back from the bag and returned to his seat. His mind spun a web of *what ifs?* The agent stared in bewilderment at Cam, the guy he'd been chasing for so long—one of the ghosts that had haunted his sleep.

"We snatched it from the freighter off the coast of Mexico. Got out clean until we were ambushed at the rendezvous point the next day. That's when we lost Trip."

"Ambushed by who?"

"About twenty hard-ons from the CIA."

"Who hired you guys?"

Cam sat silent, contemplating how far he was willing to go, but ultimately, he was ready to put all his cards on the table. He couldn't think of a single reason not to.

"Who was it, Cameron?" Rand repeated.

"It was a fella named 'Rook.' He blew in on the fuckin' wind one day and blackmailed us into pulling off a job at open sea. We figured why the hell not, nothing to lose. It was a lot of money, too." Cam paused for another taste of gin. "This Rook character was part of a mysterious order of Knights from Western Europe—The Knights of Medina."

"The Knights of Medina?"

"Yeah."

"This all sounds like a fantasy, Cameron. How much money are we talking here?"

"Millions," Cam confirmed. "Many millions." He polished off the drink and signaled for another. "The four guys Rook sent for the handoff are all dead."

"How did you and Rook communicate?"

"Doesn't matter because he's dead, too. When a guy pays you fifteen million and never follows up to receive the product...he's likely dead."

The bartender brought over their order and abruptly left with a smile.

"The body count is gonna keep climbing if you don't figure out a way to end this." Rand's attempt at resolve seemed futile.

"Trip was a good guy. He was smarter than Michael and I combined. Had a good heart, ya know." Cam took a moment to ponder a life that would never be lived out. "He left a fiancé behind. I only met her once."

"You knew his brother, Mark?"

"That I did," Cam assured through another sip of gin.

"Then I guess you were there when he died?"

"Yep. We'd been kickin' doors for months in a bunch of random villages outside Kunar. The Taliban had gotten pretty agitated, so they planned an attack on one of our Fobs in the region—"

"Fobs?"

"Forward Operating Base. We were twenty clicks north of the base at an outpost the Army had setup overlooking the valley. After the Fob got hit, we knew they were coming for our outpost next. And we were right. The Taliban surprised us before we could even get a patrol together. Non-stop mortar fire, heavy artillery and small arms pot shots. It was a real cluster fuck." Cam vividly remembered the faces of the young soldiers he fought next to that day. "We had a whole platoon of Rangers pissing their pants and squeezing off random bursts into the night," he laughed. "They were lucky Echo Team was there."

"A lot of casualties?"

"Not at first, they punched some holes in a few guys early on, but nothing lethal," Cam continued. "So, the next evening, under another wave of artillery, I gathered a small fire team and slipped down into the valley to try and untangle their positions. We made contact three or four times, little pockets of fighting here and there. When we returned to the outpost that night, everything seemed to quiet down. Guys were saying the enemy had been spooked off, but we knew better. We knew they were still on the mountain somewhere."

"And Mark?"

Cam smiled. "Mark had been fighting hard all day. And sure as shit the Tallies came back, only this time they had somehow managed to climb right up to our front door. We were fighting these dudes from ten yards away; it was ridiculous. Inbound med-evac had to abort and turn around, casualties started mounting, guys were getting picked off left and right. Mark was planted next to me, tracers flying everywhere. He'd pulled his NVGs down and was locating targets, but eventually we got pinned down behind a sandbag wall together. I had just put a burst on a 50-cal, Mark popped up and was waiting for the guy to get back on it so he could take a kill shot, but before he had a chance, he took one to the shoulder. It was like slow motion. We actually locked eyes. We were in disbelief, both stunned that he got hit, ya know. Everything stood still, frozen in time."

A long pause followed.

"Then what?" anticipated Rand.

"Then he was shot through the head. Killed instantly."

"That couldn't have been easy for you. And then to lose Trip."

"Trip died in Michael's arms...in the backseat of a Range Rover while we escaped the ambush. The kid said he wanted to go home."

Rand peered down to the floor. "I'm really sorry, Cameron. But it's only going to get worse. You have to shut this down," he implored.

"Can it get any worse, Agent Kershaw? Not only is Trip dead, but four Knights of Medina are dead. Rook is probably dead. The archaeologist who discovered all this shit is dead. And you and me? Well, we *should* be dead."

"We need do the right thing here."

"I keep hearing that. But you don't understand. My brother is being hunted down in Europe by CIA operatives as we speak. I need to figure out what the hell we've stumbled across—to see what's so important that millions of dollars and countless lives are being put at risk."

"You don't need to figure it out, you *want* to figure it out," Rand corrected.

"Either way." Cam shrugged. "My brother may have deciphered the tablet."

"Tablet? What tablet?"

"Along with the device and the photos, we found this small six-by-eight tablet. It's got symbols carved into it; we had no idea what it meant. Until now."

"Is that what Michael's message said?"

"Yes. And there's a man," Cam continued, as he pulled the photos from the duffle bag. "This man," he pointed with his index finger, "is in almost every single one of these pictures."

"Wait, wait, wait!" Rand screeched as the photos continued to drop on the table. He picked one up and studied it closely. "Is this... is this the Great Pyramid of Giza? Cameron are these... I don't understand."

"Listen," Cam whispered. "This shit was stuffed into an ancient ossuary when we took it. It had only recently been unsealed. We have no explanation."

"No kidding. I mean, how does the CIA fit in? And what the hell is *this* thing?" Rand asked, as he reached for the lightsaber in the bag.

Cam grabbed him by the wrist and held firm. "Careful, pal."

"I don't get it. If this stuff is legitimately that old, then we're dealing with some sort of ancient technology. This thing has copper wiring and steel plates," Rand observed. "And photo prints? I mean, if those are real, I'll eat my goddamn hat!" he blurted, pointing at the stack of images.

"Keep your voice down," Cam sternly instructed.

"Fine. But who's this guy you mentioned in the photos?"

"A physicist. He's retired now."

"No shit, he's retired!" Rand sarcastically gasped, as he snatched another photo. "Here he is with Napoleon's army, sooo...what...that makes him about four hundred years old? Yeah, let's fly to France and look him up."

The agent reached for his gin and took a large pull.

"Calm down," Cam grumbled. "People are getting killed. A group of weird old men paid millions of dollars and risked everything for whatever this is. But if it is what it *looks* like it is, then we're holding onto evidence of—"

"A time traveling physicist."

"If the United States government had a previously unknown piece of technology, and the ability to do something like, I dunno, change history," proposed Cam, "how far would they go to protect it?"

"It's impossible."

"But what if it *was* possible?"

"They'd kill everyone in their path to get their hands on it. As would just about every other nation in the world," Rand surmised.

"Exactly. This is important, Agent Kershaw."

"Call me Rand."

"Okay, fine—Rand. I need to figure out what this is. And there's a man in France that can tell me. You got into a gun fight with CIA agents today and were supposed to bring in a known-fugitive hours ago. It's over."

Rand sat paralyzed, drifting through space, begging desperately for his instincts to guide him. After a long pause, he checked the clock on the wall and closed his eyes. The human in him had overrun the agent in him.

"When does our flight leave?"

CHAPTER THIRTY-EIGHT

The two thugs frogmarched Michael, his face bloodied and swollen, out of the bathroom, through the corridor and down the escalator. They shuffled to the end of the platform and turned left to the DART lines. Chances were he'd simply be thrown out in front of the next train and left for dead. No cuffs. No weapon. No identification. The locals would simply chalk him up as an American drifter who fell onto the tracks.

Minutes later, the first train barreled down the track toward them. This was it. Michael closed his eyes and filled his lungs with the last taste of life he'd ever know.

He heard the brakes squeal through the air. Then they stopped. He was quickly shoved through the doors and safely onto the train, relieved to be alive.

As the DART pulled away, he continued to observe, to formulate a solution—any opportunity for escape that may present itself.

His mind drifted to Cam. *If they already have my brother, then they probably have the artifacts. In which case, I'll simply be executed*, he guessed. *Otherwise, I'll be tortured and interrogated.*

Neither scenario sat well with Michael. He had a high tolerance for pain and Cam had coached him in counter-interrogation techniques. But in this moment, Michael couldn't recall any of it. Fear had taken over.

They rode for three more stops and got off at Ashtown, where a black van awaited them in a nearby parking deck. Once inside, Michael was handcuffed and blindfolded.

As they pulled out of the deck, one of the thugs spoke sharply into a hidden mic on his wrist. "Target in possession. We're moving on to Birch Phase."

"Good," Carson replied through the tiny speaker. "I'll be waiting."

After a two-hour drive, the van wove through the small town of Kilcloon, where they soon pulled up in front of a stone house hidden deep within the forest. The estate had been used as a CIA black site for as long as Carson could remember. It would be the perfect place to carry out the next phase.

•   •   •

American Airlines 751 taxied the runway and began picking up speed for liftoff. Rand and Cameron sat uncomfortably in the fourth row of business class. The non-stop flight would have them in Paris by sunrise.

Rand had put zip ties back on Cam's wrists prior to boarding—another small element of their cover. Now in the air, Cam leaned his head against the seat as the plane leveled-off, then banked to the north. He gazed out the window at the lights of Philadelphia gleaming below.

As a boy in Hockessin, his parents often brought he and his brothers into the city for Flyers games, visits to the museums and the zoo. But his favorite sights to explore were the ones that held Philadelphia's rich history. The imprint of a nation rising to its feet blanketed the city. It was something he was proud of, it made him want to fight for the very freedom that so many others had sacrificed for. It was in his DNA—to be a shining light in the face of evil. Throughout his adult life, he'd fought for that very freedom on the battlefield and at home.

He now wondered if he would ever get to call the USA "home" again. If so, he worried, it would be from the inside of a maximum-security prison. The thought of it crushed him.

If he could somehow lose Kershaw in Paris, he'd be able to complete his objective.

Rand, however, was toiling with plans of his own. For a fleeting moment, as the 747 glided over the Atlantic, he considered wishing Cam a simple "Good luck" when they land in Paris, then boarding the next flight home. Alone.

I lost him at the airport, he'd tell them. *The CIA wasn't to be trusted and when we arrived in Paris he escaped.*

Just then, the lights dimmed in the cabin as the crew prepared for a long flight. Many of the passengers were now asleep, others were lost in a book beneath their overhead lights.

"You ever been?" asked Rand, breaking the extended silence.

"What?"

"Paris. You ever been?"

"Yeah, once," Cam replied.

"What are you hoping to get out of this Marco Damion?"

"I don't know. Maybe ask him why he's in a bunch of weird photos and hope that he has some sort of explanation as to what the device is."

Rand took a moment to reflect. He'd come so far to capture his ghosts, only to get caught up in their outlandish escape.

"What about Michael?" the agent asked.

"It's better that we're split up right now. He's fine."

"I've studied the security footage from Wynn so many times I can replay it in my head," Rand noted. "You guys were in and out so fast. And the movement—very intentional, zero hesitation. I thought for sure you *all* had military training."

"By any chance, do you have a Master's Degree in Stating The Obvious?" Cam asked with a sarcastic grin. "What are you trying to do, warm me up? An interrogation technique or something?"

"I guess you could say I'm your biggest fan. But I'm still confused."

"About what?"

"You're not the kind of criminals I normally run across. Why give the money away? I mean, people steal things to improve their station in life, not to just hand it off to the needy. That's the stuff of fairy tales. I don't get it."

"Most people don't," Cam replied. "The world outside is a lot different than the bubble most people live in. There's a completely different set of rules out there. Priorities are rearranged. And when your life is at risk, or you see anguish and innocence in the eyes of dying civilians…it changes your perspective on what's important in life. It changes you in ways that people in 'the bubble' can't understand." He took a moment and shifted his gaze downward. "The bubble means getting stressed out if you're a few minutes late to a meeting, or upsetting yourself over a scratch on your new sports car. There are children dying from cancer who don't give a shit about your sports car. There are homeless vets starving in the street that don't have a job to be late to. Villages that don't have access to clean water, whose people live in constant fear of rape and murder. It's not everyone's job to fix it, but I've chosen to help fix it. So did Michael…and Trip."

"It's admirable—what you guys do."

Cam smirked. "Then why were you trying to arrest me for it?"

"As admirable as I find it, it's still illegal. My job is to catch people who do illegal things."

"Maybe you need a new job."

"I might not have a choice."

The hours passed with little more conversation. Cam was now resting against the window with his eyes shut.

Remembering that his FBI-issued cellphone had been shut off and stuffed into the backpack, Rand slowly reached down and slid the bag to his feet. Quietly unzipping the front pocket, he pulled the phone out and held it in his hand. He checked on Cam again—*still sleeping*—and slipped it into his jacket.

Rand quietly got up from his seat and pushed up the aisle to the bathroom in the back of the plane. Standing above the urinal, he powered up the mobile. It felt like the process went on forever—a seemingly endless graphic of spinning logos. Finally, the home screen appeared. As suspected, he had multiple messages. Most of the comments were threats from Steve Brodsky.

He dialed a number and anxiously pulled the phone to his ear, then checked his watch. It was almost midnight in Las Vegas.

"Hello?"

"Steve, it's Rand, listen—"

"Oh Rand, what the hell have you done? You really fucked this up!"

"I know, Steve," he pleaded. "But the CIA has a bounty on this guy's head, he's a goddamn war hero who's been giving stolen money to dying kids, for Christ's sake. I can't just hand him over to the CIA. They'll kill him."

"Rand, it's official now. There's no turning back, the boys at the CIA have taken over. Hell, the Director of National Intelligence is involved. It's not our case anymore!"

"Fine!" Rand shot back under his breath. "But I'm making a stand, this guy is not going to be dragged to some top-secret black site and tortured. Last I checked this is America, not North fucking Korea."

"You're making a huge mistake, Agent Kershaw. You have no idea what you've gotten yourself into. Bring the Lyle kid back and maybe, just maybe, I can save your ass."

"I'm bringing him to the field office in Atlanta," Rand explained, now unwilling to give up his location.

"Atlanta? Where the hell are you?" Brodsky demanded.

Rand swallowed hard. "After that I'm calling the press. They'll have cameras and reporters all over him, and I'll watch DOJ scramble for weeks trying to explain to the American people why the CIA is trying to assassinate American civilians. There's no way I'm letting this guy disappear into the shadows of the intelligence community."

"Look, I know you're upset over the investigation. You wanted this, I know how much it meant to you and how hard you've worked, we all do. But you gotta let this go, Rand."

"I'm bringing him home—alive." Rand hung up and pressed his forehead against the wall.

Unable to find a shred of serenity, he returned to his aisle seat, debating his next move.

Another hour passed and Rand fidgeted in his seat as the 747 began its approach on Charles de Gaulle Airport. He pondered how he could get himself out of this mess unscathed. But with each passing minute, that hope drifted further and further away.

Just then his cellphone beeped. He'd forgotten to shut it down. He darted a glance at Cam—sound asleep. Rand quickly pulled the phone from his pocket, and there, sitting ominously at the top, was a text message from Melissa. He clicked it.

Melissa Dagan: *They've tracked your flight, ur a fugitive now...teams in place to apprehend u at de gaulle. RUN!*

Rand's mind raced with fear. His whole world had been upended in a matter of seconds. He tried to think of the proper authorities to call. He needed help. *Department of Justice? The FBI Director? The French Police?*

None of his thoughts made sense—everything in his mind was spinning out of control. It suddenly dawned on him that he was no longer an official member of the FBI. He'd been setup and now struggled to come up with a logical response. The CIA had framed him as a rogue agent, and the fact that he was helping a federal criminal flee the country meant he was aiding and abetting.

Surely Steve would've sorted it out with the CIA to spare my career? he tried to convince himself. It wasn't working. The reality was that Brodsky had sold him up river to save his own ass. *Who could blame him?* Whatever Cameron Lyle was involved in went well above the FBI. Rand's eyes narrowed, his pulse quickened.

The screeching of tires against the runway woke Cam from his sleep. He blinked his eyes and released a deep sigh, then peered over at Rand. Something was up.

"Agent Kershaw, you don't look so good. You okay?" he asked.

"Rand."

"Huh?"

"For the last time, it's Rand. Just Rand," he said in a zombie-like tone.

Cam looked him over with concern. He checked the zip ties on his hands and suddenly felt uneasy. Frustrated, he turned and grimaced at the window.

"I don't blame you," Cam muttered. "You're turning me in when we land, aren't you?"

Rand wasn't listening. He was in a deep trance, the wheels in his head spinning at blistering speeds. He reached between his legs and pulled the backpack into his lap and retrieved a small switchblade. He held the weapon close to his body, trying not to alarm any of the other passengers. Cam watched with confusion.

The two locked eyes as Rand grabbed Cam's wrists and pulled them close, then slashed the zip ties away. Cam yanked at the heavy-plastic bands and flicked them to the floor.

As the plane taxied to the gate, Rand discreetly pulled the 9mm from the bag, locked the clip into place and handed it to Cam.

"It's a setup. There's a CIA team waiting for us at the gate," he said hurriedly. "You're gonna need that."

"What about you?"

"They're waiting for me, too," he confided with a look of deep concern. "Congratulations, we're in this shit together now."

CHAPTER THIRTY-NINE

Michael sat in a cheap metal folding chair in the middle of a sprawling white room. Large halogen lights blasted from the ceiling, bleaching out the entire space. The wall to his left was a floor-to-ceiling mirror—a two-way with a viewing room on the other side, Michael assumed.

It had been six hours since he was brought in and tied to the chair. Not a single agent had walked through the door in that time. Surely, the idea was to disorientate him.

For Carson, six hours seemed optimal. He sent in the first operative.

Michael had been placed—by design—with his back to the door. When it finally opened, a young agent in dark slacks and a gray t-shirt walked in and circled around to face his prisoner.

"Tell me where Cameron Lyle is," the operative sternly demanded.

"I don't know," Michael mumbled, now feeling the effects of sleep deprivation.

"Tell me where the ossuary is."

"Ossuary? I have no idea what you're talking about."

"I'll explain it." The man spoke with intent and a noticeable lack of emotion. "The items you and your brother stole from the Maersk Burgundy.

The items we killed your friend for. The items that we're going to kill your entire family for. Ring a bell now, hotshot?"

Michael smiled. He wasn't going to be rattled by threats. "You're going too fast."

"I'm sorry?"

"You walk in and go straight to threatening my family? Slow down, you sound like a fucking rookie...*hotshot*."

"Threats? You think I'm just making empty threats?"

The bruiser threw a hard right across Michael's jaw. It was a perfect shot and hurt like hell. He winced in pain, then spit one of his molars out onto the clean, white floor.

After shaking his face to get the feeling back, Michael looked his interrogator in the eyes.

"You're just a military washout whose only job is to tie people to chairs and beat them up. You're a pussy...and my grandmother hits harder than that."

A steady stream of jabs followed. Michael was beginning to fade to unconsciousness, but quickly regained his strength and awaited the next round of punches. They came in volume.

•   •   •

The sun ascended over Dublin as the city came to life. It was Saturday morning and Corin Baker would normally have gone to his favorite café for a relaxing cup of coffee and a pastry. But the recent visit by Michael had ruined that for him. Today was as good as any to try the new spot up the road.

Corin snatched his keys from the counter and threw on a denim jacket. But before he could reach the door, a hard knock froze him in motion.

He quietly placed his eye against the peephole, but before he could make out anyone on the other side, the entire apartment came crashing down on him. He was thrown to the floor in a white flash.

Corin lay on the carpet as three men plunged into his apartment and slammed the door behind them. The clicking of door locks sealed his fate.

The young philologist was grabbed by the collar and pulled to his feet. "Corin Baker?"

With a deep gash across his face, Corin struggled to regain his vision. "What do you pricks want?"

A quick punch to the gut stripped him of whatever air was left in his lungs.

"A man named Michael Lyle was here. He asked you to decipher a tablet."

"Michael who?" Corin asked, trying to sound confused. "Never heard of her."

"You may think this is funny, little man, but I'll carve you up so bad pieces of you will be turning up all over Europe," the American threatened. "What did you decipher?"

"Has anyone ever told you that your face looks like a foot?"

"The joke didn't land, but the next punch to your face will—real hard."

A shout from the back room suddenly broke the tension. "We got nothing!"

"This is your last chance, dipshit. What did the tablet say?"

Corin had had his fun. The pistol tucked into the man's waistline assured him that his lack of cooperation would eventually wear thin. He wasn't willing to die for the abrasive stranger that had slept on his couch for the last three days, or the stone tablet he had been asked to decipher.

Just as Corin predicted, the pistol was swiftly pulled from the waistline and placed against his forehead. Playtime was over.

"Instructions," he finally confessed. "It was instructions of some kind."

"What did it say?"

"I copied it down on a notepad. Check my office, a purple binder on the second shelf above my desk. Just fuckin' take it."

Another man slid down the hall into Corin's office and within seconds confirmed the purple binder. "We got it," he yelled out, as he flipped through the pages and immediately found the handwritten notes.

The binder was rushed to the man holding Corin at gunpoint. The page was thoroughly reviewed, then shown to its author.

"Is this it?"

"Yeah," Corin confirmed. "That's it. I gave the other guy a copy, too. I have no clue what it's for, but that's the best I could do. I can't guarantee the accuracy, but good luck finding anyone who could come close."

He was thrown backward onto his couch as the three men hustled out of the apartment and the whole ordeal was over just as quickly as it began. Corin paced the floor, trying to gather his senses.

It's time to find a new place to live, he told himself.

•　　•　　•

Deep inside a sprawling estate in Kilcloon, Ireland, Michael focused on his breathing, trying to take his mind off the pain. He was bleeding profusely, and the last round of questioning resulted in the loss of his left pinky finger, which was now lying in a puddle of blood on the floor. There were literally pieces of him scattered around the room.

He was holding up well given the circumstances and, at long last, the ranking officer of the CIA team entered the room.

"Michael, Michael, Michael—" the burly operative ranted. "What am I going to do with you?"

"You must be the asshole in charge of this shit show."

"That I am. My name is Carson. Please accept my apologies if our hospitality has been a bit...brutal." He kicked the fingertip to the side.

"We were just the middle men," Michael explained. "This isn't my fight."

"You must be confused, Mr. Lyle. The moment you stepped foot on my freighter you placed yourselves right smack in the middle of this thing. And now you and your brother, who will be dead soon, are going to return what's mine."

"You're bluffing. You don't have Cam."

"We don't have Cam *yet*," Carson corrected. "Your brother's plane just touched down in Paris. He'll be dead in ten minutes."

"I don't believe you. He's not going to Paris."

"Whether you believe me or not is irrelevant. You see, I've already profiled both you and your brother. I've determined that you are the weaker of the two. So here you sit. Eventually you'll break down and tell me exactly where the asset is. Guys like you always crack. I want to be completely up-front with you—you're going to die here no matter what. That, my friend, is non-negotiable. But you can save your brother. I'll let him walk if you return the ossuary to me. You only have ten minutes."

"I still think you're bluffing. I really expected more out of you guys, this is deeply disappointing," snarled Michael.

"You must be way out of the loop, son."

Carson motioned toward the two-way mirror and returned to the metal door, where another operative popped in and handed him a file folder. Carson paced back to Michael and pulled a black-and-white photo from inside, tossing it on the floor at his prisoner's feet. It was a grainy photo of Cam and another man at an airport gate.

"This photo was taken twelve hours ago at Philadelphia International. The other man is an FBI agent that Cam was supposedly apprehended by, but we're pretty certain they're working together. Why that is, I have no idea, nor do I care. But my instincts tell me that my items are in his backpack. We'll know for sure in a few minutes."

"He's not stupid enough to just walk into your little trap," Michael promised. "I hope you have an army waiting for him, you're gonna need it."

"Do you guys really think you're anything more than a small band of losers? It sure as hell didn't take an army to bring *you* in. We're going to wipe your names from history and no one will ever give a shit whether you existed or not." Carson took a breath, hoping some of his words were sinking in. "Here's how this is going to work, Mr. Lyle. You're going to tell me where the items from the ossuary are. And you only have that option for another ninety seconds. If you tell me now, I let Cameron live. He can go back to his family and his old life. I promise this to you. But if you *don't* tell me, and the stuff winds up being in his backpack anyways, then as soon as I get the call that your brother's dead and we've retrieved the pack, I'm going to put a bullet in your face."

Carson let the threat hang in the air for a moment. "And finally, as a third option, if you don't tell me what I want to know and Cam's *not* carrying the items, then we kill him on the spot and spend the next two weeks torturing you unmercifully until we get what we want. Is this starting to make sense to you now?"

Carson was telling the truth and Michael knew it. He had no strategic advantage. There were no moves left on the table.

"Cam doesn't know where it is," he attempted. "I'm the only one. Let him walk and I'll tell you everything."

"Nope," Carson immediately replied. "It's not gonna be that easy. You see, one of my agents is about to walk through that door and tell me that Cam and his FBI buddy have been captured or killed at Charles de Gaulle Airport. You're on the clock."

Michael understood the art of decision making in a survival scenario. There were risks, rewards and sacrifices. Regardless of his emotions, he needed to make a decision giving him the best opportunity at success—and that success didn't always mean survival, sometimes it was simply the success of a mission. And in those instances, tough decisions needed to be made without hesitation or regret. This was one of those instances.

"So, what's it gonna be, tough guy?" Carson threatened.

Through broken bones and a bloodied mouth, a tiny grin emerged on Michael's face. "I think it's gonna be a long couple of weeks."

CHAPTER FORTY

Flight 751 rolled up to the gate. Minutes later, the jet bridge engaged and the exit door opened. Cam and Rand blended in with the first batch of passengers to exit the plane.

They paced up the jetway and prepared for battle. Before they even made it to the gate, they spotted a couple of suspiciously rugged men waiting ahead—clearly a CIA welcoming committee. With a swift lunge, they broke out of the bridge and cut right to a set of utility doors twenty feet away. The two burly operatives sprang into action and were immediately joined by four additional assassins who emerged from the crowd.

Cam went through the doors first and sprinted down a long hallway with Rand on his heels. The operatives plunged through the doors behind them and closed in.

As they approached another set of doors ahead, the hallway exploded in gunfire. Ducking their heads, Cam and Rand pushed through and spilled out into a row of conveyor belts and pulley systems. They wove their way through the maze and disappeared into a loud industrial area that looked more like a factory than an airport.

A few stray bullets punched into random luggage cases on a nearby conveyor. Rand dodged the incoming fire and bobbed beneath a swinging steel hook.

"Over here!" he yelled.

Cam held his position a few feet away and returned a burst of gunfire at the operatives who hastily regrouped and continued their pursuit. Cam then jumped over a set of thick cables and sprinted toward Rand who laid down more cover fire. The rounds missed their targets and pinged off machinery somewhere in the distance.

Now side-by-side, they broke through an exit and onto a small platform, which offered a stairwell that wound several stories down. With each lunge, Cam and Rand covered multiple steps. Hard left after hard left, they made their way into the abyss.

After a two-story descent, bullets began firing down the center of the shaft. Cam could hear the rounds whizzing past him just outside the railing. A parade of footsteps echoed through the stairwell as Cam reached the bottom. With shrapnel now ricocheting off the floor around them, Cam threw himself into the metal exit door.

It was locked.

He backed off a couple feet and fired two rounds into the doorframe. With a swift kick, it flew open and they rushed out into an open-air corridor between two buildings. In a dead sprint, they reached the end of the alley just as the CIA team filed out of the building behind them.

They were faced with a split-second decision—right or left. Cam leaned hard around the right-hand corner, Rand followed closely behind. Ahead was a loading dock with clear plastic drapes hanging from its entrance. With both arms shielded in front of his face, Cam burst through at top speed. Now inside, they both stopped. The two now stood in a bustling warehouse beneath the airport. The place was buzzing with airport employees, large airline equipment and a fleet of trolleys pulling trains of luggage containers.

"This way!" Cam dashed left toward a conveyor belt, the end of which appeared to pass through a wall in the distance—another possible escape route. Rand followed without question.

As they careened around a refueling truck, they could hear the footsteps of six men closing in. They blazed a fifty-yard dash to the end of the conveyor but were halted by a hail of gunfire, forcing them to find cover behind a flatbed luggage trolley. Separated by only a few feet, Cam motioned Rand to push further, demanding that he reach the conveyor.

Keeping his head down, Rand sprinted for the conveyor line. Cam popped around the corner of the trolley and caught sight of the hitmen charging him.

Just as they closed in, Rand released a .40 caliber storm upon the CIA team, hitting one in the leg. The other five dove to the cement floor and returned fire.

Pinned against the trolley, Cam pulled his 9mm to his chest and took a firm breath. He peeled around the corner and released five, well-placed rounds at his enemies, then slipped back behind the vehicle.

The CIA operatives scattered like roaches again. After a brief pause, one of them began advancing on Cam's position. The attacker was protected by a row of shelving along the wall. Cam took a knee and steadied his weapon. With a slide of the hips, he peeked around the front of the trolley and put three, crisp rounds into the approaching agent's chest. He then retrained his gun a few degrees left and squeezed off one more, which caught another agent in the forehead.

Cam looked downrange as he reloaded another clip—two operatives were dead on the floor, one sat behind a cargo crate wincing in pain, and two were hiding among luggage racks to his right. *I've lost one*, he worried after a quick headcount.

Just then, more footsteps began approaching from behind. Cam sunk his head in an effort to remain unseen. The steps drew closer as he pressed his head against the door of the trolley and waited, silently hoping the agent would slip past. Cam opened his eyes and saw a sixth operative slowly advancing toward him. Before the agent could get a lock on Cam, his attention shifted up the warehouse to Rand.

The assassin unknowingly pushed past Cam, slithering toward Rand, who was about to reach the end of the conveyor belt and certain freedom.

Cam rose from his knees and quietly slipped the backpack over his shoulder. In an instant, he closed in on his prey from behind. As the CIA agent raised his weapon for one last shot at Rand, Cam cracked him over the skull with his pistol. The man slumped to the ground, blood rushing from the fresh gash in his head. Number six was now accounted for.

As he stood over the sleeping body, Cam could now hear the remaining operatives continue their pursuit from a distance. He sprinted toward Rand who was now pushing through the wall ahead.

As he lowered his head and extended his stride, a sharp pain ripped through Cam's neck. The crushing blow paralyzed him immediately and he stumbled forward, trying to keep his balance and pace. It wasn't enough. He fell to the ground and slumped his head to the concrete, unable to find the strength to hold it up. His hands went numb, then his legs.

Cam closed his eyes and began to lose consciousness. He could hear the muffled sound of footsteps closing in and felt the jolt of his backpack being torn from his body. He was drifting away now, gasping for air. A blackness closed in around him as his hearing faded. The pain was now absent, but he could feel his limp body shifting as boots kicked his torso. Then, he surrendered to his fate, slipping into a coma-like sleep.

CHAPTER FORTY-ONE

A soft light found its way into his consciousness. It became brighter and brighter until Cam sluggishly tried to open his eyes. He couldn't hear and his vision was still too blurred to make out his surroundings. He could feel he was sitting upright. The sensation of motion told him he was in a car, strapped into a seat. His head rang in pain and a pulsing sting pounded through his body, emanating from his neck.

The soldier's head bobbed as he slowly regained the strength to lift it from his shoulders. He winced in pain, then blinked his eyes as his sight came back to life. Cam tried to straighten his back, but everything was too stiff to move.

Finally, with a deep breath, he turned to the left, trying to identify something—*anything*. He could see he was in a small car with what appeared to be a taxi meter mounted to the dash. Someone was driving. With a deep groan, he raised his eyes to see the man sitting next to him.

It was Rand Kershaw. The former agent's knuckles were pure white as he gripped the steering wheel and stared blankly through the windshield. They were on an interstate, dodging from lane to lane as the taxi sped through a thin pocket of traffic.

"Rand?" Cam whispered, unsure if the words were coming out.

"I'm here."

"What...what happened?"

Rand pulled a small, black dart from the console and tossed it into Cam's lap. "You were tranquilized," he said in a tone devoid of emotion.

"Then what?"

Rand kept his lifeless eyes on the road. "I wasn't going to just leave you there."

Cam noticed the blood on Rand's sleeve and began piecing together the only possible scenario. "Did you get the backpack?"

"Yes." Rand pointed his thumb to the back, where the pack rested safely on the leather seat.

Cam let out a sigh of relief, then pressed back against the headrest and closed his eyes.

After merging onto A1 South toward Paris, Rand drove the Audi ten more kilometers and exited at Saint-Denis. They wouldn't last long in a stolen taxi and needed to get on foot as soon as possible.

As the minutes passed, Cam was regaining his strength and composure. He looked again to Rand and grew concerned with the agent's emotionless disposition. He'd seen it before—battle fatigue.

"They were going to kill us," Cam tried to explain. "You had no choice."

Rand bit his lip in frustration. "You've ruined my life," he finally responded. "My life is completely over. I just wanted to find the ghosts."

"What ghosts?"

"You. You're my ghost." Rand was clearly in a state of shock. He continued his blank stare. "I've been chasing you for a year. And now, here we sit in a stolen cab—in France!—running for our lives. And the most fucked up part," he said with nervous laughter, "is that we're working together. We just took out a half dozen agents from the CIA."

"This wasn't part of the plan," Cam assured him. "It wasn't supposed to—"

"But it did. It happened."

"Rand, there's something bigger going on here. We both know it. We're in danger and fighting for our lives. There's a good chance that the most significant scientific discovery of all time is sitting in that backpack."

"No. My life is over. Your life's over, too. And you have a family." Rand struggled to focus.

"Yeah, I do," Cam agreed. "But I'm also desensitized, accustomed to sacrifice. And I know that no matter what happens to me, my family will be okay. Beyond the sadness and mourning that my death might bring, my little girls will be okay. They're strong. Hell, they've spent most of their lives preparing for me to die—ready for someone to pull up to the house and tell them their father isn't coming home."

"Do you think you'll ever see them again?" Rand genuinely asked.

"Of course! We prepare for the worst and hope for the best. But this doesn't end here, Rand. *We* decide how this ends. I'm wired up to fight to the bitter end. And clearly, so are you."

"Fine," conceded Rand. He took in a heavy breath and wiped his brow. "If we're gonna do this, we need to find Marco Damion."

•   •   •

As the minutes ticked by, Michael began to feel the effects of blood loss. Carson took notice and waved into the mirror for someone to come in and bandage the prisoner's left hand. Seconds later, a junior agent appeared with gauze and medical supplies. Michael's pinky finger was picked off the floor and dropped into a plastic bag; the agent then swiftly bandaged him up.

The medic left the room and was immediately replaced by another agent, who happened to be an attractive female in her mid-thirties with a blue business skirt and white top. She met with Carson in the middle of the room where the two whispered in secret.

Michael watched as Carson clenched his jaw and stared blankly at the floor. He was searching for something, Michael noted. Whatever she had just told him pissed him off. Carson shot Michael a threatening stare and left the room with the female agent.

Minutes later, after a quick debriefing, Carson returned alone.

"How many?" Michael struggled to ask.

"How many what?"

"How many of your assholes did he kill?"

Carson chuckled. "I'm glad you find this amusing. It's only a matter of time. Do you know that in my thirty-plus years of service, not one—not a single person—has ever gotten away from me? Many of them were much more talented than Cam, but they never lasted more than a couple of days. A very select few survived a month or so on the run but, eventually, they all fell." Carson turned his back and walked to the door. "We're all mortal, Mr. Lyle," he threatened before leaving the room.

Michael exhaled in relief. Cam was still alive out there.

CHAPTER FORTY-TWO

The black Audi pulled into the drive at Centre d'Accueil Universel Christian Church. Cam jumped out and removed the plastic taxi sign from the roof and tossed it into the backseat. He and Rand jogged across the road and quickly immersed themselves in a small crowd gathered at Parc de la Légion d'Honneur—a sprawling parkland of lawns, gardens and pathways.

In a slow, unpronounced pace they made their way around the perimeter walkways. When they reached the southern end of the park, Cam turned right, then continued up the N1 sidewalk. A well-clipped, seven-block walk brought them to the Châtillon Montrouge metro station, where Cam dug through his backpack for some cash and plugged €5 into the automated kiosk. The machine spit out two tickets and a handful of change.

A train eventually arrived and took them south to Place de Clichy—another bustling section of Paris he was familiar with.

"Now what?" Rand gasped, as they exited the station.

"Now we locate the good doctor. James looked him up online without much trouble. There's gotta be an internet café around here."

"Your brother, James? You mean *James* found Damion?"

"He stumbled onto it," Cam muttered, catching himself in the slip-up.

They began a hurried walk up Boulevard des Batignolles. Cam checked the stores along the street for anything that might have an internet connection.

"I called James when there was nowhere else to turn," he finally admitted as they hustled up the sidewalk. "I wanted him to be prepared when the CIA came knocking on his door."

"Did they?"

"Of course. But before they did, James cross-checked our photos of Eisenhower with the White House visitor logs from the day the pictures were taken, which led us to identify Marco Damion."

"Okay, so what does that mean?"

"For starters, it means Dr. Damion is about to have a lot of explaining to do."

Rand took it all in, trying to piece together a timeline of events.

"Cybercafé," Cam pointed as they came to the intersection of Rue de Rome.

Half a block up the street hung a small, dirty white sign—one in a long row of interconnected shops that dotted the square.

Rand checked over his shoulder at the stampede of tourists pacing the block. There was still no sign of a CIA team. He and Cam wove their way through a group of pedestrians and continued up the sidewalk.

They slipped into the tiny café and marched to the back, where a pair of computers rested on a long desk.

Cam slid out a plastic chair and sat down.

Before he could begin, the shopkeeper hollered from the front of the store. "Payez-moi d'abord!"

Cam froze—he had absolutely no grasp of the French language and was hesitant to reply in English. Surely, there were police bulletins out for two Americans fitting their description.

"Money, he wants money," Rand whispered with a tap on Cam's shoulder.

The bruising American scrambled to pull more cash from his backpack and lumbered to the register. He handed a wad of bills to the grumpy old

Frenchman and returned to the computer, only to find Rand typing away on its sticky, out-of-date keyboard.

"Found it. He's here in Paris. 59B Rue Voltaire," Rand said.

"How far is that from here?"

Rand hurried to find the address on a map. "Not far, we can be there in thirty minutes by train. Should I write this address down?"

"No, Rand," Cam whispered through a devilish grin. "We're international criminal masterminds. We don't write things down."

They chose a different route back to the metro station and jumped the next train to Gare de Courbevoie, five stops away just over the Seine River. They were now outside of the city, northwest of downtown Paris.

•   •   •

"We don't have anything yet, sir, but our teams are running grid checks."

If Kevin was concerned, he was hiding it well.

Carson scowled. The hidden Irish estate was dark and callous; he could think of a million other places he'd rather be. The agent had already wasted more of his precious time on the Lyles than he'd intended to. Yet here he sat, with one of the brothers bleeding in an interrogation room and another running loose around one of Europe's largest cities.

"Why is he in Paris?" the frustrated officer wondered aloud.

"We don't know. He has no known contacts there."

"We're the CIA, Kevin. We know where almost every human being on Earth is at all hours of the day. It's one goddamn international fugitive and an FBI agent! How hard is this?" he yelled, slamming a fist on the table.

"With all due respect to our team, sir, Cameron Lyle is more than well-trained—he *trained* operatives who are well-trained."

"Do I need to bring in bigger guns, Kevin?"

The junior agent knew what this meant. The blood flushed from his face. "No, sir."

"He's utilizing the metro system," Carson surmised. "He would have ditched the taxi immediately, which likely left them on foot in the northeast corridor."

"From there, they'd have easy access to the entire city," Kevin added. "That was 103 minutes ago, they could be anywhere by now. Hell, they could be out of the country."

"No," Carson snapped, thinking deeply. "They went there for a reason. Cameron's in Paris, and he's looking for something. A friend, a contact—"

"He could have just used Paris as a landing site," Kevin refuted.

"Maybe. But Cameron Lyle is trained in swift, unobstructed tactical maneuvers. He's not a counterintelligence agent, he's a battlefield soldier, trained to take the path of least resistance and strike with immediate force. Every move he makes is intentional and direct."

"And when we find him?"

"I don't want *him*."

Kevin stood confused. "I'm sorry?"

"He's killed six of our operatives in Paris and seven in Mexico. The surgical strike teams aren't working. He's just picking us off one by fucking one. And we can't exactly send in an army, he'll turn Paris into a war zone."

"So, what do you suggest?"

"Pull back the strike teams and send in surveillance. The device holds no value to him, but Michael does. Cameron will give us what we want if his brother's life hangs in the balance. Let's remove his tactical advantage and force him into making a decision."

"And you think he'll do it?" Kevin asked.

"I do. He and Michael are blood. They grew up together, they've fought together, and they stole together. Thick as fucking thieves, those two. He'll give us what we want."

●　　　●　　　●

Cam stood at the tall wooden gate of a small residence, sealed off from the rest of the world. With a stern glance at his new partner, he pushed the handle and stepped into the courtyard, then up to the front door. After a quick gut check, he knocked.

A climactic moment passed with no answer. He knocked again.

Finally, an older gentleman with a cardigan sweater and khaki pants opened the door. His white stubble was weeks old. His bifocals portrayed a subtle intelligence.

"Qu'est-ce que vous voulez?" the man grumbled.

"I'm sorry, are you Marco Damion?" Cam asked in a friendly tone.

The man's peaceful expression melted away as an awkward tension filled the courtyard. After deep consideration, he opened the door and waved them in.

"I *am* Marco Damion," he finally confirmed before shutting the door behind them. Marco noted that his two guests were either military or law enforcement—or both. "And you are?"

"My name is Cameron Lyle. This is my—my friend, Rand Kershaw. I believe we have something that you may be able to help with."

Marco stared at Cam with concern, then at the other fellow, who appeared to be sweating through his dress shirt. *These young men are in some sort of danger*, he guessed. And he knew exactly what it was.

"Yes, I believe you have something of importance."

Cam couldn't quite place the accent. It had the slipperiness of Italian with a soft Scottish cadence.

Dr. Damion escorted his guests to the study, where an oil painting of hunting dogs hung on a wood-paneled wall above a brown leather couch. A gentle breeze passed through an open window, knocking the stench from the musty furnishings.

"Please, sit," Marco told them.

"The accent, I can't quite identify it," Cam mumbled inappropriately. "You're Italian, right?"

The physicist laughed for a moment. "A mutt really. Born in Florence, raised in Edinburgh. Spent a bulk of my career in the States. I retired here almost twenty years ago."

"I see."

"Am I not what you expected, young man?" Marco joked.

"I guess I didn't know what to expect," Cam conceded.

"You're on the run," the old man bluntly pointed out with authority. "From what exactly?"

"What makes you think we're on the run?" Rand interjected.

"Two Americans. One backpack. Pulsing heart rates. And it appears you've walked further in those shoes than what they were designed for," Marco noted, glancing down at Rand's loafers. He leaned in with a look of discern and spoke slowly. "What in God's name have you brought to my house?"

"This backpack—" attempted Cam before being interrupted.

"I know what's in the backpack, lads. I'm asking *who* you have brought?" Marco darted an eye at the front door. "There are dogs on the loose, it's only a matter of time before they pick up your scent and follow it here."

"We weren't followed," Rand assured. "But we don't have a lot of time."

"Very well," Marco conceded. "Let's see it."

CHAPTER FORTY-THREE

As Marco sat calmly in the old study, Cam rustled his backpack from the floor to a mahogany tea table. He took a seat across from Marco and pulled the photos out one-by-one, then the stone tablet, and finally the mysterious metal device.

"This was precision machined, and there seems to be electrical components," Cam tried.

"Not so fast, Mr. Lyle," Marco scolded with a wag of his finger. "The tablet."

"We don't know anything about the tablet," Cam confessed. "My brother deciphered it from Dublin, then sent the translation to Philadelphia. Unfortunately, we couldn't stick around long enough for it to arrive."

"I see. And the photos?"

"With all due respect, Dr. Damion, you seem to be familiar with these items," Cam countered. "And I couldn't help but notice that you're in most of these photos."

Marco examined the photographs scattered across the table. He stopped on one in particular—taken from inside the Oval Office. "I was just a young man in this one."

"So, it *is* you?"

"Of course, it is. Don't be ridiculous."

"And the tablet?" Cam pressed.

"How did you come into possession of these items, which I assume were encased in an ossuary?" Marco asked.

"The ossuary was discovered by Dr. Diaz near Puma Punku. We were hired to intercept it on its way to the US," Cam explained. "Let's just say we ran into some unexpected hazards after retrieving it."

"If you were hired to steal it, then you were hired to return it. So why are these items sitting on a table in my study?"

Cam and Rand exchanged looks of frustration. The old man was clearly masking his absolute knowledge of the situation.

"We were hired by a group called the Knights of Medina," Cam carefully admitted. "Ever heard of 'em?"

The old man confirmed the notion with an abbreviated nod and a deep breath.

"Do you know Rook?" Cam finally asked, growing tired of the charade.

"Who and what I know isn't going to keep either of you alive, Mr. Lyle. Keeping it out of the hands of wolves, however, might."

Rand wasn't buying it. "You know what the best thing that could happen right now is, old man?" he expelled, standing up in anger. "We leave all this bullshit on the table and walk the fuck outta here and never look back! *That's* our best chance of surviving!"

"Sit down, Mr. Kershaw. It's too soon to be shitting your pants," Marco insisted.

"Do you or do you not know the Knights of Medina?" Rand demanded.

To the former agent's surprise, Cam sprang to his feet and brandished a 9mm, holding it to the physicist's head. "Answer the question, Marco. We told you we don't have much time."

Marco didn't flinch. He stared intently at the steel pistol in his face. A small fire began to roar in his eyes. "Put the gun down, Cameron. And I'll tell you everything."

Cam narrowed his brow in disgust before holstering the pistol.

"You young soldiers are so jumpy these days," Marco noted. "I am indeed familiar with the Knights of Medina. And I am saddened by the news of Sir Rook. He was a good friend."

"So he's dead?" Cam asked.

"He is."

"And you're part of this? You were part of the team that hired me, weren't you?"

"To the contrary," Marco replied. "I have been out of the game for quite some time, in fact. I only heard of Rook's passing yesterday. He was a good man."

"Then how do you know it was Rook that hired us?"

Marco deflected with a deep laugh. "Because there is only one man in the world that could coordinate the delivery of such valuable relics."

"Relics?" Cam mocked. "These are twentieth century photos and twenty-first century technologies. These aren't relics!"

"Funny how those things work," Marco scoffed.

"The photographs," Cam retorted. "Tell us about the photographs. Why are you in them and where were they taken?"

"Various places around the world," the physicist admitted. "Some I remember, some I don't."

"This one, where was this taken?" Cam pointed to the grainy image with half-built pyramids in the background.

Marco crossed his hands in his lap and sat back. "Giza, of course."

Unconvinced, Rand grabbed Cam by the arm and leaned in. "We need to talk for a sec."

Cam agreed with a nod and the two slipped out of the room to a shallow hallway.

"Something's not right," Rand hissed. "How do we know this isn't a setup? We may have just walked into the hornet's nest."

"Because we're the only people that have seen those photographs and surely the only ones to identify Damion. There's no way the CIA has put this together yet." Cam leaned over and peered into the room to check on Marco.

"Bullshit," countered Rand. "This could be a widespread conspiracy, there's no telling how many people are involved. How do we know *he's* not CIA?"

"You're right. He obviously knows Rook, maybe this is the best place to leave that stuff and just walk away. On the other hand, that means we've given up, and they'll just come here and kill him anyways. This doesn't feel like closure."

"Fine by me," Rand snapped.

"Then what?"

Rand took a moment to contemplate it. "I don't know. At this point, we go our separate ways. I don't know what else to tell you, we're being hunted by the CIA for Christ's sake. I just helped you unload your precious cargo. Hopefully now they'll leave us alone."

"And if they don't?" Cam questioned.

"Then I start my life over in Europe, I guess."

"Rand, I know this has been difficult—"

"No, you don't! What's been difficult is how much I've put into catching the assholes that committed armed robbery in my jurisdiction. What's been *difficult* is having to show up for work every fucking day knowing that all the other agents see me as a failure."

"It's over, Rand. The life you had is over. Listen, I'm going to get you a new identification and wire three million dollars to a new bank account. You're smart enough to create a new life and stay off the grid for a few years. You'll be fine."

"I don't want a new identity!" Rand shot back.

"It's time to grow the fuck up and make peace with your reality!"

After an intense stare down, Cam returned to the study to find Marco leering over the old photos.

"We're leaving, Dr. Damion," he proclaimed. "There's no point in staying involved any further. I've done my part, I have my money and now you have your stuff. We're done here."

"I appreciate your manners, Mr. Lyle, but leaving this here will only put my life in danger. Was that your objective, to simply pass your death wish off to someone else?"

"Not what I signed up for, old man. You and your friends paid me to deliver it, so I've delivered it. What happens next isn't my problem. Enjoy your retirement."

Cam and Rand made their way to the foyer and let themselves out. Escaping the courtyard, they barged onto the street and walked northbound up Rue Voltaire.

Cam felt liberated, the chains had been removed. He suddenly felt lighter knowing the items were now back in the hands of their intended owners.

As they made their way to the intersection ahead, a tall, dark foreigner sat undetected at the sidewalk patio of a restaurant, sipping cappuccino and thumbing through a newspaper.

He found it perplexing how often his targets simply appeared from thin air and presented themselves to him. And how often just sitting in one place, in a general, high-traffic area, would produce such results.

His two targets walked briskly up Rue Voltaire and turned onto Rue de Château. He stuck his face into the wide cappuccino cup as they passed by him. They looked tired and worn down.

Then, the foreigner noticed something peculiar—neither Cam nor Rand were carrying the backpack. He couldn't pinpoint exactly where they had just come from, but with a check of his watch he determined there had been a ninety-minute window of unaccounted time that they could have made a drop. The backpack could be anywhere between their current location and the Gare de Courbevoie station where they had last been seen on security camera.

His targets were now one block passed him, marching up Rue de Château. He dropped a few bills on the table and tucked his newspaper under the arm of his gray pea coat.

His sluggish pace allowed a gap to open between he and the two Americans. He kept his distance, remaining entrenched with the small crowd shuffling up the street.

Cam kept a steady pace as he motioned to his friend.

"Here, let's grab a bite and sort this out before you go."

"I don't need your money," Rand countered.

"Fine, but we both need food."

They stepped off the sidewalk and into a quaint little bistro, where only a few tables were available. Rand rolled his sleeves up and straightened his belt, then ran a hand through his dark hair and tried to relax.

Cam pulled his cap further down over his brow and ordered two, pre-made sandwiches from the glass display. They grabbed a couple bottled waters from the cooler and found a table against the wall.

Cam was ravenous. He tore through the deli paper and stuffed the warm, ham and cheese croque monsieur into his mouth, then washed it down with water.

"These things are great—*délicieux*," he said out loud.

Rand was taken aback by the careless demeanor. "Cam, I have to tell you something. When we walk out of this bistro, if you ever see me again, you'll be in handcuffs. I toyed with the idea of double-crossing you when we landed, but you're just a good guy in a bad situation. It'd be better if you never saw me again."

Cam was somewhat concerned. Rand was talking as if he was still a member of the FBI. It sounded delusional.

"Forty-eight hours. That's all I'm giving you," Rand continued. "And then I'm going to start hunting you and Michael down for the robberies. That's the best I can do."

"You *can't* go back, Rand," Cam sternly said under his breath. "You are wanted for the killing of several intelligence officers, aiding a known fugitive, tampering with evidence and interfering with a federal investigation. They'll send you to prison if they don't just kill you first. How are you not seeing this?"

"I'll take my chances."

"Fine," Cam conceded. "Fine by me."

It *wasn't* fine by him. He'd grown to like Rand and didn't want to see his new friend in danger.

"I appreciate the help and the offer. But I am what I am, and you are what you are. I'll survive," promised the hard-headed former agent.

As they finished their sandwiches, a man sat down at the table next to them.

Rand noticed the gray pea coat and jet-black hair—something he'd seen for the second time today. He dropped his head in disbelief and placed his sandwich on the table. He'd had enough of the running, the hiding, the shooting.

"You really wanna do this here?" he softly said into his water bottle, just loud enough to be heard.

"We have Michael," the foreigner quietly said into his newspaper.

Rand and Cam locked eyes. Cam slowed his breathing and casually reached for his Glock. He couldn't quite make the accent. *Dutch*, he thought.

"I wouldn't do that if I were you," the man mumbled in a slow cadence. "The device. Memorial to the Martyrs of the Deportation at midnight."

Cam's mind flashed through a myriad of potential responses, both physical and spoken. Everything inside of him wanted to blow a hole in the Dutchman's face right there in the tiny café. But strategically, he knew he had no real advantage. Michael wasn't collateral damage, he was his brother.

"Prove it," Cam finally asked into the air.

The man pulled a smartphone from his pocket and held it in his lap, just in view for Cam and Rand to easily peer over and see. With a swipe of the screen, an image of Michael sitting in a white room—bloodied and beaten—appeared.

"You motherfuckers," Cam threatened under his breath.

The tall Dutchman stood up and tucked the paper back under his arm.

"Midnight." He turned and walked to the door, leaving Cam and Rand sitting in frustration and shock.

The rain had picked up outside. Marco Damion snapped the collar of his trench coat against his neck and peered out beneath a brown ascot cap. He watched the Dutchman exit the bistro and disappear behind a passing bus and small crowd.

Chapter Forty-Four

Cam was dumbfounded, still trying to process their encounter with the Dutchman.

"We need to move. Now."

"Hold on," Rand blurted out.

"We don't have time to hold on. It's a tag-and-hunt. They're going to tail us from here, follow us and kill us. *All* of us, including Michael. The second they have the asset in sight we're all dead! We need to go now, Rand."

They jumped from the table and moved with purpose to the front of the bistro, then pushed through the door and onto the sidewalk. The streets of Paris were getting more crowded as the tourists flocked out for lunch.

Cam quickly re-evaluated their situation, which had progressed from an escape to a full-blown rescue mission. They were now firmly caught in the CIA's web. He needed to cut himself loose, recover Michael, and get off the grid as quickly as possible.

With Rand right behind him, Cam broke into a full sprint down the sidewalk and threw himself into a nearby alley. As he turned the corner at top speed, he was stopped dead in his tracks. Rand crashed around the corner and slammed into Cam's side.

There, standing like a statue, was Marco Damion.

Cam stared in disbelief at the physicist. "What the hell's going on?" he asked.

"Come with me. You're not safe here."

Cam again pulled the 9mm from his waistband and stepped up to Marco, pressing the barrel against the man's cheek.

"Bring me the backpack, Marco, or bring me my brother. I won't ask again," he threatened.

Cam no longer cared about discretion, or the fact that he was brandishing a weapon only feet from the tourists walking by. He was done with rules and best practices. He was done with all of it.

"I came for you because I don't like being hunted, Mr. Lyle. And I presume the only reason that man left you alive in the bistro is because he wants the device. I'm just saving you a step. Now don't be difficult, come with me."

Marco turned away from the gun and began pacing up the alley.

"Shit!" Cam snorted.

They followed Marco through the alley, which brought them to a well-manicured courtyard garden. Together, the men darted into another alley hidden from nearby pedestrians. At the halfway mark, Marco halted. He leaned over to grab the handle of a cellar door, framed neatly into the cobblestone at his feet. He struggled at first but managed to pull one of the metal doors open, then the other. It revealed a steep staircase chiseled from stone.

Marco led them blindly into the dark abyss below. Cam and Rand followed carefully behind, folding the metal doors behind them and disappearing into the cellar.

They continued further beneath the streets of Paris. Marco had made this trip dozens of times before, navigating each step of the ancient passageway with ease.

After a disorientating plunge into the darkness, Marco's footsteps echoed as he reached the bottom. Cam and Rand hurried to join him. Their guide struck a match to light an old lantern, revealing stonewalls of a long corridor, chiseled by hand long ago. Marco raised the lantern and pushed onward into the corridor. They quickly reached the end, where they were met by several more tunnel entrances surrounding them on each side.

The old physicist moved without hesitation to the second hall on his left. "This way," he whispered from the shadows.

The four-foot wide hallway was lined with electrical wires on both sides. After hustling into the tunnel, Marco stopped at a black metal door that appeared from nowhere. He placed his thumb on an electronic fingerprint scanner on the wall. The indicator light zapped from red to green and, after a click of the lock, Marco pushed his way through.

The doorway opened to a large underground parking deck. The place was completely empty, except for a loading dock taking up the entire right wall. Lined along the dock were four unmarked delivery vans—black with heavily tinted windows. Marco limped down a few paved steps to ground level and made his way to one of the vehicles.

"Jump in, lads. We're almost home!" he shouted.

Without question, Cam and Rand slumped into the van—Cam in the passenger seat and Rand into the rear through a gliding door.

The black Mercedes Sprinter jerked out of its space and squealed around the corner, climbing through a spiral parking deck to the city above. After a series of hard left turns, they paused at the exit and checked for traffic on Rue Sartoris.

The Sprinter darted left and accelerated toward a six-way traffic circle ahead. Without stopping, Marco careened the van into a parade of cars and broke off onto Rue d'Estienne d'Orves, where they soon settled into a clustered enclave of residential blocks.

For the next ten minutes, Marco worked his way south through the outskirts of Courbevoie and across the Seine. They were now cruising into downtown Paris. Cam noticed the tip of the Eiffel Tower cresting over the horizon.

"So, what's the score, Marco?" Cam asked, now that the intensity of the escape began to wane. "They're holding my brother hostage. I'm taking the artifacts back from you, I have no choice. And then I'm gonna forget about you and Rook and this whole damn thing."

"I understand your objective," Marco replied. "We will get you to safety and off the CIA's radar. Arrangements can be made then."

The Sprinter pressed on, southbound through Ternes and Chaillot, until they reached their destination—Musée du Vin. *The Wine Museum.*

Marco pulled the van around the back of the historic winery and into an alley that stopped at a set of iron gates. The gates pushed inward until enough room was available for the Sprinter to pass through, then creaked eerily closed behind them. Marco pulled in and parked the van in a courtyard. The men exited and followed his lead through a large wooden door, entering the grand foyer of the museum.

From there, they began weaving through another maze of hallways and passages until they found themselves at a rustic wooden bar in a fifteenth century storage room. Surrounded by an endless supply of cobweb-covered chiantis and merlots, Marco reached over and turned on the lights, then proceeded to pour three glasses of red wine.

"We're safe here," he promised.

"I appreciate you snatching us off the street and everything, but I want answers." Cam's voice was clear and stern. "The time for all this cloak-and-dagger bullshit is over. Where's the bag?"

"Yes, Mr. Lyle. I believe it is time for us to get right to it. But I cannot allow you to just walk out of here with these items. You see, surrounding this building are approximately two- to three-dozen armed members of my security detail."

"Bullshit," Rand called from his barstool.

"Perhaps," Marco shrugged. "But the odds aren't in your favor."

"They have my brother. They have Michael," Cam pointed out.

"And let me guess, they're going to kill him unless you deliver the artifacts?" Marco concluded.

"Yes!"

"Bring me the bag, it's over there," the physicist said to Cam, waving him toward a wine rack nearby.

Cam walked to the rack and retrieved his backpack, then placed it onto the dusty bar.

Marco pulled the items out one by one. Each photo carefully placed in a row in front of them. He then produced the tablet and finally the mysterious device.

"Dr. Damion, what exactly are we dealing with here?" asked Rand in a defeated voice. "I mean, what is so important about this stuff that has me hiding from the CIA in a wine museum in Paris?" He was pleading now.

"You've come a long way to be a part of this, Mr. Kershaw. My heart feels for you greatly. As it does for you and your children, Mr. Lyle." Marco was calm now, speaking clearly and from the heart. "But this device has come further than any of us combined, which is saying a lot, I assure you."

Cam listened closely, but his perceived interest was no more than a smokescreen. His mind was already made up—as was Rand's. They were patiently waiting for an opening. Marco was not about to stand in their way of bringing the device to Martyrs Memorial, located on the grounds of the famous Notre-Dame Cathedral, at midnight. Michael was the only objective, and Marco presented a clear and present danger to the plan.

"I'll start with the photographs you're so concerned with," the aging scientist began. "As I mentioned, they were taken at various points in time, at various locations around the world."

"Who buried these?" Cam anxiously asked.

"These items were buried in 792 AD. More than a millennium to you and I," he explained. "But not to everyone."

"That's impossible," Rand charged.

"Of course, it is. But physics is a world of theories and conjecture. We spend our entire lives providing guesswork for the rest of the field to study and review. And every now and then, we're rewarded when a theory is proven beyond any reasonable scientific doubt. This photograph here," Marco pointed out, tapping a finger on an image of himself and several other men posing with spear-carrying tribesmen. "This was the Huastec tribe— their culture was made up of gruesome warring factions and a brutal form of governing. But they had a remarkable knowledge of energy and physics."

Cam narrowed his eyes on the photograph, then peered over at the device. "This thing," he said as he reached for the metallic lightsaber. "What is it? And don't say it's a time machine. Our patience is running very thin, doctor."

"You must expand your mind, Mr. Lyle. These are simply photographs—the result of light reflecting against molecules in a three-dimensional capture. Physics can play tricks on you."

"The kind of tricks like...oh, I don't know...burying a twenty-first century piece of machinery in a fifteen-hundred-year-old hole before it's even invented? Or shooting photos of an ancient civilization with a Polaroid camera?" Cam was growing impatient now. It was almost time to strike.

As the two battled fiercely for middle ground, Rand shuffled through the photographs on the bar.

"I'll start at the beginning," Marco said. "The photos were taken during our process of developing the device. Or *re-developing* it, I should say."

"*You* built this thing?" Cam asked.

"Not exactly, it surfaced in the spring of 1962. I was a young physicist in Edinburgh, brought to the US to join a team of scientists tasked with re-engineering a piece of advanced technology."

"That's not the beginning," Cam interrupted. "You said it was buried in 792. Who the hell buried this thing back then?"

A smile crept across Marco's face. "Well, therein lies the problem, Mr. Lyle. The answer to your question gets a bit murky."

Cam's face said it all. He was being toyed with.

"You see, a series of events cannot be drawn in a straight line," explained Marco. "There are millions of other factors that determine the course of that line. And it is never straight, nor is it chronological."

"Wait—just wait a second," Rand thought aloud. "You said it 'surfaced' in 1962. What do you know about the castaways found on an island in the Pacific that year. The device they were carrying...is this it?" He was recalling the strange document that Melissa had told him about.

Marco nodded with a prideful grin on his face. "It is. No one knew where the castaways had come from, they seemed to appear out of nowhere, from what I was told. But yes, they had the device with them."

Cam suddenly found himself out of the loop. "Hold on, what are you guys talking about? What castaways?"

"Four men were picked up from a deserted island in '62," answered Rand. "They had a piece of technology, apparently *this* piece of technology."

"And how the hell would you know that?" Cam pressed.

"Because it was in a CIA field report attached to the Maersk Burgundy robbery file—*your* file."

"What's that have to do with me? And who exactly were these castaways?"

"Their identities were classified," Marco announced. "I know that one died shortly after their arrival. The other three were moved to a base in New Mexico. One fled a few years later, another was killed during an undisclosed accident. All but one was gone by the time I arrived, but our work on the project continued long after. We spent years trying to break the code."

"What code?" Cam was now being pulled deeper in.

"The time-space continuum, of course. We just needed to crack the code and all the secrets of the universe would be revealed. It was a very exciting time."

"Cam," Rand uttered, still seated at the bar, now examining the photographs with a magnifying glass he'd found nearby. He was mesmerized by one particular image, blinking in disbelief. "Cam!" he repeated.

"What is it, Rand?"

"This photo. You need to see this photo."

CHAPTER FORTY-FIVE

Rand held the photograph to the light above him and squinted through the magnifying glass. It showed seven, middle-aged, white men standing in an open desert with the sun brutally beating down on them: three in the foreground, four scattered in the distance.

"What is it?" Cam asked, snatching the photo from the air.

"Look," Rand said, pointing. "There's Marco in front with a few other men. And then there's *this* guy here in the back."

The details of the men were barely visible in the old grainy photograph. As Cam grabbed the lens and scanned through the image, an intense tingling sensation shot up his spine, the hairs on his arms stood up straight. One of the faces in the background was eerily familiar. It was *him*.

Rand took a step back and reached for his gun. "What the fuck is going on here?" he asked. He raised his weapon to Cam. "Why are you in that picture?"

"That's not me, Rand. Now put the gun down before somebody gets hurt."

"Actually," Marco corrected. "It *is* you, Mr. Lyle. But lower your weapon regardless, Mr. Kershaw. Our friend is unaware that it's him in the photo."

"What the hell does that mean?" Rand shouted, still aiming the gun at Cam's body mass.

"He's lying," Cam urged, as he rose to his feet, his hands slightly raised in surrender.

"Mr. Kershaw," Marco pleaded. "Cameron is telling the truth. He doesn't *believe* that it's him in the photograph...because the photograph hasn't been taken yet."

A wave of confusion washed over Rand. He appeared dangerous and unhinged, yet the pistol remained firmly pointed at Cam.

"What is that thing?" he demanded. "Tell me!"

Marco remained calm. "It is known as the Medina Device."

"So, you *are* one of the Knights of Medina!" Rand accused, as he switched his aim from Cam to Marco.

"Correct. And until last week, we were many in number. Only myself and one other remain. Our ranks were destroyed by a rather new enemy, but, nonetheless, an enemy worthy enough to bring us to our knees."

"What happened?" Rand asked, now training his weapon back on Cam.

"Carson attempted to wipe us out once and for all," Marco replied.

"Who's Carson?"

"The same rogue CIA officer who's trying to kill you. I only survived because of my position. I am, in fact, the Seneschal of the Knights of Medina, and I serve alongside our Grand Master. My identity, along with the identities of the 486 seneschals that came before me, have never been recorded or documented. And, for the last twelve hundred years we've sacrificed everything for the sole purpose of protecting man's greatest discoveries from himself. Ancient technology that some civilizations use as a means of advancement, but others use as a form of destruction. Our oath is to protect this knowledge from civilizations that are unprepared and undeserving."

Rand finally lowered his gun. Everything had suddenly changed. The walls of reality were starting to crack—the questions mounted.

"I can't allow you to simply hand this over to them," Marco warned. "I hope you can understand that, Cameron." It had been some time since he'd spoken the name. It almost felt foreign to him now.

"They're going to kill Michael," Cam argued.

"You're underestimating the power you wield," Marco corrected. "The Medina Device, at its fundamental core, is the key to the universe. It's the key to our reality."

"What the hell are you talking about?" Rand chided.

"By the fall of 1966," Marco began, "we had been experiencing tremendous breakthroughs in what is today known as the God Particle. This was forty years before CERN and the work that's being done there, which isn't exactly groundbreaking. No, the ground had already been broken long before."

"Then why wasn't it revealed to the scientific community?" asked Cam.

"It was far too dangerous. The power of particle physics is too complex for our modern-day character flaws and social behaviors. Besides, back then resources were hard to come by in private research, the big stuff was all run by the government. That's all changed now, but our research in the late sixties was unlike anything we had ever dreamed of. And it was all sparked by the discovery of the Medina Device."

Cameron and Rand listened carefully as the physicist continued in detail.

"It all starts with cosmic string, you see. It's a very distinct process of expansion in the universe. There is a hidden order in the chaos that surrounds us, an order that applies constant adaptation to itself. Our research led us to understand that nothing in the universe was random. In fact, the violent chaos of the universe proved to be a finely tuned organism. Every event since the Big Bang was executed with surgical precision. And it was all understood through the mathematics of expansion and growth."

"What, like pre-determined reality? Destiny?" Cam guessed.

"Not really," Marco chuckled. "They eventually named it the God Particle out of irony. You have to understand, we had proven that science *is* god." He took a casual sip from his wine glass. "Life itself is built from ultra-microscopic, vibrating strains, the result of which is everything you see around you. But there is so much more in front of us that we *cannot* see with our eyes. You can't see other dimensions because the laws of physics only work within our four-dimensional universe."

"You're losing me, Doc," quipped Rand.

"A lot of people initially believed there were multiple universes overlapping each other. It was the only way to make the math work. Laziness, if you ask me. But it turned out that it was *dimensions* of time and space that were overlapping, not universes themselves. It's something we can explain with mathematics but not with physics. When we began to look at the universe through the right lens, we could see what was *truly* happening. But we had been using the wrong lens prior to that. Make sense?"

"Sure," Rand replied. "You said 'cosmic string,' so what, this is like String Theory or something?"

"It is. But the biggest discovery came after we realized that the overlapping dimensions were not interacting through the laws of physics. We could calculate and measure the existence of the dimensions, but it essentially destroyed all the laws of the universe that we thought were true. Then something strange happened, we noticed that there were certain particles that had the ability to move from dimension to dimension," Marco explained. "Think of the Big Bang as a crime scene. If we could go back to it and take a snapshot of the crime being committed, we would inevitably identify the criminal. Or, in this case, the creator."

"The God Particle," Cam repeated.

"Yes, the God Particle," Marco confirmed. "We were able to recreate the Big Bang, or at least we tried. Which is exactly what the CERN team is currently doing with the Large Hadron Collider today. By the summer of 1972, we made a giant leap. Up to that point, we could only recreate the Big Bang up to a fraction of a second *after*, not the exact moment, of creation. And then...we did. And we found the maker's mark."

The words hung in the air like a surreal fog.

"That would be the single greatest scientific discovery in the history of mankind," Rand quietly noted.

"You'd be surprised," Marco cautioned.

"So, if the Medina Device is the key to the universe, how do you use it?" Cam wondered.

"I'm glad you asked. When the device was initially brought to us, it was like we had gotten the key to the house. The only problem was, we couldn't find the right house. Without understanding the universe, the device was useless. But when we saw the Big Bang in its very moment of creation, we found the architect of the cosmic string—the creator of the code. The only problem was the Law of Physics couldn't explain what we had seen. That's why we turned to mathematics. It was like trying to read Chinese with an English legend. After that, the flood gates opened, we could barely keep up with our own discoveries! We were learning more about the universe in ten-hour shifts than scientists had learned over hundreds of years."

"So, all you did was apply math to the Big Bang? And now what? You can bounce through space?" Rand asked.

The doctor was amused. "I guess you could say that. Before long we disproved Singularity and the No Boundary Theories. You see, the rate of expansion was different, time and space were *separated*. We had to completely rewrite every Law of Nature that existed prior to that. It opened doors we never thought possible. There was nothing we couldn't manipulate."

"I still don't understand," Cam stated. "What does this device have to do with the Big Bang?"

"The Big Bang turned out to be no more than the opening of a black hole. And, at the exact moment of creation, we got a glimpse into that hole. It revealed our creator."

"What did you see?" Rand anxiously questioned.

"It was another universe," Marco answered. "A living, intelligent, transcendent universe that purposely took chaotic nothingness and sparked it into a very mathematical, organized universe of fundamental constants."

"Holy shit," Cam mumbled. His eyes wandered the bar before coming to a stop at the Medina Device. "And it's all controlled by this?"

"Sort of," Marco confirmed. "There is still work to be done. But that won't happen for a very long time. The laws created by the universe are constantly evolving and being remeasured due to the rate of expansion. But from time to time, a civilization comes along that has the ability to pick up where a far previous one had left off."

"You still haven't told us what this is, and why it's so important," Rand pointed out.

Marco's eyes dove into the device, locking on for several seconds. "This device is the most powerful magnet ever created by man. It is indeed a mechanism that can transport particles to various points in the universe."

"And time?" Cam asked.

"This isn't a science fiction movie, Mr. Lyle. It doesn't exactly work the way you're imagining it. But, yes," confessed Marco. "In theory, you can transport through time. The past is merely a different point in what makes up space. You just have to find it."

Cam soaked it all in, trying desperately to wrap his head around everything. Marco had been part of a team that discovered the true nature of our universe. Clearly, in the wrong hands it could mean the catastrophic end to humanity as he knew it. But there was still the problem of Michael. And that wasn't about to magically go away.

"I'm saving my brother tonight, Marco," he said with a deflated sigh. "With or without your help."

"Cameron, let me make something perfectly clear," the physicist retorted. "In your reasoning, there is no outcome where you or Michael survive. Even if Carson hands over your brother tonight in exchange for the device, you'll both be dead by morning. They will not allow you to walk away from this. You've seen the device, you know what it is, and Michael has deciphered the tablet. You've both seen too much for them to let you live. And on the other hand, if you attempt a daring rescue of your brother, it will mean certain death for all of us."

"I don't have a choice," Cam countered. "Like you said before, there is no good outcome."

"Or maybe there is," Rand wondered aloud. "If that device is everything Marco says it is, then why don't we just zap Michael back to this room right now? Or go back and make sure none of this ever happens. I mean, unless you're full of shit, Dr. Damion, we can manipulate reality to our liking, can we not?"

"I wish it worked that way, Mr. Kershaw. Sadly, it does not."

"Then why don't you tell us exactly how it *does* work," Cam countered. "Because I think you have no idea what this thing is and you're playing games with us. We're taking the device and the photos and exchanging them for Michael. End of story."

"He's right," Rand agreed. "We're taking the device."

"The universe is a perfectly oiled machine, a beautiful organism that makes order from chaos," the aging physicist mumbled.

"You're talking in circles," Rand scoffed.

Marco smiled through his soft beard. "No, I'm talking in physics. What if I told you there was another option? Perhaps, your *only* option."

CHAPTER FORTY-SIX

Midnight was quickly approaching. The sky above Paris hung dark with the onset of clouds and a cold breeze. The streetlights of the Pont de l'Archevêché bridge produced a hazy, dotted glow through the darkness. Cam could hear the waters of the Seine River as they approached.

The three men arrived at the head of the bridge and gazed a few hundred feet to the other side. It was completely quiet, the tourists had long since left and the surrounding city blocks had drifted to sleep. Cam took the point position as they paced their way across the bridge, Rand covered the rear with his hand hidden on the trigger of a .40 caliber tucked into his jacket.

Once across the bridge, they stood at the southeast corner of Square Jean-XXIII, with the Notre-Dame Cathedral looming over them from across the lawn. The exterior lights of the cathedral illuminated the walls of its prolific architecture. To their right were the small iron gates that led to the Mémorial des Martyrs de la Déportation.

As they cautiously took their first steps toward the narrow entrance, the bells of a distant clock tower struck midnight. Its echoing ring felt ominous, daring them to continue on. With a last look around the park, Cam entered through the waist-high gates and now stood on the monument grounds.

The memorial pays tribute to the 200,000 people who were taken from Vichy and deported to Nazi-Germany during World War II. Most of those memorialized here died in concentration camps, never seen by their loved ones again. Cam could feel their tortured souls hovering in the night and silently asked for their protection.

The monument itself was surrounded by a low cement wall with inscriptions honoring the dead. Beyond the encasement, a set of staircases led down to a small rotunda. Cam and Rand drew their guns as Marco strolled to the staircase between them and stood anxiously at the top. A hush fell over the small island, which split the surrounding Seine in two. Cam stepped past Marco to the edge of the stairs and peered down at the shadowy rotunda below. It was empty.

With a silent nod, Cam shuffled his way down the steps. Once at the bottom, he was surrounded by a hexagonal wall. Glancing around, Cam noticed a dark opening in the wall to his left. It was the entrance to one of several crypts, which wove even further below the monument.

Rand quickly made his way down the steps behind Cam, followed by Marco. Just then, a figure appeared from the crypt. Cam raised his 9mm and gently rested his finger on the trigger.

To his surprise, the street lamps lining the bridge above them began to dim, then went out completely. As did all ancillary lighting that had been beaming from Notre-Dame Cathedral. The entire area around them went pitch black. The figure that Cam had seen near the crypt was now camouflaged in complete darkness. The soldier could barely see his own hand in front of his face.

A faint wind whispered through the memorial as a candle flickered to life from a far corner of the open-air rotunda. The candlelight steadied, and for a fleeting second the glow again revealed the strange figure standing in the crypt entrance.

Then—the candle went out. Complete darkness again.

"We meet at last," the voice said, remarkably closer now.

With his gun still raised, Cam shivered with agitation. His eyes tried to adjust to the blackness, he could now make out a man standing only feet in front of him. He steadied his weapon and took a small step backward.

"Lower your gun, Mr. Lyle," the voice requested. "No one needs to die here tonight."

"Where's Michael?" Cam demanded.

"He's here. Have you brought my asset?"

"It was never yours," Marco shouted from beyond, announcing his presence.

"Step closer," Carson jolted, squinting at the old physicist.

Marco and Rand took a few slow steps toward Cam, and the three now stood shoulder-to-shoulder in the middle of the rotunda floor.

"Well, isn't this interesting," Carson noted. "Dr. Marco Damion. I assume this is *your* doing?"

"Where's my brother, asshole?" Cam shouted. "I'm done playing your little war games. This ends tonight! Where is he?"

"He's right here," Carson promised, motioning to the crypt behind him.

Two men emerged from the shadows on queue. One seemed to be holding the other upright as he forced him to the center of the pavilion.

With his gun fixed on Carson, Cam glanced at the prisoner being dragged toward him. He looked badly beaten and in rough shape, struggling to stand. It was Michael. The closer Michael got, the tenser the moment became. The brothers were now merely five feet apart.

"This negotiation won't go any further until you holster your weapon," Carson said into the night.

A low fog drifted above the rotunda as they faced-off in the open-air pit surrounded by marble walls. Without warning, two more gunmen emerged from the crypt, their assault rifles at the ready. Their calculated approach and slow, precise footwork revealed a lifetime of training. Rand carefully took aim at the approaching shadows.

With a slight wave of his hand, Carson ordered the thugs to lower their assault rifles, which they immediately did. He shot a cold stare at Rand, who also lowered his weapon. Cam, however, held his pistol and focused his breathing. He steadied himself behind the 9mm, ready to light up the entire place. With every heave of his lungs he clouded the air around him with a soft fog.

After a final dramatic breath into the cold night, Cam lowered his gun.

"Very good," Carson said with relief. "Now, let's get this over with."

Cam took a long look at his little brother. Michael had clearly been interrogated and tortured; it was evident by the wrapped, bloody hand and distant look in his eyes.

"Bring him here," Cam instructed.

"The device, Mr. Lyle. Show it to me." Carson stood confident with his hands shoved into a black winter coat.

After a long pause, Cam finally turned to Marco, and delivered a knowing wink.

"Is this what you're looking for, Mr. Carson?" the physicist offered as he pulled the Medina Device from his coat pocket.

The two snipers on the roof of Notre-Dame immediately locked onto their targets in the rotunda below, as did a third sharpshooter from the gates of the monument entrance. The snipers were zeroed in, awaiting the final signal from Carson.

"Where's the rest of it?" the grizzled operative asked.

Cam dramatically threw the backpack onto the stone floor at Carson's feet.

"Thank you. Now, Dr. Damion if you would be so kind as to set the device down and walk away," Carson ordered.

"No!" Cam interjected. "Not until I have my brother."

Carson hesitated, but he was in no mood to drag this out any further. He turned and gave a commanding wave to the man holding Michael, who then thrust the prisoner onto the ground next to Cam. He landed with a gurgling thud and winced in pain.

Cam reached for his brother and lifted him from the ground. "Hold on, Michael. We'll get you outta here," he whispered.

As Carson's right hand slowly made its way up the back of his head in a deliberate movement, the snipers simultaneously eased into their triggers and released a final controlled breath, then fired.

Marco held the device outward in his right hand and pressed his thumb gently against an illuminated green button.

The four remained huddled in the center of the rotunda floor.

Then, the world suddenly stood still. The entire area was completely frozen, resistant to time and movement. The bullets from the snipers' rifles hung frozen in the air, vibrating through space, fighting for acceleration.

In a sonic boom that pulsated through the memorial and engulfed the surrounding blocks in a flash of white heat, Carson and his men were blown backward. The three snipers shuddered, blinded by the explosion searing through their scopes.

The shattering of glass from every window within a five-block radius echoed in the sky as time slowly tried to wind itself back to normal speed.

Carson lay flat on his back. He caught his breath and leaned up on his elbows, trying to make sense of what was happening. His brain fought to regain functionality. His sight had been blurred and a sharp ring echoed violently in his ears. He blinked, then blinked again. Seconds later, his hearing returned.

Through the hazy darkness, he could make out his men, scurrying around the rotunda in a frenzy.

"Carson!" a voice yelled through a muffled filter. "Carson!" It was louder now.

He shook off the concussion and stood to his feet. With a few more rapid blinks, Carson leaned forward and stared blankly at the memorial floor.

They were gone.

CHAPTER FORTY-SEVEN

The sensation was familiar—he'd been knocked unconscious a handful of times before on the battlefield. Cam felt the raindrops on his face but struggled to regain focus on the world around him. A quick body check revealed that he was laying on his back—no mortal wounds. As his vision slowly returned, he found himself staring up at a canopy of trees. He caught his breath and tried to pull himself up. Everything hurt.

Cam lifted his head and looked in every direction, trying to absorb his environment. The bitter taste of metal ran down his throat. A strange tingling sensation shot down his arm and into his hand. He held it out in front of himself and tightened it into a fist, then opened it again.

With a deep groan, Cam fought to pull himself to a seated position and turned toward a rustling nearby. It was Marco trying to pull himself off the ground next to him.

"Marco?"

The physicist's gray hair was coiled atop his head and a light stream of blood ran from his nose.

"I'm okay, Cameron."

Just then, Michael stumbled in front of them and reached out his hand to help Cam to his feet.

"It worked," Cam quietly noted. "I can't believe it fuckin' worked."

"Where the hell are we?" Michael asked, in a state of total confusion.

"We're alive. That's where we are," Marco replied.

"Rand! Where's Rand?" Cam shouted.

"I'm over here," a voice responded from the bushes. "I can't see. I think I'm blind."

Cam found him lying on his side next to a large rock, holding his ribs in pain.

"Talk to me, Rand. What's going on?"

"Where are we? I can't see."

"His vision will return soon," assured the physicist from a small clearing behind them. "It's only temporary."

After a minute of steady breathing, Rand was helped to his feet by Cam and Michael. The four men stood bewildered in the center of a thick forest beneath a sweltering sun and soft rain. The environment felt tropical.

"How long have I been out?" Michael questioned aloud.

"What's the last thing you remember?" Marco quizzed.

Michael thought for a moment and shook his head. "I was tied to a chair in a white room—"

"You don't remember being taken to Paris? The memorial?" his brother asked.

"No."

"He's suffering short-term memory loss," Marco surmised. "It too shall pass. This has been a traumatic experience for all of us."

"What happened to me?" Michael finally demanded, holding his head in pain.

"We were meeting with your captors for a trade-off," Cam explained.

Michael looked through the light rain at the thick vegetation around them. "I'm guessing it didn't go so well."

"We need to find some water," Cam directed. "Marco, you don't know where we are, do you?"

"No. Not exactly."

"What do you mean, *where* we are?" Michael flagrantly pressed. "What have you done? And who the fuck are these guys?" he yelled, sweeping his bandaged hand at the wily, old scientist and a disheveled former agent.

"Calm down, Michael," Cam gently replied. "This is Rand Kershaw, he's a friend. I owe him my life. And this is Dr. Marco Damion, a physicist. He's one of the Knights. There's a lot to unpack here, little brother."

"Did we...how did you—"

"All in due time," Marco assured. "Right now, we need to get moving."

Michael stood stunned, trying to wrap his head around the events of the last few hours. His post-concussion cloudiness cast a spell over his ability to comprehend reality. It all felt like a dream.

Cam led the pack into the pristine, vibrant jungle, searching for something—*anything*—to indicate their location. After a fifteen-minute hike through the forest, they stumbled into a clearing. The sound of the waves washing ashore could be heard in the distance. And just beyond the clearing, they set their eyes on the beautiful blue waters of an ocean.

They marched over brush and rock, giving way to sand dunes and seashells, arriving at the beach in awe, mouths agape, staring endlessly at the magnificent landscape. Then, beyond the sand and surf, something strange caught their attention. Their eyes wandered up the beach and out into the blue, where a small powerboat punched through the water toward them.

"Who's that?" Michael asked beneath his breath.

Marco stood with a knowing grin on his face, watching as the boat came to a stop on the shore fifty yards away. They could make out five men dressed in dark blue uniforms. Beyond them, where the horizon met the ocean, rested a large gray ship—a Navy cruiser with heavy battlements.

As the men in blue uniforms exited the craft and began marching up the beach, a river of shock flowed down Cam's spine. *This isn't happening,* he told himself. The visitors drew closer and it was clear they were US Naval personnel.

"I believe you boys need a lift," barked the commanding officer standing at the front of his team.

Cam was dumbstruck. He carefully examined the sailors standing in front of him.

"We just—" he tried, but nothing else came out.

"My name is Admiral Parker. We're here to rescue you. Is everyone alright?"

As the man spoke, Cam focused further on the uniforms. They were just strange enough to catch his attention. The material wasn't right; they didn't appear to fit properly. The shoes seemed dated and simple.

Cam's mind went blank. For a startling moment, he and Rand locked eyes in disbelief. His empty gaze shifted upward, over the admiral's shoulder to the large ship anchored at sea on the horizon. His pupils narrowed as he read the name written against the hull: *USS Oklahoma City*.

Cam's stomach sank, his legs became weak.

"Admiral?" he interrupted. "What year is it?"

"April, 1962. How long have you boys been on this island?" Admiral Parker followed Cam's eyes and peered over to his ship, then back at the befuddled castaway.

"We have no idea," Marco answered. "We've lost track of time."

"Well, let's get you gentlemen aboard. You could probably use a hot meal and a medical check. We can take you as far as Pearl Harbor."

With that, the sailors assisted Marco, Rand, Cam and Michael to the rubber skiff waiting in the surf.

Minutes later, a gentle ocean spray beat against Cam's forehead as the small boat glided along the water beyond the breaking waves. He closed his eyes and leaned his head back, allowing the sun to drench his tired face.

Through the rocking waters and a strong headwind, the four castaways exchanged looks that seemed to cover the entire spectrum of emotions. With each grin and nod, the *USS Oklahoma City* drew closer.

Rand's vision had now returned. The former FBI agent stared with a hopeful calm at the ocean ahead—a new existence he welcomed with open arms. He had no regrets for what he had agreed to in that dusty wine museum—something that surprised even him.

Michael sat quietly, bobbing in the boat next to his brother. He couldn't speak, unable to convert any of his thoughts into coherent words. What seemed like a tortured nightmare had somehow evolved into a twisted reality.

Following a short ride, the skiff pulled up to the guided-missile cruiser. After being hoisted to deck level, the four castaways were lifted aboard.

Now huddled on the deck, Michael turned to his brother. "Is this really 1962?" he asked.

"I'm afraid it is," Cam replied.

"But that's impossible."

"The device. It's exactly what you think it is."

A blanket of stark reality fell over Michael. "Who is Marco Damion exactly?"

Cam shot a glance at the old physicist resting nearby. "I actually have no idea."

As the *USS Oklahoma City* pulled her anchor and set out for Pearl Harbor, a small team of Navy medics gathered upon the castaways and began a series of preliminary physical exams. Cam held out his arm as a young sailor checked his blood pressure.

Once the bandage on Michael's left hand was unwrapped, he was quickly whisked off to the sick bay, where he was prepped for an immediate amputation of what remained of his pinky finger.

Another medic sat behind Marco and pressed a cold stethoscope against his back. After confirming a healthy heartbeat, the medic moved on.

"Will I ever see my family again?" Cam asked him.

"Of course," Marco replied. "Someday."

"Someday? Someday when? I never agreed to that. I can't miss out—"

"You won't miss anything, Cameron," Marco assured. "You will see your family again."

"Soon?"

"Maybe not soon enough for you, but soon enough."

"That won't work," Cam panicked. "I have to kill Carson. He's going to come after my girls. My wife! I can't let that happen. We have to go back."

"Your wife and children will be safe, this I can assure you."

"Then I'll go find him here. He's probably a teenager now, I can track him down."

"Cameron," Marco struck. "This situation is many things. What it is *not*, is an opportunity to alter history. It doesn't work like that, and the results would be catastrophic. In time, you will learn that your feelings must be cast aside. Unfortunately, Carson *needs* to exist—he's just another tiny piece of a grander purpose. And even if you try and change that reality, the universe will simply course-correct itself. There's nothing you can do to turn order back into chaos. Carson will never harm your family, and I promise your chance at revenge will come."

"And Rook?" Cam implored. "How can you let the murder of one of your Knights go unchecked? The device was meant for him, not me."

Marco knew that the truth wasn't going to come easy. "Rook's entire purpose in life was to make sure the device continued on its path—the way it has always been intended. The Medina Device was never meant for him. It was meant for *you*. It was always meant for you."

"So, we're the four mystery men who showed up in '62 in the middle of the Pacific. Why didn't you tell me?"

"I couldn't. It was all part of your master plan."

"What master plan?"

"The one you will meticulously develop," he replied with a smirk. "Please understand, Cameron, I've committed my life to preserving and protecting the secrets of mankind. History has already been written, you cannot simply rewrite it. There was never a *choice*, bringing you here has been the ultimate mission of the Knights since its inception."

"How do you know I was meant to be involved in this?"

Marco looked up at his Grand Master, finding irony in the fact that he himself was now so old, yet Cameron was so young. He'd always remembered it the other way around.

"You've been involved since the very beginning," the physicist admitted. "You've been protecting the Medina Device for thousands of years. Only, it hasn't happened yet. But you have a long journey ahead. There's much work to be done."

"What kind of work?"

"Soon you'll meet a younger version of myself," Marco reminisced. "Unfortunately, the man you see before you won't be there. But when we meet again for the first time, I promise we'll work out all the details."

Marco sat up from the deck and stood beneath the hot sun, soaking in the warmth, rejuvenating his spirit.

Nearby, Rand completed a rudimentary vision exam and was quickly released by the medics. He walked over and took a seat next to Cam.

"I really can't believe this," he muttered. "I guess I can't arrest you for those robberies."

"Why is that?"

"Because, apparently, you guys haven't committed them yet. In fact, the Wynn won't be built for another forty years. So, you've got some time."

"I'm really sorry for dragging you into this," Cam confessed with a heavy heart.

"I wasn't meant to die at some monument in Paris," Rand envisioned. "I think I like this better."

As the men sat beaten and tired on the open deck of the *USS Oklahoma City*, the admiral stood perched on a raised platform above. His captain joined him on the catwalk, still confused as to where the mysterious castaways had come from.

The two officers propped their hands on the railing and stared out into the open sea. Questions that should never be asked hung in the air, begging for answers. The captain knew that at some point he'd be told to never speak of it again. But in this moment, he simply couldn't resist.

"How did you know they were going to be there, sir?" he finally asked.

Admiral Parker considered the question with deep thought. "Because he told me they'd be there."

"Who told you?"

The admiral nodded in the direction of the tall castaway resting on the deck below.

"He did. Cameron Lyle."

Epilogue

Hyères, France – 1292 AD

Three torches maneuvered sharply through a subterranean corridor. The walls were cut from earth, the floor littered with loose stone. Several hundred feet below the tower of Saint Blaise overlooking the Sauvebonne Valley, they hurried with determination.

The labyrinth of caves seemed to lead nowhere, but the cloaked figures continued, their torches guiding every twist and turn. After a dizzying rush, they finally arrived at an open chamber.

Candles flickered along the rounded walls, illuminating the complex with a bright orange fog.

The three hooded men stood before a room of battle-hardened warriors, intellectuals and politicians. At least forty, they counted.

The tallest of the three stepped forward, flanked by his accomplices. Through tired eyes and a dusty beard, Cam pulled the hood from his head and gazed upon his audience.

"Gentlemen," he began with a booming voice. "I want to thank you for joining us this night. Our numbers may be paltry, but our power shall be massive."

The crowd remained attentive, anxious to hear the words of such an infamous warrior. They'd been beckoned here tonight by a man many had only heard of through legend.

"Some of you are Templars, some Teutonic Knights. And many of us fought together at Aizkraukle and Acre. Shoulder to shoulder, shield to shield," Cam rallied. "Others among us are scholars, pagans and Christians. Yesterday, we were knights without an order. Tonight, without order, we are no more!"

The audience sprang to life with battle cries and confirming shouts. Beside Cam, a man raised his torch above the group—a finger missing from his left hand. The warriors quieted again, hanging on every word.

"We come together here, beneath our vestige of Saint Blaise to begin a new journey!" Cam shouted. "On a battlefield unlike any we've ever known."

Rand clenched his jaw at Cam's side. He pulled his hood away from his face, revealing deep scars and gray stubble.

Cam's tone shallowed to a tranquil harmony, he was speaking with heart now. "You were each chosen for your bravery and intellect. Our mission now is to protect the greatest gifts ever given to humanity, to protect the knowledge of mankind and all that shall come from it. Our lives are no longer in the hands of any god or nation, but in the grasp of history. We are now and forever the keepers of mankind's lost wisdom. It is with great honor that I inform you, we have in our possession the lost libraries of Alexandria and Constantinople."

The men gasped in disbelief. The treasures of Alexandria had been lost nearly a thousand years ago, its existence shrouded in myth and folklore.

"And the future holds even more revelations and wisdom that will need our protection," Cam refrained.

Scanning his eyes across the room, he saw courage, honor and bravery in every direction.

Michael stood at his side with a formidable smile, his torch held high, urging his brother to continue.

"Tonight!" Cam yelled, his voice echoing through the catacombs, "We...are the Knights of Medina!"

The underground cavern erupted with a thunderous roar, the men raised fists and cheered their new Grand Master. The group gathered here tonight would forever be known as the first order of the Knights of Medina. As their cries rang untethered throughout the ground, Michael leaned in and hugged his brother.

"We finally made it, Cam. Now let's go home."

ABOUT THE AUTHOR

Photo credit: Danielle Shields

T.J. Champitto is an American novelist with a talent for suspenseful storytelling—creating fast-paced adventures that gently weave realism and science through an extraordinarily vivid lens. With his debut novel, *The Medina Device*, Champitto has burst onto the literary scene as an exciting new author who is poised to unleash more thrilling works.

NOTE FROM THE AUTHOR

Word-of-mouth is crucial for any author to succeed. If you enjoyed *The Medina Device*, please leave a review online—anywhere you are able. Even if it's just a sentence or two. It would make all the difference and would be very much appreciated.

Thanks!
TJ

Thank you so much for reading one of our **Thriller** novels.
If you enjoyed our book, please check out our recommended
title for your next great read!

Jihadi Bride by Alistair Luft

"A timely edge-of-your-seat terrorism thriller that plays on every parent's worst fears. This cinematic thriller is destined for TV." —*Best Thrillers*

www.ingramcontent.com/pod-product-compliance
Lightning Source LLC
Chambersburg PA
CBHW011955120726
47898CB00009BA/2934